GABRIELLA

A Mythical Tale of Love
and
Transformation

Judy Malloy

four o'clock press
London

This first edition published in Great Britain in 2007 by
four o' clock press - A discovered authors imprint
ISBN 978-1-906-14624-5

Available from Discovered Authors Online –
All major online retailers and available to order
through all UK bookshops
Or contact:
Books
Discovered Authors
50 Albemarle Street, London
W1S 4BD
+ (44) 207 529 37 49

books@discoveredauthors.co.uk
www.discoveredauthors.co.uk

Printed in the UK by BookForceUK. (BFUK)
BFUK policy is to use papers that are natural, renewable and recyclable products
and made from wood grown in sustainable forests where ever possible.

BookForce UK Ltd. 50 Albemarle Street London W1S 4BD

www.bookforce.co.uk

For Nicholas Adrian

PART ONE

PART TWO

They are a bright and shining people,
living in a land
where difference does not imply division;
where humans, male and female, are equal.

Where animals, and all living beings,
are treated with dignity and respect.
Theirs is a world filled with laughter and discovery,
strength and tenderness
and an insatiable desire to acquire that most inimitable of treasures,
the genuine knowledge of the Self,
both as a unique individual, yet also,
as a vital part of something much greater.

From this profound wisdom comes the absolute recognition
that no matter how diversely they see themselves or one another,
they truly know they are more the same, than different,
more united than disunited.
Therein lies the seed
that perpetually gives birth to freedom of true expression amongst them.
And the enduring peace,
which they have enjoyed for generations.

But it had not always been so. . .

PART ONE
THE MOTHER AND THE MIDWIFE

The River of Dreams

Mama. Mama,' Gabriella whispered, but there was no response. 'Mama?' Silence. Gabriella shook her Mother with a savage strength and cried out,

'Wake up, Mama. Wake up!'

Over and over she called into the night air, but there was no reply.

She gently drew her Mother closer and began to rock the woman's body, pressing the frail form of the older woman against her chest, as though to make them one, as though to lend the beat of her own heart to her Mother's silent breast. But her embrace was not returned.

They remained like this until Gabriella, exhausted, could bear the weight no longer. And then, ever so gently, she let go. Her arms ceased their fierce embrace and she slowly began to lower her Mother to the ground.

Gabriella looked down at the figure, as it lay in utter stillness upon the earth before her, and knew that the essence of her Mother had vanished.

Alone, shivering from the cold, her clothes soaking wet, she sat beside her Mother's body, staring at the flooded River of Dreams.

There once had been a time, when the River of Dreams was just an ordinary river, flowing, as it did, between an ordinary piece of land and a beautiful mountain.

And the people who lived in the land farmed the earth and were thankful for the bounty they received from it.

However, their lives were soon to change.

For, according to legend, a dark time had fallen upon the land, when the rains had ceased to fall, the once bountiful earth no longer yielded her harvest and the people began to starve. Desperate for food, they looked to the animals for sustenance. And for a while, they gave thanks for each life that sustained them.

But, as the animals of theland were not numerous enough to provide nourishment for them all, it became necessary for the bravest of men to risk travel in hand-hewn boats, across the wide waters of the river, to the far-away shore at the foot of the mountain, in search of succour. At first, they set forth with prayers and humble hearts, and it was said, they would return from the mountain each autumn with a stag so enormous, that it could scarcely be carried by eight grown men.

From year to year the mighty stags were honoured and blessed. For the meat, from a single full-grown animal, would feed the whole community. Each portion was put to good use: pelts became warm coverings; antlers and bones were hewn into tools and all was divided equally amongst the peoples. Priests blessed the hunters before they departed and, likewise, when they returned with such bounty. The animals were killed as needed, their sacrifice sustained the people of the land, and all were grateful for it. And so it continued for a number of seasons.

In time, the rains began again and with them, the crops flourished once more, making the flesh of the animals from across the river unessential for the survival of the people. This, however, did not stop the huntsmen. For the pleasure of the hunt itself had begun to outweigh its fundamental purpose. No longer did the men travel across the waters only in autumn. They went weekly, sometimes daily to track and kill.

Men, with greedy gleams in their eyes, invented new methods of laying snares and setting traps. However, the prize was no longer limited to a single great stag, as every species became subject to the pursuit of the hunters.

Birds of all kinds fell from the sky, as stones, hurled at outstretched wings, broke their gentle feathers. Starving woodland animals were lured to their deaths in mid-winter, tempted by food-baited traps designed to ensnare them. Arrows, sharpened from the bones of other animals, felled the stags in huge numbers and groups of grown men encircled small wild creatures, laughing and jeering as each, in turn, landed thudding blows upon their tiny skulls, until the animals no longer had breath.

Such desire to kill grew and grew until, in the end, it became a competition. Each year the men of the land chose seven men from amongst themselves and each strove to record the greatest number of kills. What had been an action born of necessity, became a contest fuelled by desire and driven by pride.

The Priests, once poor and humble, began to wear stoles made of fur. They ate meat each night, carelessly discarding the less tender portions. Bones and pelts that were no longer desired were simply cast away. The people, too, became fat with the flesh of the dead animals. Blessings were not spoken and thanksgiving for the sacrifice of each animal's life rarely played a part in the hunt. In these things, the mighty stag, and all other creatures from the mountain, were dishonoured.

It is said that in those days the waters of the river ran red with the life of the slain animals as the lust for blood and power began to govern the hearts of the people in the land. The relentless killings continued, until one day, after twelve consecutive moons of violence, two boats, carrying two of the ablest hunters, returned from the mountain with only their passengers inside.

The few who observed the men that day saw their usually ruddy faces had turned white as driven snow and when their boats came ashore, each hunter sat motionless within, as though frozen. When at last one came to consciousness, he spoke with a faltering voice. Wide-eyed and nearly breathless, he told them what had happened. Where stag, eagle, squirrel, ram and every other species had been seen just one week earlier, now there were none.

Every living creature on the mountain had vanished. An eerie silence was all that remained, save a gale-like wind, the sound of which had seemed to scream, 'Go, Go'; its demon howling had driven both men near to madness as they fled for their very lives.

'Only a miracle has saved us from the curse of that earth,' said the hunter. 'The Mountain is enchanted, it is filled with wickedness. Never return. Never return.'

He repeated the words over and over, rocking to and fro.

When the five remaining hunters, who had been chosen that year, heard the tale of the two, they scoffed at their weakness. Surmising the story had been contrived to cover the hunters' shame at having returned empty-handed, the five announced to the villagers that they would cross the river at dawn, the very next morning, and expose the deception.

At daybreak the villagers lined the cliffs to see the hunters on their way. As the sun shone brightly, each hunter pretended to be terribly afraid as he stepped into his own boat. Those gathered at the river's edge laughed in appreciation at the showmanship and cheered on the man they most favoured, but their jovial tones soon ended, for midway across the river a strange cloud covered the sun, causing its golden light to turn a deep, deep red.

It was nowhere near time of the setting sun, yet the sky wore colours, as though it were. The crimson heavens reflected upon the water's surface and it, too, glowed an eerie red. And then, from the top of the mountain, came the sound of a wind like none had ever heard. It howled, as if in agony, the force of it snapping whole trees that lay in its path as though they were twigs.

'Go,' it howled. 'Go.'

The hunters tried desperately to turn back to the land, but an enormous wave rose up and swamped each of their boats. The great winds stirred the waters and gusted with such ferocity that the five were blown from their vessels, like dead leaves from autumn branches, as the gales slammed their helpless bodies on to the churning carmine waters. Over and over they were pummelled until, one by one, the five men vanished forever into the depths. Each had struggled to keep his head above the surface, gasping for breath, fighting for life, but their efforts were to no avail.

With the disappearance of each man, the sanguine river grew darker and darker in hue, until it had become the colour of ancient blood. Then, when the last of the five was consumed by the angry waves, the wind immediately ceased, the cloud disappeared and sunlight cast its dazzling glow upon the river, now still and quiet, like a glistening blue mirror, reflecting the bright sky above it. No trace of the men or their boats could be seen.

The High Priest, witnessing these events, realized in horror that the mountain and the river were, indeed, cursed. In that very moment, he made a decree proclaiming that all meat, furs, pelts and any other remains of animals taken from the mountain were to be brought to the town square immediately. There they would be placed upon a huge altar, along with the hulls of the boats of the two hunters who had survived their ordeal. He ordered the men gathered about him, there upon the high cliffs, to make haste and spread the news to all those who had not seen what had happened.

And so the townsfolk flocked to the square with arms full of all that had been taken from the far-away mountain and when all the remnants were placed upon the wooden sailing vessels at the base of the pyre, a great swell of animal flesh stood heaped, ready to be burned. Ringing the makeshift altar, the villagers, eyes filled with fear, stared at their High Priest who, staying his own inner terror, took a deep breath, and removed from about his neck his most cherished fur stole.

Draping it across his forearms, he walked slowly towards the massive collection of flesh and bones. When he arrived at the altar, he hurled the stole into the air and the fur landed on the skull and antlers of a stag perched high on top of the pyre. Content that all was in place, he doused the lot with oil, set it aflame and soon, the putrid, sweet-sour smell of burning flesh filled the air.

As smoke curled skyward, the High Priest knelt at the base of the fire, rocking back and forth, worrying the long hairs of his ancient beard with his knobbly hands as he invoked the mercy of Almighty, promising holy obedience to all His laws.

Later, when hot white ash was all that remained, the High Priest drenched the smouldering mound with water, which he had also blessed with Holy prayers, and declared himself and all who dwelt in the land, pure, once more.

'Now we have offered in supplication to the Almighty that which we possessed from the evil mountain. May He have mercy upon our pitiful souls and deliver us from our misery. May He lift the curse placed upon us and keep our land safe from all further harm and sorrow. May the souls of the brave men who perished this day be lifted, with tenderness, from their watery graves by the Almighty, and may He comfort all who mourn their deaths.

'Look now to the great evil face of stone, my people,' he said, gesturing to the mountain. 'Do not flinch, look now. Look at its abominable shape carved against the sky. See that its very form defiles the entrance to the holy abode of the Almighty. It shall hereafter be known as the Mountain of Remembrance, in honour of those who have perished. Towering above us, it will serve as a constant reminder of the presence of the Evil One within this world.

'The waters which separate us from the mountain, that river, just now run red with the blood of our noble men, shall be called The River of Dreams, for it is a place of inexplicable happenings. Its very name shall remind us to remain ever alert.

'To safeguard against any further catastrophe, we shall continue to purify our lives, purging ourselves of any remnant of this curse that may yet dwell amongst us.

6

'Lest we lose sight of this high calling, we will from this day forward be called the People of The Land of Never Forgetting. For, indeed, we shall not.'

Removing the simple muslin stole from about his neck he placed it, with reverence, upon the shoulders of the man who had first spoken of his ordeal on the Mountain of Remembrance, saying, 'You truly must be a man of Almighty's choosing to have been spared such a death. I beseech you to lead us in the way of righteousness.'

And so it was that the one who had first spoken of what he had seen became the new High Priest of the Land of Never Forgetting and the second of the two survivors became his closest confidant. They became known throughout the Land as The Two and, together, they ruled with a severity born of darkest fear.

There were some in the Land, however, who had believed all along that the wanton killing of the animals had been meaningless and cruel. They had despised such brutality. For a time these men and women spoke out, saying that the deaths of the hunters had been no curse at all but, rather, the hand of Creator intervening on behalf of the innocent. But their convictions were met with disdain and their tongues hideously silenced; for in the Land, at that time, all manner of expression, other than that advocated by The Two, was quashed.

Those who knew the power of herbs for healing and the language of trees for blessing were killed, the special knowledge they possessed dying with them. The few remaining enlightened ones, who survived, grew silent, hiding their wisdom, fearing for their very lives. They suppressed their deep beliefs and denied the truths they most cherished. Worship ceased to be a joyous celebration of Creator, and became instead, a strict and sombre adherence to the rules and teachings of the Priests, who claimed they were doing all they did in honour of the Almighty.

They taught that men were made in the image of the Almighty, that they were superior to women; and because of their supremacy, not only women, but children, animals and the earth were to be in submission to them.

The people were no longer permitted to look at one another, but were commanded to keep their heads covered and bowed low. They were not allowed to question the Law or the manner of its interpretation and they were never to venture forth beyond the boundaries of their Land.

Most specifically, they were forbidden travel to the River of Dreams and the Mountain of Remembrance, which loomed beyond it. From the Land, only the summit of the Mountain was visible, its craggy facade etched indelibly upon the horizon. Although nothing, with regard to the Mountain or the River, had ever been specifically written upon the pages of the Great Book of the Law, the holy men referred to them often and invoked them as constant reminders of the presence of evil and danger.

And so it was that the mantle of the High Priest was passed from the One Who Had First Spoken to his eldest son, who passed it to his eldest, who passed it to his, until, many lifetimes later, in one fierce push of blood and water, a child was born in the Land of Never Forgetting, eyes wide open, brightest blue, fully focused, and yet with a far-away gaze. It was a girl.

THE BIRTH

When the Midwife received the little child she gasped, for the baby had no left arm. Instead, on the upper portion of her tiny back, above the curve of ribs, protecting her rapidly beating heart, was a grotesque lump. This mass was different in colour and texture from the rest of the infant's body and had the appearance of many petals of skin all overlapping one another. It looked like a hideous, pulsating flower of flesh, something other, but this growth was clearly part of the child and clearly unnatural.

The Mother cried out, 'That is not my baby,' rejecting it upon first sight and, pushing the child away, she begged the Midwife to keep the horror of it secret from the Father. The infant, remaining oddly quiet in these first moments of her life, made no sound or cry and hardly moved at all. Yet she needed no audible expression for the two women to take notice of her, for she commanded their attention with the intently focused gaze of her beautiful pale-blue eyes.

The Midwife had never seen such eyes as these. In the whole of her experience, no child had ever been born with the ability to stay its vision. But this child did exactly that, and more. She seemed to perceive all that was happening around her and with her eyes she responded.

How harsh the scene must have appeared that night as it unfolded to her newly-born soul. The Mother's face filled with horror, rejecting her. The ancient Midwife, holding her at arm's length, expressed a similar look of disgust; hers masked with ever so slight a degree of pity, as if staring at some poor wild animal that had been maimed. At first none of the child's immediate needs were met and it is difficult to know how many moments passed in this manner.

The silence was uncomfortable for the women but no words could dispel the darkness in their spirits. All seemed a horrible dream. What had once

9

been an expectant and joyful atmosphere grew heavy, as the cheerful, blazing fire died down, leaving the air in the cottage to grow cold, as though reflecting the Mother's heart.

As the last of the logs upon the hearth collapsed in a puff of ash and spark, a sudden rasping, ancient scream cut through the night air causing the Midwife to race to the window, the child clutched within her arms. The Mother followed and all three saw, to their amazement, the form of a huge owl, silhouetted against the silver disc of the roundest moon. With enormous wings outstretched, it flew low to the earth and then made seven circles in the air above them before flying into the forest behind the cottage. Its appearance on this night seemed to awaken something in the child and she began to cry.

Hers was a mewling, whimpering cry. There was nothing demanding or harsh in its nature, yet her expression aroused both Mother and Midwife. By now the infant had grown cold and her once pink skin was deathly pale, her little frame shivering in an effort to keep itself warm.

Rallying their spirits, the two women moved quickly in order to overcome their confusion and initial disgust, for there was much to be done. The Mother reached her arms out towards the Midwife saying, 'Hand me my child'. As the Midwife gently wrapped the little baby in a woollen blanket and lowered the child to her Mother's breast, the Mother whispered and gently stroked the tiny one as she gazed into the pools of blue, which were her daughter's eyes.

With the baby attended to, the older woman busied herself, stoking the fire and preparing some food, while contemplating the appearance of the magnificent bird. It had been years since she had seen an owl of such proportion and its visitation this night was no coincidence. Of that, the Midwife was sure.

Later, after a nourishing supper of thick vegetable soup and brown bread, with the child asleep and warmed once more, the women began to speak.

'I do not know what to do,' said the Midwife.

'What else can you do?' the Mother replied. 'She is as she is.'

'I know. Save for her left side she seems a beautiful, special child. She is perfect in all manner of things.'

'You know as well as I...' the Mother began but the Midwife interrupted her saying, 'Her cry awakened my heart and a tenderness for her has stirred within me. I must protect her.'

The Mother heard the woman's words but felt she needed to speak with reason for all their sakes. 'You know as well as I,' she continued, 'Her misshapen form bodes badly for each of us. It is difficult enough that I birthed a girl-child and not a son; but in her disfigurement, blame will be assigned. You will be condemned as Midwife with an evil nature, I may be judged as having been unfaithful or she will be seen as unclean in her very creation. They will not share your compassion for her and my husband will, of course, abandon me. Their hearts will not be wakened, for they will not see her as we do.'

The conversation ceased and in the stillness that followed, the child stirred against the Mother's chest. Her eyes opened and she looked up gently; first at her Mother and then at the Midwife. It was as though she knew what they were saying, as though she understood, and when she had looked upon them both, the baby closed her eyes and returned to sleep once more.

'What, then, shall we do?' asked the Mother, feeling her skin bumpy with raised flesh that accompanied the shivers going up her spine.

After a long pause, the Midwife answered her with a sigh, 'She, like no other, has been born with eyes wide open, on the night of the roundest moon, in the bitter cold and darkest dark of the shortest day. The screeching cry of the night-eagle, the great grey owl, has awakened the spirit within her. All is to be heeded. We must keep her malformation a secret for as long as we are able. It should not be too difficult, as it is winter, and, if ever we need to journey out of doors, we will swaddle her in a manner that will conceal her body. We will celebrate her birth and plan her naming ceremony as though nothing untowards has occurred.'

'Let us request that her Naming Day takes place in early spring,' she continued. 'This will give me time to ponder all these things. I will report that her birth was a difficult one and that I will remain near you both to provide support for her first months. In this manner, your husband will not return to his home. It should not be too much a concern for him, as men leave the care of women to other women.'

'And then what? What will happen after the naming? Can we keep her deformity hidden forever?' asked the Mother.

'No,' the Midwife responded. 'No, it will most surely be something which cannot be hidden forever; but I sense from the depths of me, that it is my duty and my privilege to protect her until her Naming Day. It puts both of us in grave danger not to report this to the High Priest, but I can do no other. I shall not be part of her death; I shall only be part of her life and of her living.'

As the Midwife said these last words she felt a growing conviction, a summoning of a deep and unknowable truth, for something within the bright spark of this baby's crystal-blue eyes had reignited a passion, a wisdom, which had long lain dormant in the old woman's soul.

And so it was that the Midwife found the courage to defy the authority of the Land. Together, the two women made a pact to break the Law, each knowing full well that imperfect babies, born in the Land of Never Forgetting, never saw a second morning.

The Priests seemed indifferent to the punishment of women and the killing of children when births were not the norm. They were able to justify their actions with platitudes about 'protecting the pure of heart' and 'eliminating evil' and carried about the Book of Law, which was full of rules and all manner of correct behaviours, which had to be abided by. No one, other than the Priests, was allowed to read or touch the Book, for it was written in an ancient language unknown to the common people. It was proclaimed as the Word of the Almighty, but its content could vary quite radically in translation, depending upon the High Priest interpreting it.

Until this moment the Midwife herself had been too frightened of the harsh penalties to dare defy any of their edicts, but this night had extinguished the dark ignorance fuelled by fear.

The light within the child emboldened both women and each was prepared to suffer death so that she might have life.

～

The following day, the Midwife dutifully reported the birth to the High Priest and, as the old woman had anticipated, little interest was aroused for it was a girl-child. Likewise, as she had predicted, the Father did not object when it was suggested he stay away in order to allow Mother and daughter to recover. And so it was decided that three cycles of the moon would pass and on the day, following the night of the third roundest moon, the child would be presented at her Naming Day.

The short days and long nights were unseasonably warm and the little cottage, nestled in the evergreen trees, was filled with love. Fires in the hearth sparked and sizzled; the air was sweet with the smell of freshly baked bread; new clothes were sewn and the Midwife brought her beautifully coloured yarns to the cottage and began to weave a garment for the child to wear on her Naming Day.

The Midwife knew many things about the gifts of the earth, the healing properties of herbs and plants, the special wisdom of the trees and the powers of certain stones. She had learned long ago to extract a bounty of beautiful colours from nature, which she used to dye yarns, and from them she wove luxurious garments that became especially valued by the Priests. The brighter the colours, the more elaborate the patterns, the greater the desire of the Priests to wear them.

She was valued, too, for her ability to ease the pains of childbirth. Although in her youth she had tried to share her vast wisdom in secret, as she grew older, fewer and fewer sought to know the significance of these things. What good was such knowledge to a people so frightened by the wrath of the Priests? It was well known that anyone who taught or studied

13

the ancient truths was harshly punished, even killed, if they dared to do so.

As the baby grew in size and curiosity, she shared the common needs of infants; but seemed different than any the Mother and Midwife had known. Beyond the obvious deformity of her left side, there was something else, something quite unique, almost mysterious, about this child. She smiled and giggled often and the Mother drew nearer to her with each passing day. In the early hours of the dawn, the two would hold each other closely, opening to the new and deepening love between them.

As if in keeping with the blossoming affection between Mother and child, the barren earth began to unfold and, as is the way of all seasons, the only constancy was change. Each evening the sun lingered longer in the sky and each morning the cock crowed, just that bit sooner. The harsh winds eased and the snows melted, giving way to the gentle rains of spring.

As the Naming Day grew closer, the Mother began to feel a growing sense of fear. Even the joy of spring did little to lift her spirits. *Perhaps we are never sure of the future but only pretend we know what will occur in order to keep our fears assuaged,* she mused. She often looked upon her child, sleeping peacefully in her cradle and, as feelings of overwhelming love brought tears to her eyes, she knew that she, no matter what the future, had made the correct choice in protecting her.

Time did not pause for the Mother's love, but hastened on with alarming rapidity until at dawn, on the day preceding the night of the third roundest moon, the Midwife left the cottage, telling the Mother she needed to prepare for the morrow.

Upon her return, she was carrying a hazel wood rod on her right shoulder, attached to which was a heavy sack. In her left hand she held a black ash basket, which contained a delicately wrapped package, decorated with the first of that year's pale yellow primroses. Lowering the rod to the floor of the cottage, she held the package out to the Mother with both hands. The Mother gently removed the flowers, taking care to not damage them, and opened the gift. Inside was the most magnificent fabric she had ever seen.

The Midwife had fashioned it specially, for instead of having sleeves

14

this garment was designed so that it could completely enfold the child, fastening up the front with buttons made from the carved wood of the rowan tree. The fabric was soft as a newborn rabbit and the threads woven by the Midwife were of such exquisite colours the Mother was reminded of a rainbow; crimson-red, orange, yellow, green, sea-blue, and lastly an indigo-coloured hood. Each hue blended almost magically into the next, so subtle the weave, it seemed more one colour than six.

The Mother's eyes filled with tears as she thanked the Midwife for her generosity and kindness, but each of them knew it was gratitude for so much more. They had comforted each other well in the preceding weeks and each had learned much about themselves. It had been effortless in many ways, but perhaps this was because they were not really learning anything new, but rather, remembering all they had long forgotten.

Seven Sacred Trees

That evening, as the sun passed below the western horizon and the roundest moon became visible in the east, the Midwife instructed the Mother to clothe her baby in the rainbow-coloured garment, place her in the basket of black ash and follow. Picking up the heavy bundle, strapped to the hazel wood rod, she hoisted it to her shoulder and took them along a winding path, which led deep into the forest, behind the cottage, where pine, fir and hemlock grew. Here the air was crisp and fresh with the scent of spring.

The three were silent: Mother and child following close behind the Midwife. When they arrived at a small clearing beneath a thicket of trees, the Midwife lowered the hazel wood rod to the ground and carefully untied her satchel. She gestured to the Mother to set the basket and child down beneath a large fir tree, as she opened the fabric that was attached to the hazel wood rod and drew out all that it contained.

There were forty-nine small white pebbles, gathered from the banks of the River of Dreams; seven highly-polished sticks of the wood of seven trees; kindling; dried fungus taken from a paper-white birch tree; and a large drawstring pouch, identical in colour and texture to the child's newly-woven garment. The Midwife raised her eyes towards the sky and said aloud:

Holy One, please hear my prayer
Let my voice ring through the air
Shine on us your heavenly face.
Bless this earth, this healing place.

And with those words she took the hazel wood rod and drew two circles on the ground. The two circles overlapped in the middle, forming a third, distinctive shape between them. Reaching down, she took a single white stone in her left hand, held it before her, hand extended towards the sky and said:

Whitest stone from River's edge
Witness now, this holy pledge.
Circle 'round this blaze of fire
Save her from the funeral pyre.

Hear us now, Eternal Grace.
Hold us in your sweet embrace.
Give your gifts to light the way;
Preserve her on her Naming Day.

The Midwife then gathered up the remaining white pebbles with her left hand, seven at a time, and set them along the lines traced in the earth by the hazel wood rod. Seven times she repeated this action, beginning at the union of the circles at their southernmost point and, moving from west to east, she distributed all the pebbles around the circumference of both circles. After digging a small trough where the two overlapped, she placed the flat piece of birch fungus within it, red side facing upwards, rotted side to the ground.

Upon this, she placed the kindling, which she had collected from the seven trees. Taking up the seven lengths of polished wood, she placed them, one at a time, in spoke-like fashion, radiating from the centre of the entwined circles and spoke these words:

Ash to keep your pathway clear,
Help you listen, Help you hear.
That within and that without,
Helps you grow. No need to doubt.

Beech, the wood transports you back.
Gives you knowledge that you lack.
Learn to trust all that you know,
Look to lessons long ago.

Blackthorn, tree of winter's days,
Blossoms, at the sun's first rays.
Outside forces are at hand,
Hold your earth now, heal your land.

Elder, tree of quick repair,
Heals its branches without care.
Creation story never ends;
What is broken always mends.

Strongest Oak tree, towering high,
Branches reaching to the sky,
Hold her feet on solid ground,
Help her roots be strong and sound.

Pine, oh tree of constant green,
Please remind her what she's seen.
Awake in her an inner guide,
Let her heart with you abide.

And lastly, Willow, graceful tree,
Let her learn of life from thee.
Cycles, rhythms, ebb and flow,
What is joyful, once was woe.

After she had spoken, the Midwife paused, studying all that surrounded her. Above the great canopy of evergreen, guardian trees, the sky's light was beginning to deepen, revealing shades of mauve and blue. The air was thick with the fragrance of pine needles and the musty green scent of fern and bracken. And from far away they could hear the haunting song of a solitary blackbird. From behind the branches of the great fir, the First Star, all-alone, shone brightly, as though watching from above, all that was below. Its steady light not yet masked by the brightness of the moon.

Within this heightened stillness lay the tiny child, wrapped in her protective rainbow garment, nestled in the black ash basket set down beneath the towering fir tree. Beside her, was the Mother, drawn and pale, her brow deeply marked by unending worry. Opposite them, on the other side of the two white circles formed from the forty-nine pebbles, stood the ancient Midwife, hazel wood in hand. And between them, the seven branches of wood, fanned out like rays of summer sun; seven gifts from seven sacred trees, bestowed upon the child this night.

All was as it should be. Picking up the rainbow-coloured pouch, the Midwife untied it and drew from within pieces of pyrite and flint. Holding the pyrite in her right hand and the flint in her left, she knelt at the union of the circles and lifted them both towards First Star's light,

Gifts of stone, your Spirit lend.
On this night, all darkness end.
Guide my hands, create the spark,
Illumination; leave your mark.

With more strength than one would imagine the old woman to possess, she began to strike the pyrite with the flint. Large sparks began to float down to the edge of the dried fungus underlying the kindling. As pieces of stone broke away from the pyrite, the Midwife was careful to keep the fungus clear so that sparks might land upon it. Soon, her strokes became rhythmical as her body rocked from side to side, as though keeping time to a melody only she could hear. The sweat on her brow became visible as her efforts increased. And then, in an instant, a large spark made its way on to the tinder. She stopped her rocking and quickly leant forward, blowing, encouraging it to burn.

The spark, which had at first seemed so fragile, grew in strength, as small flames began to ignite the twigs she had placed upon the fungus. Feeding the fire with larger and larger pieces of kindling, she coaxed the flames and they began to burn the seven branches of sacred wood, at the centre of the two adjoining circles of pebbles. When she was confident that the fire had enough strength to continue without further assistance, she placed the pyrite and flint safely back within the rainbow pouch. The glow of the fire lit up the faces of all three as they gazed upon it. Each seemed transfixed by its extraordinary power and warmth, and all was still, save for the Midwife gently feeding the unburned portions of the seven polished sticks into the heart of the flames.

When the last of each of the sticks was ablaze, the baby began to coo and her voice sounded forth in the night air with sweetness and delight as she gazed on Mother, Midwife and fire. The roundest moon, now fully risen, cast a silvery glow upon the trees above and the earth below, making the golden light of their fire seem brighter still. As the last of the seven sticks was consumed, the golden blaze flared upward, as though a gust of wind had risen inside it and then, all was quickly reduced to a pile of glowing embers.

The Midwife beckoned the Mother to gather her child and approach the circles. When the two women were stood directly opposite one another, the Midwife lowered her head ever so slightly to Mother and child and reached to the earth for her hazel wood rod, with which she stirred the ashes, dispersing the remaining heat. When all was extinguished, she placed the rod back upon the ground and reached once more for the rainbow pouch. From within, she drew two small pottery vials with waxen stoppers and a bowl carved from the wood of a yew tree. Placing one of the vials on the earth alongside the hazel wood rod and, holding the other aloft, she removed its stopper, held it skyward, and said:

Water, come from River of Dreams,
Add your gift to moonlight beams,
Moisten hardened hearts of men,
Let them see Life once again.

Not with outer vision, nay,
But with heart's eyes let them say,
Though your form brings earthly fear;
Still, we long to stay quite near.

When this had been uttered she poured the water into the wooden bowl. Taking the second vial, she removed its stopper and, likewise, held it towards the sky with these words:

Salt, the gift of sun on sea,
Safeguard all that's meant to be.
Keep alive the life within
Her most mortal, wounded, skin.

Blend again with waters pure,
Forming tears to help obscure
Sight, which may condemn and harm.
Change their hate, to love. Disarm.

Holding the container of salt above the wooden bowl she poured its contents into the water and then, taking the bowl into her right hand, the Midwife knelt upon the earth and reached into the cool ash with her left. Seven times she reached into the ash, gathering the charred remains of the seven sacred trees and placed them in the bowl as well. This, she then placed gently upon the ground, at the meeting of the two circles, at the southernmost point. Holding the hazel wood rod with both hands, the Midwife stirred all that was within the yew tree bowl in a slow and deliberate manner until a grey paste had formed. Lifting the bowl skyward once more, she said:

Ash and Beech and Willow fine,
Blackthorn, Elder, Oak and Pine.
Burnt together on this night,
Light the way for her birthright.

Blend with water and with salt,
Let her mark be not her fault.
Let her live her mortal life,
Free from judgment, free from strife.

We offer you our sacrament,
Knowing she is Heaven-sent.
No more guidance from a tome,
Heal our hearts now. Lead us Home.

As she prayed this last prayer, the Midwife asked the Mother to lift the child from the basket, and, slowly the Midwife began to unfasten the rowan buttons, allowing the rainbow garment to slide from the infant's left side, revealing the peculiar flower-like shape beneath, which glistened, in the light of the moon.

Immersing the bony fingers of her left hand into the bowl until they were completely covered with the grey paste, she placed them gently upon the child's deformity, slowly making the shape of one full circle upon it, until all was completely covered. The moist grey poultice dried instantly as she blew on it softly. Fastening the buttons of rowan once more, she closed the rainbow-coloured garment about the child, who had made no sound at all.

With eyes closed, the two women stood alongside one another, holding the precious child between them. That night, in that moment, the stillness seemed unfathomable. And yet it was so. When the two opened their eyes to look down once more, they found the child's eyes closed and her body swaying, ever so gently.

Without speaking, each knew it was time to return home. The Mother placed the baby back inside the black ash basket while the Midwife gathered her hazel wood rod and tied the fabric to it once more. The bundle was much smaller now, as it contained only the two empty vials, the yew tree bowl and the rainbow pouch, which held the flint and pyrite.

In continued silence, they made their way back to the cottage, along the silvery path, which led from their evergreen sanctuary.

THE NAMING DAY

D awn on the child's Naming Day arrived to the song of a robin, open-throated, cheerful and full of merriment; its response to the glorious morning sun was nothing short of joyous. The baby began to coo as if part of some sort of happy duet whilst the older women attempted to get on with all that was required.

Within the spirit of the Midwife, a sense of calm was pervasive; it was not a forced stillness, but rather a deep certainty that all would be well. However, no such peace was available to the Mother. She had slept restlessly; tossing and turning until the early hours, her thoughts raging with fear that all would be discovered.

'We must work diligently to look happy and contented,' the Midwife encouraged her. 'I know it is difficult, but we are her only earthly hope this day.'

Feeling nothing but love for her daughter, the Mother continued with her activities in an effort to stay her fears. Gently washing her child with warm water, she was careful to leave the poultice untouched. Rays of light streamed into the centre of the room; it was a perfect beginning. *Perhaps it is an omen of good fortune*, the Mother thought to herself as she gently massaged the infant's skin with rose-petal oil, its aroma filling the little cottage with a delightful scent. Placing the exquisite rainbow-coloured garment upon the baby she fastened the rowan buttons, leaving nothing but her daughter's face exposed. Part of the bodice was the same pure blue as the child's eyes, which today were more astonishingly clear and bright than ever before.

After the Mother had nursed her child, the two women ate a meagre breakfast together, then cleared the dishes and had just put them away when the bell began to ring out, calling the villagers to the square. The time had come. Looking first at the beautiful child and then at each other, The Mother and Midwife bowed their heads and spoke a silent prayer. When each finished, they squared their shoulders, placed the little babe within the basket of woven black ash and made their way towards the town.

By the time they arrived, the square was nearly filled with villagers. While naming ceremonies were traditional for children, the High Priest had made attendance mandatory only for the naming of sons. So, ordinarily, there were few gathered for the Naming Day of a girl-child, however, from the numbers congregated, it was plain to see that tongues had been wagging.

As the two women approached the edge of the square with their treasure, the crowd separated to create a human aisle, allowing them to proceed; Mother and child first, followed by the Midwife. As the three passed amongst them, gasps were heard from those assembled, 'Look at her eyes,' said one. 'How heavenly her gaze,' whispered another. Similar expressions of rapture accompanied the trio as they moved towards the High Priest, who awaited them, along with the Father, at the far end of the square.

The Priest had chosen to wear a black robe adorned with a solid white stole, his vestment appearing particularly stark against the bright sky of a spring morning and the little child wrapped in rainbow-coloured fabric. The Father seemed aloof and almost disinterested in the whole event. A girl-child's birth was no blessing for him, her Naming Day a mere formality. In fact, initially the two men seemed more interested in a private conversation they were having with one another than in the arrival of the child. 'Welcome the beautiful one!' shouted a voice from the back of the crowd. And at this, the Priest peered into the basket to see what all the fuss was about.

For the Mother and Midwife, the events which next occurred seemed to take place in a manner slower than actual time. The Priest inclined his head politely down towards the child, more out of habit than interest; then looked up quickly to ensure that his congregation had seen him do so; but immediately, as though drawn by an unseen force, his gaze returned to the child. His eyes rested upon her and he seemed powerless to do anything other than hold fast as she gazed at him in return. His face was now rapt with attention and his cold and distant attitude began to soften, becoming almost tender.

Moving his right hand to his chest, with his eyes riveted upon her, he proclaimed, 'A gift we have been given this day. How rare to see such light in one so small. Welcome her, all of you. Welcome this precious child.'

The crowd was abuzz with talk and exclamation. 'This is a girl-child; what is the High Priest saying?' said a man at the front of the square and further back a women whispered, 'I saw a light surrounding her head, I knew she was different.' Someone close by replied, 'What does it mean? Has he gone mad?' There was near cacophony throughout the square when suddenly the Priest's voice boomed out as he asked the Mother, 'What name is given?'

The Mother slowly drew close to him and whispered the name into his ear.

'Aptly chosen, truly true,' he exclaimed. Holding out his arms he gestured for the Mother to place her child within them. Again, the villagers gasped and the hearts of the two women began to pound within their breasts. This had never happened before. Girl-children were not touched by the Priests; for they would hold only sons as they lifted them heavenward, announcing their names for all to hear.

As if reading their minds, the Priest bellowed forth, 'A purity exists in her. Within her eyes I have seen light as never before. Today we join together in celebrating this miracle, this life.' And with those words the Priest motioned again for the child to be handed over to him.

Slowly the Mother lowered her basket to the ground, gathered her daughter and surrendered her into the arms of the High Priest. Looking down at the child, he stared at the mysterious beauty of her crystal-blue gaze and then in a loud, clear voice he prayed; 'Father of power and might, Maker of all that is good and perfect in our world, we gather here to bring before you another of your children, formed by you, for your glory and service. Today we present, in supplication, your own. Receive her now.' He then placed both hands beneath her tiny body and lifted her high above his head saying, 'We name you…'

Suddenly he screamed.

With an agonized guttural tone he cried out, 'No. No. You are no child of the Almighty,' and dropped her from his grasp nearly eight lengths in the air. She fell to the ground with a sickening thud as a horrified gasp came from the crowd. 'She is maimed. She is imperfect!' he bellowed forth. 'Something evil has here transpired.'

Rainbow cloak was torn from her body, rowan buttons ripped from the fabric. The violence of this action rolled the baby on to her stomach leaving her little face pressed into the earth beneath her. But she made no sound.

'There, there it is,' shouted the Priest. 'There is the sign of the sin.' Necks craned to see what the Priest was pointing at. Those nearer the front of the crowd began to scream; a woman fainted, and murmurings began anew as the evidence became clear. Visible to all, on the left side of the baby was the lumpy mass of pink flesh, which had an odd grey pastiness within its slight indentations. The entire deformity pulsated. All were frozen in horror. All were silenced.

It was the Father's voice, demanding retribution, which eventually fractured the eerie quiet. 'Kill them all,' came his blood-lusty cry. 'Kill them all and remove this evil from amongst us.' His voice freed the tongues of the others gathered together, 'They must perish,' they shouted. 'Burn them,' came the cries of the villagers, their words clouding the sunny day with fear and hatred.

In the midst of the chaos, the Priest, as though driven by a force greater than himself, rolled her body over with the pointed toe of his boot. This simple act allowed their eyes to meet once more. She looked up, without a whimper, and gazed into the deepest part of him. Upon seeing her face once more, his visage grew soft and open and great tears began to well up within his eyes. Until, at last, he could contain them no more, and his great sorrow began to stream down his cheeks, silencing the vicious cries of the mob. All eyes were upon him, but his were only for the child.

After what seemed an age, the Priest garnered his strength and forced himself to look away from the infant, who lay nearly naked upon the earth before him. In tones no stronger than a whisper, he said to all who observed;

'Sin has been committed here. They must be punished.' He did not look at the baby again but instead turned his focus to Mother and Midwife, as a cool indifference returned to his eyes. 'You two hags have conspired to deceive this holy congregation. Since you made this decision with such seeming ease, you shall have the opportunity to make another. Decide between yourselves whose worthless life will end in a blaze of fire, in this place, at this time, on the morrow, whilst the other two bear witness to her shame.'

Turning to the villagers, in his most pious tone, he said, 'One of these will pay homage to the Almighty in the form of her death tomorrow morning, here in this square, beneath the dark, tormented shadow of The Mountain of Remembrance. Every citizen is commanded to attend and when the screams for mercy and pity come forth from the flames of judgement she has created for herself, each of you will be reminded that the only punishment for wilful disobedience against the Law of the Almighty is death.'

At this he sneered, and with his hand he gestured that those congregated should create a pathway enabling the Father and himself to pass through. They began to walk, when suddenly the Priest turned to address the women one last time, 'Do not attempt to escape. Your cottage will be guarded throughout the night. If anything unusual occurs, if any is not present upon the morrow, it will result in the death of all three. You shall have no chance to run. You shall find no place to hide.'

The Father cast a final look of disdain upon the two women and spat upon the face of his naked child before following the Priest, who was, by now, making his way through the crowd with great haste. Heads shook and tongues clucked as they exited the square.

When the Priest and the Father had gone, all others did likewise. Not a single person came forth to offer comfort or support. Within moments the village square was abandoned, as were Midwife, Mother and child. In silence, they lifted the baby from the ground, wiped the spittle from her face, covered her exposed flesh with her rainbow cloak and placed her once more inside the basket. As the three began the walk back to their little cottage, curtains twitched, shutters banged and doors were closed as they passed by. They were no longer welcome.

27

The short walk seemed to take forever. Once home, free to converse, the Mother spoke first, 'It has happened; it is my worst nightmare come into being.'

'Why, then? We are safely held,' replied the Midwife, 'for this was what I most hoped would occur.'

'Hoped? Hoped for this?' exclaimed the Mother.

'Oh, yes. It is perfect in every way,' answered the Midwife.

'How could you think this perfect?' came the Mother's response.

'My dear child, the punishment is relegated to one, not three. Therein lay all blessing,' she explained with a sweet smile, exuding peace.

'Any death is too much to bear,' the Mother protested. 'The ceremony in the woods, your prayers, your petitions; they are all unanswered, all for naught.'

'Oh, no. No, that is not true. My prayers have been completely met; answered by Creator beyond wildest imagining. Tears came to the eyes of the Priest just as I had asked. He saw only the light within her, the magnificence of her creation. Every person gathered there today saw this. Even now, he could not deny what he bore witness to with his own eyes. It is thus reflected in his judgment. His decision was that one should be killed. In this, the other two are spared. Do you not see?' she asked.

The Mother looked upon the older woman, with her silvery hair and piercing green eyes, and said, 'I must confess I am unwilling to die. My daughter occupies all of my heart and my desire is to remain near her, to love and guide and protect her as best I can.'

'Of course it is, dearest soul. It could be no other way. I have no children of my own and feel my purpose upon this earth has been fulfilled in the birth of this child. She has re-awakened my heart, long grown numb, and reminded me of a path I travelled years ago, but had abandoned as the Priests and the Law grew in strength. I permitted fear and silence to govern my destiny. This child, with her bright eyes and gentle spirit, has brought me home to myself once more. Allow me to die, in order that you both might live. I have no doubt that my earthly ending is, in truth, only the beginning.'

The two women embraced and so it was agreed.

THE SACRIFICE

D awn arrived much as it had the day before with robin's song, blue sky, and bright warming sunshine. Breakfast was prepared and eaten, baby fed, dishes cleared, washed and put away. Memories of all that had occurred since the little one's birth occupied each of the women's thoughts.

Rather than the rainbow garment, the baby was clothed in a plain muslin cape and the Mother wore a dark brown dress and placed a scarf on her head. The Midwife chose a hooded robe of deep violet, a finely woven linen skirt and a blouse of purest white.

When they were nearly ready the Midwife said, with a sense of urgency, 'I feel the child needs her name given this day, before all else.'

'Yes, oh yes,' whispered the Mother.

The Midwife reached for the little one and lifting her into the air, much in the same manner as the High Priest had done, she said:

We welcome you, oh tender child
To this, your life on earth.
We give great thanks to all of Heav́in
For your most precious birth.

Within your eyes a fearsome light
Breaks forth with 'naught but love.
Reminding those who gaze on you
That all are from above.

Go forth, proclaiming what you know.
Hold fast amidst the storm.
Your journey here will far exceed
The limits of your form.

And so, we raise you heavenward,
Rejoicing in your name.
Sweet Gabriella, brightly shine,
'Til all the world's aflame.

Gabriella, how precious the name sounded when spoken aloud; Gabriella, how precious the child. All was still, all at peace, until the bell began to toll. Tears came to each woman's eyes as they gazed upon one another. How cruel it seemed to have to say farewell. Embracing one last time proved difficult, as neither seemed willing to release the other. In the end, it was the Midwife whose immense love summoned the strength to do so. She held the Mother at arm's length and said, 'It is time.'

She pulled the amethyst hood on to the crown of her head, its vibrant colour contrasting richly with her glistening, silver tresses. Taking up the hazel wood rod, the old woman opened the door for the Mother and Gabriella, who was once more being carried in the basket made of black ash. When the two had left the cottage, the Midwife paused to place a large pouch, made of the rainbow fabric, upon the table, alongside the hearth. Touching it with outstretched hand, her lips created the shapes of unvoiced words, as though in silent prayer. When she finished, she joined Mother and child, closing the door behind her and the three began their unbearable walk into the village, the Midwife leading the way.

As they rounded the final curve of the path, before they reached the road that would lead them to the square, the Midwife turned to the Mother and said, 'I have left a gift for you upon the table, near the hearth. Know this, now and always. You are loved, and all life is everlasting, filled with gifts beyond our comprehending. In these truths, give thanks, unceasingly, every moment, of every day.' Without waiting for a reply, she turned her face towards the town and continued to walk.

They heard the villagers before they saw them. Sounds of hatred, mixing oddly with glee, filled the air. As they approached the masses, a hail of rotten fruits and vegetables came at them. Each step was punctuated with abusive words and spittle. Animal dung was rubbed on to their clothes and their flesh. Humiliated, and nearly overwhelmed by the anger of the mob, the three were pushed and shoved as they tried to make their way towards the High Priest. Sometimes the women lost footing and were kicked as they struggled to stand up once more.

Half crawling, half walking, they arrived exhausted at the feet of the Priest, who was standing on a makeshift platform alongside the funeral pyre. He was clothed in a brilliant red robe, his vestments peacock blue, both of which were the handiwork of the Midwife. Beneath the great platform to his left were dry pieces of wood soaked in oil, on top of which was erected a stake, where the sinner was to be tightly bound. Around its circumference, men with black hooded masks held lit torches, awaiting the Priest's command.

'What have you decided?' he demanded.

'Take me,' said the Midwife removing her hood and raising her bright green eyes to look up directly into his.

He quickly looked away and declared to the people that the Midwife was a witch. 'Her evil hand defiled the child's flesh, causing it to wither in such a grotesque manner. Now she must die, an offering to the Almighty, who settles for naught but perfection.'

'Witch. Witch,' the people began to shout. 'Burn her. Burn her. Burn her. Burn her,' grew the chant from the bloodthirsty crowd.

Without hesitation, carrying the hazel wood rod in her right hand, the Midwife began to climb the precarious pile of sticks. She lost her footing often and tumbled more than once to the bottom, only to be forced to begin her climb once more as the violent mob hurled pebbles and rocks the size of angry fists at her, inflicting pain upon the old woman, over and over again. Dazed, the Midwife struggled to make her way to the top of the pyre. Streams of deep red trickled down her brow on to her breast, her life-blood leaving its crimson mark upon her garment of purest white.

When at last she arrived at the top, she wiped the blood from her face with the back of her left hand and took a last and lingering look at Gabriella. The child was focused completely upon her and in the light of the little one's eyes the Midwife drew strength, the rage of those gathered in the square becoming nothing more than a distant drone to her.

The Priest gestured to the crowd to cease the throwing of rocks as two of the hooded men made their way up the pyre in order to bind the Midwife to the stake. As they began their ascent, the Midwife held out her arm and proclaimed, 'There is no need to bind me. I shall not move from here.' She touched her chest with the hand holding the hazel wood, and then extended both arms before her, hazel wood rod resting upon her upturned palms, as if in silent offering. When this was done, her gaze returned to Gabriella. And she felt nothing but love.

The Priest seemed taken aback by the strength of her voice and her lack of fear. He followed her gaze until his eyes, too, rested upon the child. Again, as had happened the day before, his visage softened and for a moment it seemed as though his tears might begin anew. But he forced his eyes away from the baby to focus, instead, on the Midwife.

He sneered at the bony figure of the silver-haired old woman in her bloodstained garments.

'We shall see, ugly hag. We shall see you writhe in the agony of the eternal flames that shall forever surround your wretchedness. There will be no escaping the wrath you now shall know.'

And then, following a single gesture of his hand, the hooded men lowered their torches. Flames touched the oil-soaked logs, the smell of burning wood permeated the morning air and smoke began to rise.

But this smoke rose in no ordinary manner. Rather than dispersing into the sky, the smoke gathered together, creating a sort of coiling haze just below the Midwife's body. Once there, it began to swirl with the force of a cyclone. 'You see,' he said to the crowd, 'bear witness. She is a witch. This is the dark cover of the Evil One coming to carry her once more to the depths of His torment,' cried the Priest, but few heard his words of judgment, for his sonorous tone was muffled by the roar of the billowing cloud of smoke.

Far overhead, ominous thunderheads began to form above the Midwife; lightning slashed at the horizon, ripping through the blackness like knives. As the intensity of the flames and the thick swirling smoke rose higher and higher, the villagers grew quiet and fearful. But the Midwife remained serene, even as the flames, nearing the top of the pyre, clawed at her feet.

Suddenly, from the depths of the immense cloud directly above the Midwife's head, came an unearthly scream and out of the raging storm appeared an enormous grey owl, its talons outstretched towards the Midwife. Swooping down, it landed on her at the very moment the smoke and flames engulfed them both.

Seconds later, with a great flapping of wings, the owl ascended from the cloud of smoke, hazel wood rod held firmly in its grip. It flew higher and higher, over the rooftops of the houses in the Land of Never Forgetting, across the River of Dreams and was last seen scaling the heights of the Mountain of Remembrance.

The cloud, once charcoal grey, became a hideous black and rain began to pelt down. Instinctively, the people covered their heads, but it was unnecessary, for the downpour fell only on the funeral pyre. Within seconds, the fire was extinguished; the embers sizzled and sparked until a great gust of wind arose, clearing the smoke. And when the wind settled down at last, no trace of Midwife or flame remained.

In silence, the townsfolk and the Father left the square, casting wary glances in the direction of the Mother and the odd child she was cradling. So intent was their gaze upon the two, that few noticed the shape of the

High Priest, his once regal form now collapsed in a heap at the base of the pyre, his forehead pressed to the earth beneath him. The few that did mark his presence, assumed he was deep in prayer and continued on their way with haste.

Something inexplicable had happened this day. All had born witness and each, in their own way, vowed never to speak of it again.

The Escape

In the few days immediately following the death of the Midwife, all was quiet, perhaps too quiet. The grief of the Mother weighed heavily upon her and Gabriella, too, seemed filled with sadness, her once nearly constant giggles replaced with only silence, or an occasional cry to communicate a need. In these moments of her child's expression the Mother was reminded that although the Midwife was no longer with her, Gabriella was. Gabriella was alive. And this she knew, her daughter's safety, was the great gift of the Midwife's sacrifice and in that knowledge she began to find comfort.

As if reflecting the lightening of her spirit, Spring, little by little, found its way into their cottage, the brooding mornings and quickly fading light of wintry afternoons giving way to brighter sunshine. On the days there was rain, it was soft and gently prompted the barren earth to bring forth not only primroses, but snowdrops as well. Tiny green leaves, just barely visible, hinted at the later arrival of lilies of the valley and foxgloves. All the plants were beginning to push their way from the dark earth, towards the sky, towards blossoming.

On one particularly magical morning when birdsong filled the air with sweetly sung melody and the sun shone so brightly it caused the dew to glisten like diamonds, the Mother knew she could no longer remain indoors. She simply had to go outside, into the air, into the day. Beyond her desire to stretch her body and feel the fresh morning, the Mother needed things from the market, and she knew, as they would certainly not find their way to her, she would have to go and get them. Although the moon had completed two full cycles since the Naming Day, the Mother did not relish the prospect of a visit to the village. Still, it had to be done.

Not wanting to draw too much attention to herself or her child, she dressed in a pale brown blouse and skirt and tied a scarf of matching fabric over her golden curls and began to prepare Gabriella for their outing. For her child, she chose the plain muslin garment designed by the midwife, knowing the rainbow-coloured fabric would be immediately recognized. When satisfied she had disguised them as best she could, she placed Gabriella in the basket of black ash and walked to the market.

Her heart was racing, but she encouraged herself to keep going. *I have been forgiven; the High Priest has accepted the sacrifice of the Midwife as payment for our deception. I have nothing to hide. I have nothing to fear.* She repeated these words over and over to herself as she walked along the path into the village. As she drew near the edge of the green, her inner thoughts were met by outer sounds and it readily became clear that they had been recognized almost immediately. They were greeted with hisses and the clucking of tongues, the abrupt banging of doors and sudden silencing of conversations, in mid-sentence. Some people even spoke aloud to her saying, 'You are not wanted here.'

'Evil woman, friend of the witch,' the Mother heard them say, but continued walking. *I have no need to be frightened, they can say things, but their words cannot kill Gabriella or me. The High Priest's proclamation on her Naming Day will ensure that. We are safe.* Head high, her precious child held closely to her, she continued to make her way to the market.

Once there, the Mother found no one would look at her, no one had a word for her, and most certainly, no one offered to trade with her. She went from cart to cart and at each, she was met with downcast eyes or hostile stares. At the last of the carts there was a craggy-faced woman selling dairy products. She, unlike all the others, took pity on the Mother and handed her a sizeable lump of hard cheese saying, 'I will take nothing for it, as I want nothing from your hand. But have it and stay away from this town and all of us. You and your child are no longer welcome here.' Her ancient, raspy voice was loud enough to be heard by all those gathered in the market and there was no disputing the finality in her tone, the abruptness of her words.

The Mother took the cheese from her and thanked her for her kindness as hot tears began welling up. Determined not to allow anyone to see her in this manner, the Mother placed the cheese in her basket, alongside Gabriella, squared her shoulders and made her way back through the village. Once she knew she could no longer be seen, her grief flowed in great floods. *I have done nothing wrong. I have given birth to a beautiful little girl-child, who has the misfortune of being born without an arm. This was nothing of my doing, nothing of the Midwife's doing, no reflection of Gabriella's nature. How can other people not see the truth in this? How can they not see her beauty? How can they be so blind?*

As her thoughts raced, she picked up the pace of her steps and found herself at her cottage in very little time. As she turned up the path, which led directly to her home, she had to catch her breath, for the door was ajar. She was quite certain she had closed it behind her, but it was now definitely open. She slowed her steps and approached, calling out, 'Hello. Hello. Is someone here?' But there was no answer. She paused to listen and, hearing nothing, moved closer still. Although she saw only the door out of place, the Mother had a growing sense of sickness in the pit of her stomach. She knew all was not right.

Standing directly outside the cottage, she looked through the window and saw, to her horror, the devastation within the walls where once she had felt a modicum of safety. Racing to the door, she pushed it open. Only then did she fully see the violence that had been wrought upon them. Most dishes were broken into little pieces, all cooking pans had been taken from her, the stools had been smashed, the bedclothes, save two blankets, ripped to shreds, her clothing had been cut into strips with a knife and Gabriella's rainbow garment was torn into small pieces with such aggression that it left the Mother fearing for their very lives. *Who would do such a thing? Why would anyone do this?*

She doubled over in pain as though kicked in the stomach, feeling the wind had been knocked out of her. Head reeling, feeling faint, she forced herself to take a drink of water and its gentle coolness refreshed her slightly. Taking a torn piece of skirt, she dipped the fabric into the water and wrung the excess out, then placed the cool compress on her neck, her wrists, her forehead. This she repeated a number of times until the dizziness left her and her strength began to slowly return. With little choice she began to clean up the rubble of her belongings, now mostly useless. She fought against feelings of terror and concentrated on removing from her sight the ugliness that hate had created. Behind the cottage, she piled all the broken pottery and furniture, salvaging what she could as she discarded the items that would no longer be of use.

As she placed the final piece of what had been the indigo hood of Gabriella's Naming Day garment on top of the mound, she remembered the final gift of the Midwife to her and ran inside to see if it was safe. There, buried under the oats at the bottom of the grain barrel was the rainbow parcel, untouched, just as she had left it.

Why she had thought to hide it was now even more compelling. Seven days following the Midwife's death, the Mother had received very clear instructions, from within her own spirit, to keep the pouch safe from sight and this had been the safest place she could imagine. *How grateful I am to have followed those feelings* she mused in the growing shadows of the day, hiding the pouch once more in the depths of the barrel.

Oddly, their food had not been touched. Whoever ransacked her property left all that was consumable, destroying only what little comforts she owned, again reminding her, in an altogether different and much more obvious way, that she was reviled.

After that day, afraid to leave the cottage for fear of what might happen in her absence, the Mother and Gabriella never ventured further than the tiny patch of land in front of it. For a child still in a basket, not yet walking, it was nearly enough.

There were even occasions when the Mother, whilst playing with her child, observing her discovering her toes and lips, eyes and nose, watching her twist her strawberry-coloured curls around her tiny fingers while she was nursed, in these tender moments, she could almost forget her plight, utterly absorbed in the love she felt for Gabriella.

In a way, she found it a great relief to have her child, for the little one's demands were constant, almost predictable, and she, more often than not, could meet them. There could be no slipping into sorrow or feeling pity for her circumstances with Gabriella's spirit nearby. Her giggling curiosity and her beauty served to be a remedy for all that could easily have plagued the Mother.

Another full cycle of the moon passed in this manner and, save the dwindling supply of food, the Mother felt reasonably secure once more. It would not be possible to live another winter without food, but it was not yet even summer and she did not have to worry about that quite yet. Time had a way of healing things, she knew, and perhaps it would help heal her situation as well.

But it was not meant to be; for the events surrounding the death of the Midwife had fast become the stuff of whispers, the seeds of gossip had been sown and any hope the Mother had placed in the passage of time and the fading of memory was quickly lost.

For mysterious occurrences tend to gain intrigue in the minds of people who place high value on only those things that can be explained. And fear begets nothing but greater fear.

One night, when the sky was blackest black, no light of moon to pierce the darkness, the Mother heard sounds outside her cottage. She thought at first it was an animal, but after closer listening she recognized the sounds as human footsteps and from the occasional muffled whispers, she knew there was more than one of them.

As she lay in her bed, fairly holding her breath, she knew these were people who had chosen to come by cover of night, people who did not want to be seen.

The very thought made her pulse race and her mouth grow dry. She instinctively gathered Gabriella to herself and quickly tried to hide as best she could, choosing to wedge herself between the bed frame and the wall, opposite the window and door. Grabbing her two blankets from the bed, she lay trembling beneath them.

It was then that the assault began.

At first she could not make out the sound, a kind of small thudding against the outside of the cottage, and then the object making the sound made its way inside. With a great crash a large-sized stone smashed into the wall above her head and landed on top of the blankets covering them. *Let out a sound* she thought and out came a cry of pain, although she had felt none. As she lay on the floor, her daughter clutched to her breast, stone after stone was hurled into the cottage, aimed directly at the bed, exactly where she and Gabriella had been fast asleep only moments before.

With nearly every stone she released a moan and Gabriella began to cry in response to her Mother's seeming distress. As the Mother's false cries of pain diminished in intensity, so, too, the number of stones being thrown. After a short while, the Mother gently placed her hand over Gabriella's mouth to silence her and, making no further sound herself, as quickly as the onslaught had begun, it finished.

The Mother heard the muted whispers of men's voices and footsteps walking away from the cottage into the woods. She was trembling, her palms were clammy and Gabriella was clinging to her in fear, but she knew that she had outsmarted them. Her heart was still pounding and with each quickened beat she heard *Go! Go!* Her inner voice fairly screaming for her to stay no longer in this place.

It was clear to her that she and her child were not merely avoided, but despised. Killing the Midwife had not released Gabriella and herself from condemnation; theirs would be merely deaths of another sort.

Knowing this would never change, in the early hours of the morning of the longest day, the Mother began to pack. She placed as many of her earthly possessions as she could into long pieces of muslin. Bowls, cups, spoons, candles, flint and pyrite, her two woollen blankets, the rainbow pouch containing the Midwife's unopened gift and the remainder of her food; all of these she wrapped into two large satchels made from the torn cloths, which she strapped to her body.

Next she placed her child within a larger piece of cloth and fashioned a sort of fabric cradle, tying it firmly to her body as well. When she was quite certain that Gabriella was secure, the Mother picked up the black ash basket the Midwife had made for her and, looking more pack horse than woman, she left the only home she had ever known and never looked back, not even once.

Her journey took her into the evergreen glade behind the cottage, past the circles of white stones that marked the site of the pre-Naming Day ceremony and alongside a little brook that she had never followed before. On and on journeyed Mother and child, to a part of the forest, thick, not only with pine and hemlock, but deeply canopied with birch, elm and oak. Dazzling deep pink blossoms of the foxglove fairly glowed within the shadowy recesses of the dark woods and the gentle yellow of the primroses brightened what might have been gloomy undergrowth without them.

As she followed the babbling brook which by now had become a stream, its spluttering, splashing sounds brought a smile to her lips and the Mother found a peace she could not fully explain. Birdsong added winged melody to the gaiety of the water's dance and the sunlight, glimmering through the leaves upon the branches above her head, painted a picture of light and shadow upon the earth beneath her feet. Every breath felt fresh and full of moisture, full of life. All of these things conspired to encourage her and keep her on her path.

Although her circumstances had grown unbearable, the Mother felt she was not running away. She knew from her depths that, rather, she was moving towards something. From deep within her chest, somewhere behind the bone between her breasts, she had felt a growing urgency, a very insistent message, hastening her departure. The feeling had begun after her trip to the market and had each day following, grown increasingly strong, culminating in the harrowing experience of the previous night's attack. The constancy of it had demanded her response and now, walking in the quiet refuge of this ancient forest, she knew she had listened well.

The Mother did not mark how long she walked in this manner, or notice the changing terrain of the ground upon which she travelled. So deeply engrossed in her thoughts was she, that she never saw the trees beginning to thin, revealing a bright sunny sky above them. On she journeyed, lost in contemplation, oblivious of the steep incline of the land beneath her feet. Up a sharply graded hill and then across a meadow of buttercups and clover she continued, still mindful only of her inward journey.

With eyes looking mostly downward, at her feet, she appeared to be studying her every step but, in fact, she was focused on nothing at all and as a result, she was unaware of what truly lay ahead of her.

The day progressed in this way until the sun had risen past its highest position. Her climbing continued ever upward and the small stream she had followed from behind her cottage had grown much larger and now it coursed through a ravine far below her. The once green earth beneath her feet was fast becoming rocky and uneven. Of this, too, she saw nothing.

Nearing the highest point of her climb, the Mother's foot tripped on a large protruding stone and she was sent tumbling forwards. Instinctively she put both arms around Gabriella to protect her from harm. In so doing, she let go her grip upon the black ash basket and it went somersaulting through the air and disappeared out of sight. Startled from her reverie, the Mother, seeing that Gabriella was safe, brushed herself off and stood up.

Immediately, she fell back to her knees, staring, aghast, at what lay before her. No more than five steps away from where she knelt, the earth abruptly ended. She was perched on top of a high plateau, where, far far below lay a vast body of water and, just beyond that, a huge mountain. From the shape of its summit, the Mother recognized the Mountain of Remembrance, and although she had never seen it, she knew the water at its base had to be the River of Dreams.

Making sure she was a safe distance from the edge, the Mother stood up and looked back in the direction from whence she had come and saw that there was nothing visible of her little village. All she could see were the tops of the trees in the forest she had passed through. The light upon their leaves was a deepening gold and from its elongated angle she could tell she had travelled the whole of the day.

Turning back once more to face the imposing Mountain, the Mother found she could scarcely breathe. She had never imagined she would ever be so close to it; never dreamt it could be so beautiful. In the glow of the setting sun, its surfaces both reflected light and cast shadow simultaneously; the lingering sunbeams, like the chisel of a sculptor, carving an ever-emerging form.

Breaking her gaze upon the Mountain, the Mother gathered the few belongings scattered in her fall, save the ash basket woven by the Midwife. As she could not see it, she assumed it had fallen over the edge of the cliff. Too tired to explore any further, she found herself unable to move as she sat on the earth, eyes riveted once more, on the shape of the Mountain.

Behind her breastbone the familiar pounding began anew as the ancient story of the Mountain of Remembrance and the River of Dreams flooded her mind. The tale of the five who had drowned in the waters; the disappearance of all creatures from the Mountain; the winds that had howled and moaned and filled the sky with darkness; and then, the appointment of The Two, who had survived their ordeal, as the High Priests of the people. They had made new laws and codes of behaviour in order to purify the Land of Never Forgetting and their Law held fast to this day.

All these thoughts rushed forth from the deep recesses of her mind as she sat gazing up at the forbidden Mountain. These same men had instituted the laws that declared her child imperfect, unholy, not of the Almighty. And this was the same Law that had taken the life of her beautiful friend.

Lifting Gabriella up from the pouch of muslin she gave her suckle. And as she looked at her daughter, seeing her curls of red-blonde hair, her sky-blue eyes, feeling her skin, soft as summer rain, the Mother knew that this Law could not be the truth. As a woman, she had not been permitted to study the ways and teachings of the Almighty. Services of worship, centred on the writings contained within the Great Book, were forbidden to women, who, she had been taught, had no souls, had no minds to train.

What little she had learned had come in the form of Holy Laws to be obeyed while in service to men, who ruled in His name. Until the birth of Gabriella she had never had reason to question or doubt this authority. However, in the final splendorous moments of this, the longest day, she found herself doubting everything she knew.

Eating some of the cheese and bread she had carried with her, she sat quietly still, never averting her eyes from the Mountain. When she finished her food, she felt too weary to take another step. So, under a twilight sky, on a cliff-side high above the River of Dreams, she rocked her child in her arms, singing a lullaby the Midwife had sung:

Tiny little baby, time for sleep.
Not another sound now, not a peep.

May the twinkling stars within the skies,
Dance a gentle dance before your eyes.

Rest, oh precious child, in silv'ry dreams.
'Til the dawn returns with sunshine beams.

She sang the words over and over, perhaps as much to herself as to her child, until the stars, indeed, danced a gentle dance, coaxing them both to sleep.

THE BRIDGE

True to the verse of the lullaby, the dawn did return with sunshine beams. Having slept well, the Mother felt restored, if somewhat stiff and sore from the effort of her heavy-laden walking. She stretched her arms and legs and took great inhalations of the crisp dawn air into her lungs. All was fresh and clean, the smell of new beginnings.

The Mother first fed Gabriella and then herself and, now thirsty, wondered how she might obtain water. She could not go back, she could not go forward. *I cannot remain here,* the Mother thought. *I have come this far, there must be a way and I will find it.*

Picking up Gabriella, she decided to explore. First she walked to the edge of the cliff overlooking the River of Dreams and, careful to keep well back from the overhanging edge, she looked for any hint of a path or trail leading down to the shore below. Nothing. Traversing down to the shore of the River of Dreams on her own would be improbable and with Gabriella and all her possessions strapped upon her back, it would be impossible.

Moving from there to the edge of the plateau, which overlooked the ravine, she did likewise. Again, she saw nothing. Then, walking back upstream for a short distance, with the Mountain now directly behind her, the Mother saw something she had obviously missed in the twilight of the evening before. Two great poplars, leaves aquiver, stood on either side of the ravine, their trembling foliage fairly whispering in the breeze, *Come here. Look here,* they seemed to say.

Making her way cautiously to the tree on her side of the ravine, she could see that attached to the base of it was a rough-looking ladder of heather rope which tumbled over the steep edge into the depths below her. Cautiously peering down she saw that it became a bridge, which spanned the ravine in a most precarious-looking manner. On the far side, was another rope ladder, which traversed a steep wall of rock towards the second poplar tree to which it was tied. Beyond this, was the beginning of an obvious trail.

The pounding began again in the Mother's breast. This was the way. She knew it. *You must hurry. You must hurry,* a voice inside urged her.

It seemed as though the bridge was in a complete state of disrepair and the half logs that passed for stepping places looked as if they would break away with the slightest weight. But it was the only way forward for her. The very thought of attempting such a crossing made the Mother tremble with fear; she did not like heights: climbing trees or hills or anything high above ground had never appealed to her at all, but in this moment, her feelings seemed irrelevant.

She simply had to go on, for she remembered with a sudden jolt of panic that the High Priest frequently sent men to guard the River of Dreams and, if they had discovered her missing, rather than dead, they would not be far behind. There was no time for further delay.

Running to gather all of her belongings, she folded them, once more, into the fabric satchels and tied them upon her body. With Gabriella she did likewise and then raced back to the poplar. *Hurry. Hurry,* came the voice once more but the Mother did not want to hurry. She did not want to move. With all that she had strapped on her body she felt heavy and unbalanced and she could not imagine crossing a rickety bridge. She sat herself down and leaned against the trunk of the tree to quiet the argument within her own mind. Just as she did, she heard voices. This time they were not within herself, they were coming towards her and they were the voices of men.

She could not be discovered with her child so close to the Mountain and the River, it would mean the death of them both.

Without a thought of testing the strength of the rope ladder, the Mother walked briskly to the edge of the ravine, dropped to her knees, took hold of the ladder and began to climb down.

The first few steps were difficult as the ladder swung outwards to compensate for large overhanging rocks. Each time the Mother placed the fullness of her weight upon the rungs of heather rope, bits of earth dislodged and tumbled to the depths below.

She began to panic; her breath grew shallow and irregular, she felt dizzy and sweat poured profusely from her brow and her palms, causing her to nearly lose her grip with every step. As she wiped them dry, one at a time, on her skirt, she tried to remain composed by counting her steps. *One, two, three, four,* she silently counted until she reached *twenty*.

It was on the next step down that her foot touched something much more solid and she let her arms unbend just a little further from the rung she was holding, to test that it was sure footing beneath her. To her relief she found it to be a small ledge. She knew she could now let go of the rope and rest, but just as she was about to do so, she heard the men's voices once more, much closer this time. So close, she could recognize them. They were the voices of the eldest son of the High Priest, the Father and one of the High Priest's guards.

'She could not have come too far. She is but an ignorant woman with a deformed child. Where could they possibly hide?' said the Father.

'I am not sure of that. I am certain only that we will find them and fully rid our land of the evil contained within them. I knew they would eventually flee and so they have. I cannot imagine why they should have left in such a hurry,' answered the eldest son of the High Priest, in a tone of mock innocence, which elicited laughter from the other two.

'This is the evidence we have been hoping for since the day the hag-witch was burned on the pyre,' he continued. 'When we find them, these two will be soon reunited with their sister in the eternal darkness of the Evil One and purity in our Land shall be restored.'

The men laughed with such hollow empty tones it caused gooseflesh to rise upon the Mother's skin. As she pressed her form tightly against the embankment in a desperate effort to make herself less visible, her heart pounded so loudly she was sure they would be able to hear it. She gripped the rope more and more tightly, until the knuckles of her hands became white with tension.

Gradually the voices of the men grew faint and for a moment she relaxed. Then a shout came from one of them, 'Over here.' She froze, *Have they seen me?* she wondered, clutching the heather ladder in desperation. Again came the cry, 'Over here.'

'Look what I see, there at the edge of the River of Dreams. Is that not the basket she carried the child in?' asked the guard. The other two affirmed that it was so and agreed that they should retrieve the basket as proof of their deaths for the High Priest, which they did.

'What a foolish woman,' came the voice of the son. 'It is now obvious that she reviled our Law in attempting to cross the River of Dreams. She has been punished for her disobedience, not only for this, but also for hiding a malformed child who should have been left to die. In her actions she has offended the Law of the Almighty.'

Their voices came closer to her once more and she heard the guard ask, 'Could she not have crossed the bridge of rope?' To which the son retorted, 'Few strong and able men manage that without plunging to their deaths. How could it be possible for a woman and her demon child to do so?'

His comrades agreed and as they joked about the watery fate of the Mother and Gabriella their voices gradually faded into the distance. *Have they not seen me?* she thought, trying to calm her breath. *Or are they above me even now, looking down, silently taunting me as they lay their snare? Am I, could I be, shielded from sight by the protruding rocks?*

She grasped the ladder more tightly still, terrified that the men were standing above her, waiting for her to make a single move.

And in this way the Mother remained, until well into the lateness of the day, when, at last, drenched with the damp of panic, and with every muscle in spasm under the weight she was shouldering, she could bear it no more and let go her grip with a deep moan. Her body crumpled into a heap upon the ledge below her and there, curled upon her side at the bottom of the ladder, at the beginning of the bridge, she at last looked up.

She could see nothing but a great outcropping of stone above her. In each direction she looked the stones blocked her view. *If I cannot see past them, they*

49

will not have seen us, she thought, resting in the knowledge. And so, there she remained.

Gabriella began to cry but her pitiful mewling was not heard, for all listening ceased as the Mother retreated to a place far inside herself, to a place where she could not be reached.

It was only when the sun was beginning to set that the Mother finally summoned forth a last vestige of courage, awakened by the persistence of her child. The voice of the little one was distressed and nearly hoarse with crying as the Mother's eyes finally opened to look down at her precious daughter. Compelled by love to try anew and realising that Gabriella's cries must not have been detected, the Mother thought they might be safe for the time being and so, after comforting her discontented child as best she could, she slowly stood up and faced the bridge.

Her head reeled as she studied the span before her. Although she had descended twenty-one steps, each a fair distance from the one preceding it, the Mother found she was still high above the water below. The log slats on the bridge itself were nearly as wide as two body lengths, but they had sizeable gaps between them. With no rope on the sides to guide or balance her, the bridge lay completely open to the depths below.

In the deep gorge, with the last remnants of the day's light fast fading, she knew she could not safely sleep on the tiny ledge she stood upon, nor could she risk detection on the morrow.

Yet, she could not bring herself to take a single step. From a hidden place, deep in her soul, came her own voice asking. *Help. Could someone please help us?*

Beginning at first like a whisper and growing louder with each moment, a great sound, like a mighty wind, began to take shape in the air above her head, startling the Mother, who looked to see from whence it came. A great owl had appeared with huge silver-grey wings that stretched wide across the sky. It had golden eyes, focused only on her, as it flew down towards the bridge from the poplar on the distant bank. The bird's magnificent strength and enormous size stirred something deep within the Mother, reminding her of the owl that had appeared at the Midwife's burning and on the night that Gabriella had been born.

Swooping close, the owl perched in the middle of the bridge, staring directly at her. When the Mother returned the gaze of the bird, it rotated its head to look upon the wall of the ravine directly behind it. It looked at the Mother and then, again, at the wall. Over and over the owl repeated this pattern, as if to tell her it was time to go. In the rapidly fading light the Mother knew she could not make the crossing in any form of darkness and seemed to falter once again.

As if sensing a growing urgency, the owl flew closer yet to the Mother, and without averting its gaze, it perched on the bridge, five logs away from her as though willing her to begin. Somehow in the comfort of the owl's presence the Mother found the courage to take a first step. It was not easy, for her weight caused the bridge to sway and bounce. With each subsequent step, the movement of the bridge increased and the further her distance from the wall of stone behind her, the greater the swaying of the bridge became. It took all of her concentration to steady her balance, calm her mind, and continue on; always, the owl remained before her with unwavering constancy.

Nearly half way, the Mother slipped on a moss-covered piece of wood. Instinctively she leaned to her left, her arms, rigid with fear, clutching at the air as she tried to regain her balance. She managed, somehow, to remain upright; but, again, her body froze and would not move.

She was terrified.

The owl flew close once more and its insistence seemed to spark a light inside the Mother, *She gave her life so that my child and I could live. I must not stop. I must take these steps for her sake. I must honour her.*

Eyes fast upon the winged creature, she walked slowly, and carefully, the rest of the way to safety. Arriving at the far side of the bridge, the owl did not pause but instead quickly began to climb the steps of the ladder above her, one at a time, as if to set an example for the Mother. *Count. Count once more*, the Mother thought to herself. Guessing the number to be the same as before, she began, *one, two, three* and so on until she reached *twenty-one*. There at the top of the ladder was another pair of strong ropes, lashed to the trunk of the second poplar tree.

With great relief, she pulled herself up until her entire body was resting on solid ground. Crawling upon all fours the Mother made her way to the tree and there beneath it, she gently untied Gabriella and all the other bundles from her body. Holding her child tenderly she rocked back and forth, as tears of relief trickled down her face.

She had done it. She had crossed over.

With her eyes now accustomed to the gloaming, the Mother could see that the path, leading away from the poplar tree, travelled down a small hill, at the foot of which was a freshwater pool. With wobbly legs and nearly overwhelming exhaustion, she made her way towards it, knelt down at its edge and, cupping her hands, drank her fill. Taking off her boots, she put her blistered feet into the welcoming coolness of the water and she found herself feeling revived and refreshed enough to nurse her hungry child. Later, when both were satiated, the Mother carried Gabriella up the little knoll to the great poplar where, beneath the quiet whispers of a gentle breeze playing upon its leaves, the two fell deeply asleep as the owl, perched high above them, kept a silent vigil.

THE COTTAGE IN THE WOODS

After a long and dreamless sleep the Mother woke to the golden melody of a thrush, which was perched exactly where the owl had been the night before.

The brilliant song of the winged messenger heralded the dawn, giving the Mother ample time to gather her things together once more and prepare for her continued journey, but she found herself strangely unwilling to move. She felt she had done enough carting and carrying, forcing her tired body towards an unknown goal. However, as she looked back to the other side of the ravine she had crossed, she could see how precarious her present location was.

Although the bridge had been difficult for her to traverse, men, unencumbered, would most certainly give chase if they caught sight of her. Having been presumed dead by the three men who had come looking the day before might give her a little more time, but she knew she could no longer remain visible to anyone on the opposite side of the ravine. With new determination and the slightest sense of hope, she tied her belongings and Gabriella to herself once more and began to walk.

She noticed almost immediately how different the soil was beneath her feet. It was dark, nearly black and filled with moisture. In the Land, the earth was more the colour of clay pots, sandy and much drier. Other than that things seemed quite similar with oak, pine and chestnut trees and she recognized the familiar songs of birds she knew. As she walked on and on, out of the corner of her eye the huge facade of the Mountain remained constant against the horizon.

Pausing only to feed Gabriella, the Mother kept on her way. She did not know where she was heading but her feet seemed as if guided and when the sun reached its near highest point in the summer sky, the Mother saw before her a distinctive path. It was large and flat enough to allow carts, animals and people to traverse it with ease. As it was worn nearly smooth she suspected it was, indeed, used as a pathway for people in and out of a village, and at the very thought of other people, the Mother felt a growing wave of panic. She had spent so much time thinking of those behind her she had not given any thought to those who might be before her.

As the path widened and grew ever more defined, the Mother felt she had no option but to continue. *Perhaps things could be different here, on this side,* she thought. *Perhaps these people see things in a different way.* She took a deep breath and walked on.

In the far off distance she began to perceive the shapes of rounded roofs against rolling hills and a distinctive line of trees that most likely surrounded a village square. Her chest began to pound. She longed to walk towards it, to trust that all would be well, but as her heart raced, her feet slowed.

She could now just barely see the summit of the Mountain, as great trees on either side had begun to line the path. The once bright sky became cloudy, warmth and light turning to cool shade. She could see less and less clearly and lost all sense of direction in the growing darkness of the path. *I must find another way. There must be another way. Please help,* she muttered, to no one in particular.

Then, in that very instant a dark cloud, that had been covering the sun, shifted, allowing sunlight to pour through the branches of the treetops high above her. Two gigantic oak trees, warmed by this kiss of sunshine, cast their shadows directly to her left and her eyes traced their long bold shapes on the earth. There, as if simply waiting for her to discover it, was an overgrown, yet traversable, footpath.

As abruptly as it had been revealed, it seemed to vanish, as another cloud covered the sun. The Mother rushed closer to what she thought she had seen. There indeed, before her, was an overgrown trail leading away from the well-travelled path and into the forest. Stepping upon it, with Gabriella held closely to her, she began to walk more deeply into the woods. Blacker and blacker the way became as a deepening silence created a sense of unease within her.

And then, directly ahead of her, she saw a shaft of light piercing the gloom. In such darkness the tiny strip of sunshine was a bright beacon urging her on.

Suddenly, the forest was no longer dominating the sky and she found herself in a clearing completely surrounded by dense trees, which were thickly covered with lichen and moss. In the very centre was a tiny little cottage made from heather and daub, which had a thatched roof, also made of heather. The thatch was well worn and the whole place looked as though it had been abandoned for ages. There were large pieces of granite suspended from heather ropes that criss-crossed, forming a lattice shape along the steep angle of the roof.

These were still neatly in place anchoring what was left of the thatch. The roof itself was shaggy and overgrown, clearly now a favourite nesting place for birds. Two tiny windows bordered the entrance to the front and between them was a group of tightly bound heather twigs: the hurdle door. The Mother could see that its shape fitted perfectly within the doorframe. The little house looked neglected and unhappy for it.

'Hello,' the Mother called out. There was no reply.

Again, in a somewhat louder tone, she called, 'Hello, is anyone here?'

But no one answered. Quite slowly the Mother walked towards the house and arriving at the threshold, she lifted the hurdle door, shifting it to the right. With a great thrashing of wings, a small grey bird flew out, just missing her head, making her heart skip a beat.

'Oh me. Just a collared dove, nothing to be frightened of,' she said aloud, trying to calm her spirits.

Stepping through the door and into the cottage she found the air smelled damp and musty. Looking up towards the roof, the Mother could see nearly as much sky as thatch. There was a central fire pit but nothing had been burned in it for a very long time. Clearly, no one lived here any more.

Do I dare make it my own? she thought, for in her village, any passing wanderer, without recourse, was allowed to claim a deserted property.

Although she had never thought very well of the Law, or the people that made use of it, now, finding herself desperately in need of a home, the Law suddenly seemed a very sensible thing.

Looking around the small cottage she saw there was a large pot, with its stand, which could be set over the fire; a ladle; a knife with a sharpening stone; and a baking board made from clay. Tucked to one side, she could make out the remnants of a bed, with large logs cut and shaped to make a frame designed to contain soft and fragrant heather to cushion sleep, but its contents were now dry and brittle. In another of the corners was a large heather broom and next to it, a neatly stacked pile of dried peat for fuel.

There was clearly much to be done to make the little cottage habitable, but as she had only one goal, to create a new life for them both, this cottage seemed a gift from above.

Returning outside to the fresh air, they supped: Gabriella from her Mother's breast and the Mother from the small parcel that contained the remainder of her cheese and bread.

When she finished eating, the Mother began to explore behind the cottage. There, in the last hours of daylight, she found, to her delight, a well, with a large stick placed across the opening attached to a rope. Pulling heavily on the rope a bucket emerged from the depths, filled with clear sweet-smelling water. Using a roughly carved wooden ladle, which was tied to the side of the bucket, she drank and drank to quench her thirst.

Beyond the well, she noticed a patch of earth, which at some point had obviously been cultivated, but was now grown wild with nettle and weeds. Just beyond it, she saw a smaller structure that looked like a shack. When she looked inside she discovered a hand plough; a small axe with a slightly rusted blade; a linen sheet for broadcasting seed; large baskets for gathering turf; and, lastly, an unused spade.

It was as though all had been prepared, awaiting their arrival.

The Mother had never been much good at growing things. *How I wish I would have paid more attention to the Midwife and asked her more questions. She knew so much about all of these things,* she thought, feeling a growing sense of fatigue and despondency come upon her.

I need sleep, she thought, and decided that Gabriella and she would remain outside their newly-found home, away from its musty interior, beneath a ceiling of stars. Once again, wrapped in the woollen blankets she had carried so very far that day, the Mother and her child found rest.

When she awoke, aided by the bright light of a new day, the Mother inspected the inside of her cottage once more. There was blue clay for a floor, with a few flagstones placed in the heavier wear areas near the hearth and the hurdle door. Looking at the patchy roof, she knew that the obvious hole in the centre was designed to accommodate smoke and sparks from the fire, but she could now see clearly that the roof was in tatters. Much would have to be done to render it capable of withstanding the heavy rains of winter that could so easily flood the interior. *Still it is a roof over our heads and I shall make it a home,* she thought, while walking behind the cottage to look at the overgrown garden. *It will require immense work to prepare this ground.*

Seeing all that had to be done, the Mother felt nearly overwhelmed, but thinking she must begin somewhere, she decided to make the roof her priority. With that in mind, she walked to the small shed behind the cottage and collected the hatchet and the largest of the gathering baskets. Then, strapping Gabriella to her once more, the Mother followed the path behind the little house and went in search of heather, which she knew must be plentiful and not too far away. Within a few moments, the Mother found what she was looking for. Beneath a grove of chestnut, beech, holly, birch and hazel wood trees, there grew a profuse thicket of heather and broom.

Working steadily she lifted divots of heather from the earth and laid them in her basket. She chopped some of the taller bushes to make twigs that could be shaped with a knife into sharp pegs. With these, she could firmly secure the new divots into the existing thatch. And when her basket was nearly full, she paused to catch her breath. The sunlight, shining brightly through the leaves of the trees, created a flickering pattern on all it touched. It was exquisite.

Gathering all that she had collected, she walked back to the cottage and found herself beginning to doubt her decision, for she had simply no idea where to start. As a child she had often seen her Father thatching roofs and learned much from watching him, but she had never tried a hand at it. *How am I to begin? How will I even get on to the roof?* she thought. *How can I get on to the roof?* The Mother returned to the small shed behind the cottage and found, to her amazement, a ladder leaning against the far wall. She was sure she had not seen it the day before. How odd.

It was a rickety old thing: two longish pieces of wood with bits of log for rungs, held in place with carefully shaped heather root pegs. She dragged it to the front of the cottage with a smile on her face, untied Gabriella from the makeshift cradle of fabric, gave her a quick kiss and laid her gently upon the earth.

Remembering as best she could, she began by carefully lifting a number of the thin sods and placed them in long straight rows, so that they might more easily dry in the warm sunshine. And then, again to her amazement, and without delay, she knew exactly what to do next. Bottles: small tightly -bound bundles of heather twigs would have to be constructed. These she planned to tuck into the existing thatch at the wall-head, thereby creating a new covering of fresh heather. And lastly, using the knife she had found, she carved twigs into sharp pegs; with these she would secure the new divots.

After filling her pack with divots and tools she leant the wobbly ladder against the edge of the cottage and up she climbed. It was not nearly as frightening as she had thought it might be and, in fact, she felt no fear at all. Careful to check that the roof itself could hold her weight, she opened her pack and began to make the repairs in methodical fashion: lay the divot, place the peg, secure by tapping with the spade; lay the divot, place the peg, secure by tapping with the spade. Her method became rhythmical as the light grew longer in the sky and, later, when the sun had started to set, and she was climbing down the ladder for the last time that evening, she was proud of her accomplishment and felt rather clever, indeed.

Stepping through the hurdle door into the cottage, she looked up at her roof. The only light she could see was that entering through the centre hole above the hearth. She had repaired the roof and she had done it well, but as there was still a pervading smell of damp about the place, she decided that they would remain outside.

After she had nursed Gabriella, the Mother took a refreshing drink of cool water from the well and, as dusk turned to night, she could still feel a lingering warmth upon her sun-kissed face. It had been a satisfying day's work that deserved a good night's rest. And so it was the two of them slept once more under the stars.

FINDING FOOD FROM THE EARTH

With the dawning of another bright and sparkling day, the Mother fairly leapt from beneath her blanket, knowing there was so much yet to be done. Whilst the divots had all been placed correctly, there was still the matter of the bottles of heather to be secured. So, following the pattern established the day before, beginning at the right, moving always to the left, the Mother made her way along the fringes of thatch, tucking the small bundles of heather along the roofline to form the eaves. These she knew would carry any rainwater away from the walls, windows and door and keep the inside of her home dry and warm. Lifting the stone weights one by one, she tucked and tapped the bottles into place.

It was less arduous a task than the previous day's and she found, to her surprise, that she had completed it by midday. After returning the basket, hatchet and ladder to the shed, the Mother looked up at her newly-thatched roof and thought the cottage looked much improved for her care.

Now, it was time to work inside. Knowing that a fire in the central fireplace was essential to help alleviate the damp, the Mother found her pyrite, flint and birch bark and, using pieces of the dried heather bed for kindling, quickly managed to start a fire, which she stoked and prodded to life. Soon it was crackling merrily as she placed small pieces of dried turf upon the growing flames. It was not long before the interior of the little cottage was transformed by such warmth and cheer.

Picking up the broom, she swept every inch of the floor. She discovered two three-legged stools and a few extra dishes; pulled the remaining heather from the bed frame, added it to the fire, and decided she would gather more to make a new one. Her heart was filled with expectancy and confidence. She had never thought she would be capable of anything more than cooking, cleaning and perhaps birthing a child.

It was not long before the mere thought of cooking prompted grumblings in her stomach, loudly reminding her that she had eaten nothing for nearly a day. Walking out behind the cottage to the overgrown patch of earth, she hoped she might find something edible, but all she could see was a jumble of leaves and plant stems, nothing that looked remotely appetizing at all. With a growing sense of hunger, the Mother tried in vain to remember the Midwife's words of wisdom about plants and tubers but they seemed all too distant and vague in her memory. She simply had no idea what to do.

Mustering her strength, she strapped Gabriella to herself once more, picked up a small basket and decided to continue looking for as long as it would take. She walked into the gloom of the forest, past heather and broom, further and further along the path. There, as the trees began to thin, she happened upon a small brook and with a sense of amazement she spotted a host of raspberry bushes growing thickly along its banks.

With the warm afternoon sun flickering through the leaves, the bright red fruits beckoned to her like jewels and she fairly ran towards them, eagerly picking great handfuls. When she had eaten her fill, and saved some in her basket for later, she plunged her juice-stained hands into the babbling waters of the brook and drank until her thirst was quenched, the residue of her feast quickly vanishing in the cool, clear current.

The day had brought her all she needed. The earth had provided for her in a manner that filled her heart with gratitude and a profound sense of peace. She had sought and she had received.

Walking along the path, back to the little cottage, the Mother thought about this. *Is it possible to simply ask and truly receive?* As she pondered, the Mother realized she had been instructed all along to pray for her needs, but rather than trust that her prayers would be heard, or her needs met, she had grown up believing that she needed to behave in a certain manner in order for her prayers to be answered. In her mind she had come to equate perfect behaviour, in accordance with the Law, as set forth by the Priests, as the only hope of receiving favour from Almighty Father. Now, none of this made any sense.

I have protected my daughter from a Law I felt I had to defy, she thought. *Even though the Midwife sacrificed her life for this choice, I, myself, feel I am held safe in this decision. There was help in being hidden from the men and with the difficult crossing over the bridge; there is a cottage here in the woods with all that we could ask for; there is water when I thirst and now this bounty of ripe fruit has filled my stomach and given me strength. It is all to be partaken. All is gifted to me, freely given; I have earned none of it. I have broken the Law, yet I am not being punished. Rather, I am being blessed.*

Her thoughts faded and a sweet peace filled her mind as she arrived back at the cottage. It felt as though a new story was beginning within her, as though all she had been taught in the course of her living was somehow being transformed beyond recognition.

The Mother untied Gabriella from around her own body and held her closely. Gabriella, with her gentle, almost serene nature, had surprised and delighted her, these past few days especially. She had fussed and made her presence known only when hungry, uncomfortable or in need of attention. Other than for these, her little spirit had remained calm and still. 'What a miracle you are,' the Mother said to her child. Gabriella, sitting upon her Mother's lap, gazed into her eyes for a long while and then smiled a most dazzling smile. The two remained in this manner until the sun began to set.

Later, as they closed their eyes to welcome sleep the Mother whispered, 'If you can hear me, Creator, thank you for all you have done and are doing. Please help me with the garden, if you see fit.' And off to sleep they drifted.

During the night the Mother's sleep was interrupted. She found herself in the cottage, seated upon one of the three-legged stools. A knock upon the doorframe caused her to look up. There, standing at the threshold, was the Midwife. She looked stunning. A cape of vivid green, which matched the colour of her eyes, adorned her person and there seemed to be a bright light forming a circle around her body. Her silvery hair, long and silky, reaching down to her waist, caught the luminescence and her entire being seemed to shimmer.

'Is it you? Is it really you? asked the Mother, as tears of disbelief rolled down her cheeks.

The Midwife slowly nodded her head in affirmation.

'Come in. Come in, my friend. I thought I would never see you again,' gasped the Mother.

The two sat closely together and the Mother invited her to partake of the raspberries, as they were all she had to offer. When they had dined, the Midwife said, 'The season of berries is short. These will not be enough to keep you strong and healthy. Go past the place of the berries at the stream, until you find a stand of bulrushes. Take the flowering heads of these each day. Cut the roughest parts away and boil in a kettle of water, suspended above the flames. When the pod is soft to the touch of a knife, remove it and, holding it with a cloth to protect your fingers, cut the soft flesh of the pod from the core. That contained within, will provide you with sustenance.

'There is also another bounty you have missed that I shall tell you of. You can harvest the fiddlehead ferns that lie deep within the shade of the forest. Take only those which measure less than the length of your first finger, for they will be sweet and tender. Boil these in water and season with the new-growth leaves of wild leeks that can be found in the shade near the stream.' Standing up, she kissed the sleeping Gabriella upon her forehead and left abruptly.

The Mother called out to her, but the sound of her own voice merely woke her from a deep sleep. *It was only a dream*, she thought. And yet it had all been so real, she felt as if she could have truly touched the old woman's shining face with her hands.

In the soft half-light of early dawn, she saw only Gabriella close beside her. Picking her up to nurse, the Mother ate the last of the raspberries and planned to pick more, later in the day. In fact, as the season for berries was usually quite short, she decided she would harvest them every day for as long as she could.

The thought echoed the words the midwife had spoken in her dream and caused her to remember it in greater detail. As she had to find other food, she decided to explore further along the brook, as the Midwife had instructed. *It will do no harm to walk a little further along the path,* she thought, *and in any case I have little to lose in trying.*

When it was light enough to travel safely, the Mother and child set out once more and this time she saw hundreds of fiddlehead ferns growing freely within the woods. They had always been there, of course, but it was as if she was seeing them for the first time. *I will harvest these on my return,* she decided, as she continued on to the raspberry bushes. Eating only a few this time, she saved handfuls for later. Then, with only a moment's hesitation, and a slight degree of unease, she continued on her way, beside the brook, walking ever deeper into the forest.

As she followed the flowing water, the Mother noted that the brook had begun to angle quite sharply to the left and there, just beyond the bend, the Mother could see ahead of her a large area of marsh. And, just as the Midwife had foretold, it was thick with bulrushes. Walking carefully upon the boggy earth, mindful of where she placed her feet, she soon found she could easily reach the flower heads, which stood all about her, nodding in the breeze. Gripping the entire head of a bulrush with one hand, she held and twisted, until it snapped off in her palm. Placing the first into the basket she did so with four others. Giving thanks, she carefully made her way back across the marsh, causing waterfowl, and a host of small birds, to scold her and flurry away as she walked towards the brook.

In the deep shadows, alongside the bank, again as she had been instructed in the dream, the Mother spied wild leeks and, touching their long green leaves, she recognized their familiar smell. These too, she added to the basket. *How is this possible?* she thought as she began to walk back towards the cottage. She paused once more, to collect a number of fiddlehead ferns that she could see growing beneath a giant oak tree. Carefully she measured each new yellow-green growth and harvested only those no longer than the length of her first finger and when she had picked two large handfuls, she placed them alongside the wild leeks and headed for home.

As she prepared the bulrushes and started the fire, just as she had been instructed, she wondered if all of it was simply pure chance. Every time she tried to dismiss the events as happenstance, a voice from within her demanded that she see what had truly happened. By now, she was quite certain that the dream had come very specifically for her, and yet, she had no way of explaining how all that she had been told had come to be.

Having lived her life in a village where anything inexplicable was linked to evil, rather than good, she found the reality of her present circumstances difficult to embrace. *Perhaps it does not matter. Perhaps my only responsibility is to listen and to follow the instructions I receive,* she whispered to herself and, with an intensity that surprised her, the Mother made a vow to do just that.

When the water had begun to boil, the Mother placed the bulrush heads inside and then, after a few moments, when the outside coverings looked ready to burst; she removed them from the pot. Scraping the fleshy portion from the hard inner core, she tasted them and found them satisfying, rather nutty and with a texture that seemed like bread. Saving some for later, she placed the leeks and fiddleheads into the still boiling water and these softened quickly in the heat. She removed them both, tasted the spicy leaves of leek and the sweet, chewy fiddleheads and declared her feast delicious, having saved her raspberries as the perfect ending to her meal.

The entire banquet had been given to her by Creator; and, at least for now, the fruits of the wild had sustained her; and in turn her milk had sustained her child. 'Thank you,' the Mother said, not really knowing any longer to whom she spoke.

Now that food had been prepared, the cottage was beginning to lose its smell of damp and mildew. There was still much to do: heather would need to be gathered for a new bed, work still needed to be done. *Not today, though,* the Mother thought, smiling to herself, *not today.* Five bulrushes, a bowl of greens and a handful too many raspberries had filled the Mother completely. Her stomach had not been so contented in months and it was all she could do to keep her eyes open. So she walked outside to the front garden of her little cottage where, with her arms wrapped lovingly round her child, she slept.

Hours later, the Mother woke as the sky was beginning to darken. Once this would have frightened her, but no longer. *Night is simply the other side of day,* she thought, but strangely, in spite of the fact that she had rested most of the afternoon, she felt more wearied than ever. It was as though the months of fear and sorrow had at last begun to unwind from a place deep inside of her. She stayed awake just long enough to feed Gabriella and rinse the dishes she had used for cooking and eating.

This was all she could do before she fell back asleep beneath the stars and her warm woollen blanket.

Again, on this night, her sleep was interrupted by the Midwife, appearing in a dream. Dressed as before, all emerald and glowing, she praised the Mother for listening well and then instructed her further. Firstly, she was to make the heather bed, as she and Gabriella would need shelter soon.

'Rains, mighty ones, are coming, but you must not worry,' the Midwife said with a loving smile. 'These rains will soften the earth behind the cottage and allow you to make furrows in the soil. Stubborn weeds will be more easily removed, preparing the way for things to grow beyond your wildest imaginings.'

Secondly, she was to take the largest of the baskets to the places she had harvested in the woods and gather enough food for five days.

'This will be plenty of provision,' said the Midwife. And lastly, 'Two buckets of water should be drawn from the well. Fill the kettle and fill two bowls. Within one bowl place the fiddleheads and leeks; with only a small covering of water, this will keep them fresh from day to day. The second is for your own drinking needs. Start your fire upon your return from gathering the heather for the bed. Place the kettle above it, even if you are not cooking. For the circle of sky within your thatch will allow rain to pour into the kettle; but the kettle shall protect the flames from extinguishing. Have no fear, for the water from the kettle will never overflow.

'Be at peace now. All is well.' And, just as she had done the previous night, the Midwife left abruptly with a single kiss for Gabriella and not another word.

W aking early the next day the Mother knew, before opening her eyes, that the sky would be cloudy. The intensity of the Midwife's presence in her dreams, coupled with the events of the previous day, made any doubt impossible. Quickly she fed Gabriella and gathered the tools she would need to harvest the heather for their bed. With child strapped to her side and all the baskets hooked over her arms she walked to the heather as quickly as she could Once there she cut the plants, nearly at the base of the stem, dozens of them, until her baskets were filled and then returned home, but what she had gathered was enough for only part of the bed, as the upper portions of the heather were still young and not quite bushy. Back she went and repeated the process again, all the while the clouds darkening above her.

When she had finally emptied the second lot of heather on to the cottage floor she did not pause. Food had to be gathered, and quickly, from the look of the brooding skies. Walking past the heather and broom, clutching the largest of the baskets, she began to run for the marsh of bulrushes, where she spared no time plucking the heads of the plants from their spiky stems. The Midwife had told her to gather enough for five days of provision. Thinking that five heads been quite filling, the Mother snapped off twenty-five of the puffy brown ovals and placed them in her basket.

Passing the stream on the way back to the cottage, she picked all the raspberries that could be easily reached and quickly went to the wild leeks, adding their spicy new leaves to her basket. Lastly, in the growing darkness of the forest, she harvested enough finger-length fiddleheads for five days and with her basket piled high, she raced home to the cottage.

What else? the Mother asked herself. *I know there is something else. Water, you need water,* came her answer. Firstly, she carried the kettle to the well and filled it as she had been instructed and then did likewise with the two bowls.

She placed the kettle on the stand above the fire, directly beneath the roof's opening, and put the greens into one of the bowls. She had done it. All that she had been told by the Midwife, she had accomplished.

Pausing for a moment she noticed that there was now an eerie silence all around the cottage. There was no birdsong, no buzzing of insects, no wind. There were no sounds at all and although it was only midday, the sky wore the cloak of night. Glancing at the corner of the cottage, the Mother felt grateful there was a stack of turf large enough to sustain a fire for five days, and knew there was still more in the shed, if needed. She busied herself with pyrite, flint and the making of the fire. Soon it was crackling and the cottage felt cosy and warm; but above her, the ominous sky weighed heavily. Discomfort and unease began to plague the Mother's heart. All was ready. She had been told to have no fear and yet she did. Deep within, she felt little but terror.

What else? What else can I do? she thought, forcing herself to action. 'I'll make the bed,' she declared out loud. And thus the Mother put her frightening thoughts at bay by occupying herself with a task: she shaped the heather to a uniform length and packed it into the frame, piece by piece, flower side up. Once the heather was in place, she arranged the two woollen blankets upon it and, as she straightened from her task and secured the hurdle door, the heavens opened, casting a torrent of rain down from the skies. These were no ordinary rains. These were like none the Mother had ever seen. This was a deluge.

Sheets of rain pummelled the cottage and the leaves on the trees added to the tumult with a loud percussive thrumming. Even though the Midwife had told her in the dream that it would happen in this manner, the Mother found herself gasping in disbelief at the intensity of it all. Hour after hour the drenching rains continued. To her amazement, just as the Midwife had predicted, the kettle protected the fire and contained all the rain that fell through the hole in the middle of the roof. *By now it should have overflowed again and again,* she thought.

After she fed Gabriella, the Mother prepared a meal for herself. As it was so dark inside the little cottage she decided, for the first time since she had arrived, to light one of the candles she had carried with her. The glow of its gentle flickering light added to the glow of the fire, and together they cast a golden hue on all that was inside the little cottage. They were safe and dry, and once again, in responding to the wisdom contained within the gift of the dreams, the two of them had been provided for.

'Thank you, Creator. Thank you for the rain and for leading me in preparation for it. Hold us closely this night and help me know the way,' the Mother said out loud. And with a single breath, she extinguished the candle, placed another piece of turf on the fire and curled upon the newly-made bed with her child. The torrential rains continued, creating a sort of watery lullaby and within moments the Mother was asleep, Gabriella fast by her side, smiling, eyes wide open.

It was as though no time had passed and when the Mother awoke, nothing had changed. *How odd to have the sky remain exactly the same shade of all pervading blackness,* she thought as the rain continued to pour down. It seemed Heaven itself was weeping upon the earth below. On and on it continued with no lull, no lessening, no variation.

With neither sun nor moon to guide her, the Mother lost all sense of day and night. At first, she felt alarmed and invented various means of attempting to mark the time. One turf log burned for so long; walking the length of the cottage and back twenty times took a little less; chewing each portion of food fifty times, even less than that.

But after numerous efforts, she realized she had no greater sense of the actual time than when she had begun and it occurred to her that measuring time was perhaps only her attempt to feel she had control. In fact, the truth was quite the opposite; she was in control of nothing, save what she did in each moment. In preparation for these rains she had been given counsel and she had followed it. Although her actions had prepared her for the storm, nothing she could do would stop it or influence its severity.

As the terror of losing control began to leave her, something new came in its stead. A gentle sense of tranquillity and wellbeing began to flow into the deeply hidden places where her tightly-coiled energies had been held.

Gradually her need to accomplish tasks, to follow prescribed rules, to avoid her inner disquiet, was replaced by a stillness in her mind that was deafening. It was as if the rains, which were softening the earth outside, had also began to soften those places in her that had grown hard and calloused in response to all that had happened in her life. Gradually, almost imperceptibly, the parched and thirsting corners of her spirit began to moisten and she felt huge salt tears pour down upon her face as she acknowledged a gratitude for which she could find no words.

Gabriella looked lovingly upon her, unperturbed by the rain. In this time, the Mother actually knew the depth of her child's love for her and it took her breath away to experience the purity of it. She found it difficult to stay her eyes upon her child's, as though the love between them was almost too much for her to bear.

Moments became timeless. With no real external clock of sun or moon, the Mother began to respond as her body saw fit. She slept when she was tired, ate when hungry, drank when thirsty. She did nothing because it was supposed to be done, in a certain way, at a given time; but, instead, followed only the rhythm set by her internal desires and needs.

Sometimes she would light a candle and simply stare at it, noticing that the light on the taper had different colours and varying degrees of intensity. Following out from the hot blue centre of the flame, through the orange halo, to its periphery of molten gold, she would study it, wondering at what point she could no longer see its boundary. *Where does the glow of the candle end and the light of the fire within the cottage begin?* she mused. Light became her focus. Light was all that mattered.

After one such moment with the candlelight she felt hungry and began, as usual, to prepare her food, but to her surprise she saw that there were only five bulrushes remaining inside the basket. *Surely the rains will be ending soon,* she thought, but then felt saddened, for this seemingly unending time, of no time, had begun to comfort her.

Blowing out the candle, she lay back on the bed and followed the wisps of grey smoke spiralling towards the ceiling until her eyes became heavy with sleep. But her sleep was not to be without interruption, for that night the Midwife came once more. This time she seemed much larger than the Mother remembered and there was a fierce sense of urgency in her emerald eyes.

'My dear one, the rains are soon to finish,' she said. 'You have done well to heed my voice. Now will come the next step upon your path. The gift I gave you before Gabriella's Naming Day is now ready to be opened. Within the pouch, you will find gifts of life and sustenance: seeds ready for planting.

'First, however, you will need to prepare the earth so that it may receive them. Tomorrow, upon waking, walk behind the cottage. There you will discover the earth to be moist from the rains. In the small shed there is a special tool to help you remove all the overgrowth and dig channels in the softened earth. Seven of these must be dug, each the entire length of the plot of earth. Dig six trenches leaving two large steps between each, and for the seventh, walk five full paces before turning up the soil. Once this has been completed, place the seeds I have given you in the freshly-turned furrows. Within the one large pouch, you will find seven smaller. Use one pouch's seeds for each of the seven channels.

'As you look at the garden patch from the cottage, place the seeds in this order: the seeds in the red pouch are to be planted in the first trench on your left, followed by the seeds from the orange, yellow, green, aqua, blue and lastly, white, in the trench furthest to your right. Space each seed equidistant from the next, according to the number you find within each pouch. When all the seeds have been sown, gently cover them with soil. Once this has been completed, stand before the earth, arms outstretched, and speak this prayer:

Open earth. Receive this seed.
Encourage growth and banish weed.

From the unseen depths within;
Miracle of life begin.

All potential, dormant, still,
Free from human wrath and will,

Let the moist protective loam
Be your shelter; be your home,

Until this soil opens wide
To free the hidden gifts inside.

Herbs and tubers, fruits and grains,
Blessed by sun and blessed by rains.

Abundant may our harvest be,
We humbly leave our prayer with Thee.

'Do these things and your garden will grow. Hold fast to this miracle and do not forget the wonders that will occur. Watch and be amazed. Nurture this patch of earth and know that all that grows within it will provide for you. Give thanks each day and never forget from whence has come this precious gift of life.' With these words the Midwife again vanished abruptly and the Mother awoke, startled by the brightness of the morning sunshine which poured into the cottage.

She leapt out of bed and ran outside. Just as the Midwife had foretold, the once hardened and inhospitable soil had grown soft with the rain and, there, indeed, in a dark recess of the shed was the tool with which she could work the land. After seven rows were made ready, according to the Midwife's instructions, the Mother returned to the cottage to collect the large pouch the Midwife had given her; untying the knot, she found within it seven smaller pouches, again, just as the Midwife had foretold. At the top of each row of earth she placed the unopened seven, furthest to her left she began with crimson red followed by orange, golden yellow, forest green, aqua, indigo blue and purest white.

These she opened one at a time, carefully assessing the space between the seeds and gingerly pressed each into the upturned earth. When she had placed the last of the seeds and covered them with a blanket of soil, the

Mother spread open her arms and repeated the prayer the Midwife had spoken. She had no idea how she had remembered all the words, or if she had remembered them correctly, but it did not seem to matter. The seeds had been planted, her heart was open and, once again, she had trusted her dream. All the while, Gabriella lay quietly upon the soft earth, her bright blue eyes sparkling as she observed.

The Mother had laboured well into the day and she was hungry. So after she had nursed Gabriella, she walked the now familiar path towards the bulrushes, which seemed more plentiful than ever. These, she knew, would sustain her, until her own garden began to grow.

And grow it did. To her amazement and delight, tufts of green began appearing within days. The Mother found this to be miraculous. The seedlings were growing at a remarkable speed. Each day she repeated the prayer of the dream, sometimes using the exact words, sometimes using her own. Whichever she chose, her days began with an invocation to Creator to care for her garden, to care for her child and to care for herself. It was a new way of praying. Prayers had always been listened to, as Priests prayed them for her.

Now, it was her own thoughts, petitions and thanks being offered, in her own voice. She felt a deep sense of belonging to a Divine Power, whose grace and benevolence sustained and guided her.

As the Mother and her garden flourished, so too did Gabriella. Each day she found a new sound; she discovered her own tiny feet and hand, her face, her Mother's hands. With growing interest she studied all that surrounded her, swiftly perceiving that there was a world separate to her. Where she ended and it began became more and more evident. Her little body grew larger as she found the strength to sit upright all on her own and soon she became eager to walk, using everything she could find as support.

On one clear sunny afternoon, as the Mother was sitting behind the cottage, surveying the growth of her garden, Gabriella was standing, keeping her balance by touching the wall of the cottage. When suddenly, there was a cry of delight, and, as the little girl drew her hand away from her support, she walked slowly towards the Mother. 'Mama' came the words as she took her first steps towards the woman seated before her upon the earth. Tears of joy and love welled up in the Mother's eyes. Gabriella, her daughter, whom she had named, had just done the same for her.

The days grew hotter and the plants in the garden taller and stronger. The Mother studied them eagerly, for she was unsure of what she had planted. She had not recognized the seeds when she had sown them, but as the young vegetation became visible, she began to identify familiar shapes. On the left, the seeds taken from the red pouch were clearly becoming lavender plants. Next to these, valerian, followed by carrot, squash, bean and cabbage.

From the seventh pouch had come the fewest number of seeds and the Mother could now see why. Those planted in the seventh furrow were apple seeds; fruit trees were growing in her garden, seven of them, side by side. Each day they seemed to grow nearly a foot in height as buds formed and blossoms came. Soon, bees flew between the flowering trees and there appeared upon the earth between the sixth and seventh rows she had planted, the telltale green of the potato plant. To her amazement she realized that there were potatoes growing beneath the ground and she had not put them there. *How can this be?* the Mother wondered.

THE HARVEST

Life was abundant and gracious; Gabriella began to run and play between the rows of garden plants. Bulrushes, berries, nettle and wild peppermint for tea, everything they desired was provided from nature. As plants needed staking, the Mother found long sticks in the forest and sunk them into the earth to provide support for the climbing strands. By the time the days were growing shorter, after only two full cycles of the moon, the Mother was harvesting beans, pulling up carrots, digging for potatoes and gathering bundles of lavender to perfume the cottage and deepen her sleep.

The apples were not yet ready to pick; but the trees were covered with fruit. *There will be a harvest this year. How it is possible, I do not know; but it is so,* she reflected.

Gabriella's growing body was less satiated with only her Mother's milk now but the bulrushes seemed to fill her desires. These, along with cooked carrots and smashed potatoes, added variety of taste for them both. As summer gave way to autumn, the Mother found her garden had yielded far more than she and Gabriella could possibly eat. Apples, squash, beans, carrots, potatoes, cabbages, valerian for a calming tea, and lavender with its relaxing qualities; every crop had produced an enormous harvest.

Perhaps I can exchange some of this bounty for goods, thought the Mother, but the very idea of leaving their haven in the forest filled her with dread. The reality of seeing other people was frightening and yet, she knew that soon Gabriella would need bigger clothes; they would need more turf for the fire, flour for bread, oats for porridge and all manner of supplies for the colder winter days ahead.

Her mind was uneasy with the memories of all that had occurred in the village she had left behind. How could she risk exposing herself and Gabriella to judgment once more? She had no idea how the people of this village would react to them and felt torn between the decision to go and trade, and the desire to cloister them both away, in the safety of their little cottage, deep in the forest. *Still, perhaps there is nothing to be frightened of at all,* she thought, deciding to choose love over fear. *There are, after all, things Gabriella and I need.* It was as simple as that. Until this moment they had been provided for with amazing generosity. Surely going into the village would be no risk.

Steadying her thoughts with her belief in all the goodness she had known since leaving the Land of Never Forgetting, the Mother made plans to carry as much as she could to the nearby village to trade, but first she felt the need to explore. Rising early the next morning, she fed Gabriella and, after satisfying her own hunger, she strapped her daughter into the fabric once more. She was much heavier now and the Mother needed to support her with both arms to offset the weight the child placed upon her shoulders. As an afterthought, the Mother decided to take along with her a few samples of her garden's bounty. Picking up the largest of the baskets, she filled one side with carrots, cabbages, potatoes and beans, then placed bundles of lavender and a few valerian roots on the other. Laden, once more, she set off along the footpath that had first led her to the cottage.

The way through the forest was now so overgrown that she had to concentrate with nearly every step and found herself looking down at her feet far more than in front of her. So it was with a sense of surprise that she felt her foot touch the wider road leading to the village. Looking up, she saw the very top of the Mountain of Remembrance and the sight of it caused her to gasp. Since arriving at her new home, she had thought less and less often of the Mountain and the River of Dreams.

How quickly she had put the teachings of the Law from the Land of Never Forgetting behind her. Remembering now gave rise to familiar feelings of fear and she quickly diverted her eyes to quell them. As she did, the Mother

77

could see that the little village at the base of the hills beyond was actually much closer than she had remembered.

Taking a deep breath she continued walking, but due to the weight of both basket and child, the Mother had to pause frequently to regain her strength. The closer she got to the village, the more rapidly her heart pounded within her breast. She knew that Gabriella's deformity could not be seen, for with her child pressed safely to her, it was completely hidden, there was nothing to fear. And yet, she could not keep calm herself. *What if it is discovered? What if it all goes wrong?* The voices within began to fairly shout at her. *Go back. Go back where it is safe. You are a foolish woman to risk both your lives. Stay in the woods, alone and safe. Stay put, where no one will know.*

She could hear voices on the road, coming her way. *Run. Run*, her inner voice screamed at her. Quickly, the Mother darted off the road and into a thickly wooded area where she crouched behind the trunk of an ancient beech tree. Waiting for the travellers to reach a place where she could no longer see them, she regained her courage and, after looking in both directions, returned to the road. When her feet hit the surface she ran, as fast as she was able, towards the path that would lead her back to her cottage. Voices, she could hear voices on the road behind them again. *Where is the path? Where is the path?* the Mother thought and she began to panic, for she was unable to find it.

'You. You there,' came the sound of a man's voice behind her. Like a frightened animal the Mother froze in her tracks.

'You. Where are you going with that food?' asked a second male voice. Forcing herself to respond, the Mother replied, trying to sound as sure as she could.

'I was looking for a market where I might sell my vegetables. I am in need of things for my child and myself as winter draws near.' The men, bearded, and in robes of pale grey, came closer. One of them was rolling a medium-sized handcart, hewn from oak. 'May I inspect your wares?' asked the first who had spoken. The Mother nodded and, trying to suppress her trembling hands, she placed the basket before him.

'These are big and healthy. I will buy all of them,' he said with a low-pitched voice. 'We need them more than you can know. There has been extraordinary rain, the likes of which we have never seen before. All our crops have been flooded; save for a few grains, there is little else.' He stared at her overflowing basket and then he looked at her intently with eyes of palest blue. Finally, he said, 'I do not recognize you. Where are you from?' The Mother looked down, not knowing what to say. She paused, 'I am from the Land beyond the ravine. My daughter and I were left desolate when we were abandoned and I have come this long way to find a manner in which to support us.'

'I am sorry for your loss,' the second man said with a kindly tone. 'You have been wise in coming this way, for you will have no trouble finding buyers. Have you more to trade?'

'Yes. Oh, yes.' The Mother answered with a more confident voice.

'The market takes place in three days time, so you may come to the village then. You will surely gain all you are seeking, as will those who find their way to you.' With that the two men reached to their waists to untie the moneybags, which were attached to their belts. 'We will buy all you have today. Will two bits of silver from each of us suffice?'

Even though it seemed a very large sum of money, and more than equitable, the Mother thought of something she would rather have. Averting her gaze from the men, she replied, 'It is exceedingly generous; however, as the way is long for me to travel with child and harvest, would you consider trading your cart for the goods? In exchange, I will give each of you twice this much again on market day.'

The two men looked at one another and then the first to have spoken said, 'Yes. This we will do. I made this cart myself, so it will not be difficult for me to replace it.'

With that the Mother handed them the basket filled with produce and said, 'Return with this as a measure and I will make good my promise in three days time.' The two men bowed a little bow, smiled at Gabriella, who smiled back at them, and then went on their way with the basket filled with food, delighting in their good fortune. When they were well out of sight, the Mother untied Gabriella and strapped her securely into the wagon and began to roll the cart, which moved with remarkable ease, towards home.

THE MARKET

For the next three days the Mother prepared. She picked the reddest, most luscious-looking apples within her reach and then shook the higher branches of the trees for more; she gathered potatoes, carrots, squash and cabbage and rinsed them clean in the water she had drawn from the well. On the third day she cut down some beans and fashioned bundles of lavender with rope made of heather. Lastly, she dug the tender root of the valerian plant; for she knew its curative properties could relieve distress and sleeplessness. It would fetch a good price. By nightfall on the eve of market day, the wagon was filled to the top, save one empty space, reserved for Gabriella.

Rising with the sun's earliest wash of colours, the Mother fed Gabriella and then herself as usual. Strapping her daughter into place, she took hold of her wagon and guided it along the bumpy path with little effort. She was quite proud of her resourcefulness in having asked for it, rather than silver, as payment.

Fearlessly, this time, she made her way from the cottage feeling it much less treacherous now that she had met the two men who had rewarded her so handsomely.

As she drew closer to the village she realised with a shudder that it all looked very familiar and a sense of deep anxiety began to creep in upon her. Forcing herself to stay calm, she recalled the remarkable journey she had taken to arrive at this far-away place, to build a new life for herself and Gabriella. Here at the base of these hills, she could not see anything of the River of Dreams. And the summit of the Mountain of Remembrance itself seemed smaller still and far away in the distance. *I am in a new place. It is a new life I am now leading,* she thought, over and over again.

But her fears deepened as she pushed her cart through the village. For there, opening out before her, at the end of a row of little houses was the village square. Stemming back her tears, she remembered all that had happened on Gabriella's Naming Day, and that led her thoughts to the memory of the ghastly pyre that had consumed the Midwife. Taking a deep breath, she steadied her nerves, trying to keep her tears of sorrow at bay.

There were a number of sellers already in the square: a woman with woven cloth and needles; a man with a stash of eggs and cheeses; another with several large bags of oats and barley, but, just as the two men had said, there were no vegetables to be seen. A man pushing a cart filled with turf logs arrived, as did another with smoked meats. All seemed calm and the Mother found a place to set the weight of her cart down amidst the stares of strangers.

For a long time no one spoke to her, no one welcomed her at all and she began to feel increasingly awkward, believing that she must look such an incongruous sight, a stranger in a strange place. At first, the Mother thought they were staring at Gabriella, but she soon realised they were not nearly as interested in her as they were with the food piled high within her cart.

Still, no one came close. All seemed indifferent until a bell rang out, signalling the start of market day, at which time more villagers made their way to the square. But again, none came her way.

Just as she was losing hope of making any trades at all, the two men in grey robes appeared with an empty cart and the Mother's, now empty, basket and they seemed to be familiar to everyone present. Greeting those gathered in the market, they made straight for the Mother. They presented her with her basket and, as she had promised, she filled it four more times, twice for each of them.

'This woman comes from a distant land,' announced the man who made the carts. 'The crops there were not destroyed by these terrible floods of our summer. She, and her harvest, are an answer to our prayers,' he said, addressing the suspicious villagers.

Within minutes so many people had made their way towards the Mother that she had to ration her supply until all of it was gone and the Mother traded well for herself in return: two small bags of grain, one filled with barley and the other with oats, twenty turf logs, fabric sufficient for both a new robe for Gabriella and also a skirt and apron for herself, a needle and a spool of thread, a bar of soap, ten candles, twelve eggs and a wheel of hard cheese. She did not much care for the taste of meat, so from the meat vendor she negotiated one piece of silver in exchange for a mixed bag of potatoes, apples and carrots and more beans and cabbages than she could count.

By midday, as all her produce had gone, she decided to return home. Wheeling her way back through the village she felt gladdened as encouraging shouts came through doors and windows. 'Will you be back next week?' the voices asked. 'Why, yes, yes, I will be back and I do have more to offer.' The villagers were truly delighted with their good fortune and they called out to her with promises of bread and cakes and all manner of things that could be traded for. *They are hungry*, she thought, *and I shall feed them.*

As she made the final turn from the village, she saw the men in grey once more. 'We have been very rude not to say how beautiful your daughter is,' said the cart maker. 'What name has she been given?' he asked.

'Gabriella,' replied the Mother.

'Ah, it is a perfect name for one with eyes the colour of the Heavens,' he responded.

'We shall see each other again next week, Creator willing,' he said, bowing to her again, and with a slight nod of his head, he departed.

When the Mother was certain she would be seen by no one, she wheeled the cart down the path to her cottage. Once home, she lifted Gabriella from the cart and gave her a big hug. She had been as good as gold for the entire duration of the morning. Sitting quietly at the market, she had observed all that took place, but had never fussed or made any demand.

Now she toddled about with glee, exploring absolutely everything, her little legs happy to be moving again. Keeping an eye on her inquisitive daughter, the Mother began to unload the cart, feeling grateful for all she had been given. That night she prepared a feast of eggs, cheese, warm apples and a succulent combination of squash and carrots, which made Gabriella gurgle with delight.

And so the next week and every week until late autumn, the Mother and Gabriella returned to the village square, the cart heavy-laden with fruit, vegetables and fresh herbs. With each progressive market day, the villagers seemed drawn, not only to the bounty of the earth, but also to the bright light in Gabriella's eyes. The villagers came to visit her like bees to honey. Wherever the Mother set her cart to rest within the square, the people flocked.

Perhaps, at first, it had been to barter for the Mother's bounty; but it soon became evident that they wanted to bask in the presence of this child with the unique, unearthly beauty, as well. And the Mother took great joy in both.

For the first year of Gabriella's life, all was at peace. The Mother's heart was light and she felt increasingly amazed at her blessings. The child's spirit sweetened with the passage of time and they played together and laughed often. And then, after the initial season of planting and reaping, the Mother harvested not only full-grown plants but also seeds and tubers for the following year. These she placed upon the earthen floor of the cottage in a cool dry place to await the warmth of spring once more.

Following a mild winter the days grew longer and the earth softened to receive the fertile seeds. The Mother planted all that she had kept and swiftly invoked the Midwife's prayer as best she could. And, as before, all was well. New growth flourished and the harvest was bountiful as summer grew nigh.

Preparing her cart for travel once more, the Mother realized, to her disquiet, that Gabriella had now grown too big to be strapped to the cart, as she had been the previous year. *What am I to do?* Old fears, long kept at bay, flooded her mind as she began to worry about her child and so, convinced that her daughter's disfigurement could not risk detection, she decided to travel to market alone. *Of course, I will tell them that she is safe at home,* she thought. *But how can I keep her safe?*

THE BINDINGS

By the early hours of the first market day that year, the Mother had found her solution. She took pieces of muslin and bound Gabriella's legs together, gently strapping her right arm to her torso with a further length of fabric. Then, with a very long piece of muslin she began to wrap her child from her toes right up to her neck and laid her upon a soft fleece in the centre of the floor of the cottage. There no harm would come to her if she rolled from side to side.

Gabriella gazed, wide-eyed with fear, at her Mother, without speaking a word, and the Mother, with tears rolling down her cheeks, said, 'Mama is protecting us from harm Gabriella. You are unique and very special. Some grown-ups do not understand these things. Mama loves you and will always protect you.'

The Mother, now certain that her child could not injure herself whilst she was absent, gave her a kiss upon the brow and with a final 'I love you', she turned her back and wiped away her tears. Gabriella called out, 'Mama. Mama', with cries that soon became sobs, but the Mother did not turn back. *I know this is the correct thing to do. I know we will be safe this way,* she said to herself, clenching her fists as she raced to the cart. She was desperate to distance herself from the cries of her child and it was not long before all she could hear was the whispering of the trees and branches all about her.

Upon arriving at the market, villagers hastened to trade with her, for she was eagerly remembered from the previous year. And as quickly as she was able, the Mother sold all she had brought. Those gathered around her asked after Gabriella and their questions were satisfied by her well-rehearsed answers. With a forced smile and a quick wave to the villagers, the Mother turned her cart towards home with haste, feeling pained at what she had done to her child.

When she was sure she was the only person travelling on the wider road from the village, she knew it was safe to veer into the forest. Once there, she fairly ran down the overgrown path for home. Approaching the cottage, she set down the cart and pushed through the hurdle door, fearing the worst. There, just as she had left her, was Gabriella.

'Mama,' she said. But there was no smile this time, only the puffy red eyes of a child, who had been crying, for far too long.

Quickly removing all of the binding, the Mother held her child to her chest and hugged her.

'Mama has been to the market and traded for all we need. You have been Mama's big helper. What a good girl you have been to stay here and keep us both safe,' she said with a big kiss, unwrapping the last of her daughter's little torso, freeing her right arm.

Gabriella flung it about her Mother's neck saying, 'Mama's big helper'.

'Yes, my beautiful girl. You are Mama's big helper,' she replied, swinging her round and round at a dizzying pace until they both collapsed in a giggling heap on top of the pile of fabric that had bound Gabriella only moments before.

And thus it was they began their new life together.

As each harvest season ended, the Mother continued to gather seeds for the next year's planting. Winter was spent mostly indoors and in spring, when the hardened ground softened enough for planting, the entire cycle would begin anew. However, for each of the next seven years, the sun shone more and more brightly and the rainfall drastically diminished. The soil hardened and it seemed to her to have turned to stone. And all the while, the harvests she yielded were growing smaller and smaller as the earth grew strangely parched and depleted.

Each market day, Gabriella was bound with the muslin and left inside the cottage, lying upon the fleece in the middle of the dirt floor. She would stifle her cries until she thought her Mother was far enough away that they could not be heard.

Gabriella hated market days. They had become full of fear for her. She did not understand why she had to be tied up and left upon the hard earth floor week after week. Each day she would count the sunrises and sunsets knowing that when the seventh occurred, she would be bound again. It was the being alone she so despised and anticipation of these days sent great waves of panic and a kind of sickness through her little body each and every week.

On one market day morning, Gabriella could bear it no more. Instead of her regular practice of waiting for the sun to fully rise before she began to cry, Gabriella, bound and lying on the fleece, could no longer contain her rising terror. She began to howl and scream shortly after her Mother left the cottage. She sounded more animal than child, except for the intermittent 'Mama' which pierced the early morning air.

The Mother, now nearly upon the road to the village, hearing her daughter's bloodcurdling screams, tore back through the woods towards the cottage, leaving her cart on the path, well hidden from view.

She raced into the cottage screaming, 'What are you doing? I was near the road when I heard you. If I can hear you, so can others. We must keep our secret. We must never let anyone know where we live; we must never let them see you. You are beautiful, my precious Gabriella; but I am the only person in the world who can see you as you truly are.'

Gabriella was now sobbing uncontrollably; all the Mother had said was no longer enough; none of it made any sense to her at all.

'Why? Why, if I am so beautiful, do you hide me away?'

'I cannot stop for this. You must obey.'

Gabriella stared at her Mother as though she had never seen her before and began to scream, 'No, I want to be untied. I want to be free. Take me to the market in the square with you. Please untie me, Mama. Please do not leave me alone any more.'

'There is no time for this, Gabriella. I must go,' she said fiercely. 'We need things desperately, the garden is producing less now and I must arrive at market first, in order to trade for what we require.' Her words were met with louder wailings from Gabriella.

'Stop this,' the Mother demanded. 'Stop it! Stop it! Stop it!' she repeated as she shook her child violently by the shoulders. Gabriella cried louder still and then the Mother slapped her child with a stinging force that left a bright red mark, the exact shape of her hand, upon her daughter's left cheek.

'I have no time for this. Now, you be quiet. Do not make me strike you again.'

Stunned into silence Gabriella whispered 'I will obey.'

The Mother, wiping away a single tear from her own face, grabbed a further length of muslin and tied it around her child's mouth, sufficiently well to muffle her cries. 'There. Now your voice will not be heard. This will keep you safe.'

As she stood at the hurdle door, she looked down at Gabriella, gagged and bound from head to toe.

'Never, ever forget that I have sacrificed everything for you. Do this now for me.' And with that she left.

It was the first time in Gabriella's life there had been no kiss goodbye.

Gabriella heard her Mother run down the path towards her waiting cart and longed to follow her. She tried to quell her feelings but it was no use. Great tears welled up within her eyes and poured down her cheeks. Muted sobs came through the muslin gag as Gabriella cried and cried and cried.

Why was I ever born? she wondered.

I have cost my Mother everything. It is all my fault. I must be a good girl. I must be a good girl. The exhaustion of her outburst and her Mother's brutal response had left her drained of all energy and she fell deeply asleep.

MIDDLENIGHT

In a dreamless state she slept, exhausted, until she was awakened by the warmth of sunlight upon her face. Something was different. She listened. *Breathing, I hear breathing.* She looked towards the door on her right, nothing. Then she looked to her left and let out a muffled yelp. There, lying between her body and the hearth was a dog, sound asleep.

She struggled to sit upright and her movements caused it to wake. The dog sat up as well and gazed at her with his deep brown eyes, came closer and rested his forehead upon hers, nuzzling her tenderly. Then he licked her cheek, in the exact place where the Mother had slapped her.

In this gentle act, Gabriella was comforted. Although she could not speak, Gabriella's thoughts were communicated in the depths of her bright blue eyes. She thanked this lovely creature for his tender care on this day and tried to tell him how much she loved him. The fear of being left alone, the pain she had felt for so long lessened, as the dog drew close to her.

Suddenly the dog's ears pricked to attention. He licked Gabriella once more, as if to say goodbye and bolted out of the cottage. Understanding his language immediately, Gabriella quickly lay down once more and pretended to be asleep.

The Mother came racing into the cottage and hastily removed all the bindings. 'Oh, Gabriella. I am so sorry.'

Warily, Gabriella replied, 'I know Mama, I know.'

Her Mother sunk to the floor, the fullness of her weight heavy against her child's tiny body and sobbed. 'It is so lonely being the only one to care for you. Please forgive me. Please forgive me.'

'I forgive you, Mama. I forgive you,' whispered Gabriella.

And as the night grew darker, Gabriella rocked the older woman tenderly in her embrace until sleep came to her. Gently covering her Mother with a woollen blanket, she set about unpacking the items from within the cart, which numbered hardly anything.

Gabriella watched as her Mother drifted further and further away from her. And, in an attempt to help, she began to prepare their meals, gather what little food she could, clean the house and wash their clothes. And each night she would stroke her Mother's forehead, releasing her into a restless sleep.

The fact that the garden was producing less and less was now obvious to those in the village as well. Most weeks the Mother came back from market day with her cart filled, not with goods she had traded for, but with only the ill-looking produce she had tried, unsuccessfully, to sell.

Often their evening meals were accompanied by silence, broken occasionally with questions asked by the Mother, for which there were no answers. 'Why is this happening to me? Why is it all changing? Everything was so beautiful. Why is my garden no longer growing? Why am I being punished?'

As she asked the questions, expecting no response, her eyes would dart wildly about the room and she would wring her hands as though the answer could be squeezed from them. After finishing her meal, leaving Gabriella to clear and clean, the Mother would pace the floor from one length to the other whispering 'Why? Why? I should never have listened to those dreams.'

'What dreams? How can I help Mama?' Gabriella would ask, over and over, until the last of the dishes had been put away. 'Never mind, now. These things are not for you to know. I must protect you. Be a good girl, Gabriella. Be silent and hide yourself away. This is your greatest gift to our little family,' she would say, with a slightly forced smile and a glance in her child's direction. But Gabriella noticed that the Mother's eyes no longer seemed to actually see her at all. It was as though her Mother's once animated face had become a mask; a mask with a fixed smile and an oddly unfocused gaze.

Every market day, Gabriella was tied and gagged as usual but both were unnecessary, for she no longer cried out and had no desire to run away. The child's only ritual on these mornings was to ask Creator to send the dog with the deep brown eyes to her and each time she prayed her prayer it was answered with the appearance of the dog.

In her heart she named him Middlenight, in honour of his shiny black coat. He was big and strong, yet gentler than anything she had ever known. Market days, once filled with such dread and sorrow for her, had fast become the days she most longed for. Middlenight was her first friend. She yearned to stroke him; but as that was impossible, she settled for the sensation of his brow upon her own, his warmth next to her body and the deep cocoa-coloured eyes that held her to the depths of her being. And thus it continued until the eleventh year of Gabriella's life.

THE DARKNESS

In this year the garden produced hardly anything at all, apples did not ripen, most of the vegetables had root rot and the rest were small and shrivelled. The Mother's sorrow had caused her to cease nearly all activity. She had not even gathered seed to plant after the last year's harvest. The oppressive heat of the summer suns had parched the earth leaving them hardly the means to survive and, much to Gabriella's dismay, on the very first market day the Mother remained at home. She had nothing to sell, nothing had grown and now, without the market days, Gabriella realized, to her dismay, that she would no longer see Middlenight.

It seemed the only thing growing in the harvest season of Gabriella's eleventh year was the sadness within the spirit of the Mother. 'I have worked so hard, all of my life. For what?' she cried to the sky above her. 'I tire of the struggle. Who will come and lessen my load? When does my reward come for all I have done? I have a child with only one arm. She is too costly. She has always been too costly.'

Suddenly aware of what she had said, the Mother, now sobbing, looked at Gabriella and said, 'I love you, more than life itself, but my burden has become too great for me to bear. I ask for help and none comes. Years ago, dreams came to me in the night and within them I found help and guidance; but now I know it was all a lie. Now I only toss and turn, sleep evades me, I am so very weary. My life is nothing but a curse.'

When her ramblings finished, she looked at her daughter, studying her from head to toe in a manner that made Gabriella uncomfortable; but the little girl felt too frightened to move or turn away. The adoring look she once knew had become a deeply suspicious stare. It was as though the Mother did not recognize her. She stared and stared at her child, as if in horror.

In a very real way, Gabriella had begun to believe that she was the cause of all of her Mother's sadness. She tried to be good but despite her best

94

efforts, her Mother often slipped into a shadowy world of melancholy where no amount of her child's light could comfort her. It was as though every sorrowful memory the Mother felt was heightened by the mere sight of her. Gabriella knew she was different. It was obvious that she had only one arm; but the Mother had always told her that it made her special. *How could my being special cause so much pain?* she asked herself over and over.

One night, after her Mother had looked at her for a long while in a detached, sad sort of way, Gabriella mustered the courage to ask the question that had troubled her for as long as she could remember.

'Mama, how is it that I have only one arm?'

Through the fog of her own thoughts, the Mother did not hear her child.

'What did you say?' she asked in a vague and indifferent manner.

Gabriella took a deep breath and repeated her question, 'How is it that I have only one arm?'

The Mother turned to face her daughter, her eyes dull with pain and her tongue heavy and said, 'I do not know. The Law taught that it was a sign of evil, in you, or me or the Midwife who helped bring you forth. This I cannot believe. I know this deformity, this, which makes you so very different, is not of your doing. Yet, this is the way Creator chose to make you. I wish it were not so. So many times I have wished it were not so. From the day of your birth I have struggled with this, perhaps now you are old enough to hear your story.

'When your misshapen form was given to me, at first I did not claim you as my own. I did not want you near me. The Midwife and I left you well alone. Quiet you were. You never cried out, never made a sound until an owl screeched overhead. By the light of the roundest moon we saw that owl make seven circles above our cottage, before flying away. The cry awakened something in you and you made a whimpering sound.

'It was only then I truly looked at you, at your eyes. Blue, so blue they were, like the colour of the sky. I felt only love and could do nothing other than protect you from your fate by hiding your deformity from the High Priest and from your Father.

'On the eve of your Naming Day, the Midwife led us into the evergreen forest behind the cottage in which you were born. There she lit a fire and prayed prayers for your protection, but they failed, your deformity was discovered on your Naming Day, in front of the entire village. With this came condemnation. We had hidden the truth from the High Priest and one of us; myself, the Midwife or you, was to die by flames, to pay the price for that sin. We had to choose who it would be. In the end, the Midwife decided it would be her. She knew in her heart that it was I who could care for you best. The following day, on top of a pyre, she was consumed by raging fire, but even her death did not restore you to wholeness.'

Gabriella looked on, wide-eyed, as the Mother continued her story, 'Although we were allowed to live, your body caused fear in the villagers. I was abandoned by your Father and rejected by all who knew me. They tried to kill us in the night and that was when I knew I had no choice but to move on. I journeyed here, made a home for us, planted the seeds, a gift from the Midwife before her death, and all was beautiful for so long. But now, the rains have stopped, the earth is barren and I am tired. I am so very tired and there is no one who can help.'

As she spoke these last words her voice grew flat in tone, the flame in her eyes went out and the once bright light within grew dim and vacuous. Gabriella's left side, for the first time in her life, began to ache with a pain she had never known.

'Mama,' she cried. There was no response. 'Mama, I am sorry I was born,' she said reaching out with her arm, but her words fell on deaf ears as the Mother stared straight ahead, focused on nothing at all.

The short days and long nights of winter passed with the Mother rarely speaking, rarely moving. Her only activity from time to time was to walk with small halting steps, marking the inner perimeter of the cottage. As she shuffled along the dirt floor, in a breathy, whispered voice, mutterings would sometimes come, as before, 'Why has this happened to me? Why was she born to me? Why am I being punished?' Her words grew more and more stilted and each time she spoke she said less and less until, eventually, the only word was 'Why?'

As her speech grew shorter, so too did the path of her steps. Smaller and smaller became the pattern she made upon the earthen floor, the room closed in upon her as her spirit wound into itself more and more tightly. In the end, when she could no longer move, she simply curled into a ball and lay down upon the heather bed, where Gabriella covered her with a woollen blanket and stroked her temple tenderly, just at the point where the hair meets the skin, until, at last, the Mother fell into a fitful sleep.

Gabriella would do her best to take care of her, but most often her efforts were to no avail. The Mother had retreated deep inside, to a place only big enough for one.

THE OWL RETURNS

The winter nights were long and bitterly cold. As Gabriella had not been taught to make a fire by herself, she kept vigilant watch over the one her Mother had last made, careful to keep it alive. Unable to do much more than gather sticks and twigs to feed the flames, the fire was most often very small, as she did not burn too many of the peat logs, knowing she would need them to last. The small pieces of kindling helped somewhat, but on one particularly cold night she began to shiver from the lack of warmth.

Frightened by what would become of her and feeling so alone, great salty tears began to splash down her cheeks. Then, like an answered, but unvoiced prayer, Middlenight arrived at her side. Gabriella was overjoyed, as she had not seen her friend since the market days had ended with her Mother's decline.

His big brown eyes met hers and somehow his very spirit warmed her. He snuggled near, his black coat bringing warmth, his strength lending support. As it was the first time Gabriella had been unbound in all their time together, she was at last able to stroke his shiny coat arm. Middlenight responded to her gentle touch by drawing closer still and the two fell asleep together, before the fire that cold winter's night.

The Mother had disappeared so completely that she took no notice of Middlenight's presence at all. The dog, sensing this, remained constantly at Gabriella's side throughout the rest of winter.

Nearly two full cycles of the moon passed in this manner before the days began to grow warmer and the nights shorter. For food there was hard cheese, a small number of potatoes and turnips, porridge oats and the tiniest portion of dried meat. These Gabriella rationed between her Mother and herself. Most often the Mother refused to eat, despite Gabriella's coaxing.

When she pushed the rejected food away, Gabriella devoured her Mother's portion as well as her own, knowing she needed to remain strong. From these meagre provisions she fed Middlenight as well. And although she truly savoured the dried meat, she offered most of it to him, mixing it with porridge oats, as she could see it was his favourite.

Middlenight responded to her generosity with gentleness and a profound understanding beyond any Gabriella had ever known. He observed her every movement: comforted her when she tossed and turned; nestled her until she could sleep; licked her face to wipe away her tears; and often nuzzled her, placing his forehead directly upon hers, as if to banish any harmful thoughts from her mind.

The Mother no longer saw, nor heard her daughter at all and she lay on the bed, day after night after day, lost in her own rambling conversations, replaying out loud random scenes from her past, often asking what it would be to live any life, other than her own. Spoken words became a confusion of moaned and grunted sounds.

The only constant in her behaviour was the insistent rubbing of her left palm with the fingers of her right hand. Always she worked one against the other, as if trying to rid herself of a pain only she could perceive.

Seeing her Mother in this way frightened Gabriella. It caused her heart to pound and tears to flow nearly every day.

'What can I do to help, Mama?' she would ask. 'Look Mama, tiny snowdrops are pushing their way to the sunshine; can you see them? The sky is blue today, blue as a robin's egg, Mama. Can you hear her singing the song of the morning?' In response to each question, Gabriella received silence.

Nothing but silence.

To ease her loneliness, Gabriella began describing all that she saw to Middlenight and his shining cocoa eyes followed her every move and gesture, his ears pricking up with the inflections of her voice. In many ways, he was now the only companion she had in the world, reassuring her that she was heard, that she was understood, that she was alive.

Each evening, before bed, it became her ritual to report on the shape of the moon and the quality of the sky as she thanked her Guiding Lights, the stars, before kissing her Mother and snuggling up to Middlenight for warmth.

One night something remarkable happened as Gabriella stood, gazing at the sky from the window. She looked upon the heavens and said, 'Roundest moon against pitch-black sky with thickening clouds, edged in silver. Rain may live in those clouds, Mama. Rain may be coming. Thank you Guiding Lights for protecting us this day. Thank you for the rain, which might be on its way.' As she walked towards the bed to give a kiss to the Mother, a sudden screech pierced the night air with such violence that Gabriella raced into the garden to see what could have made such a sound. Middlenight, as always, was fast at her side.

Together they scanned the sky and saw nothing, but then, as they turned towards the cottage, two wonderful events occurred. Firstly, they saw, in the frame of the door, the Mother, standing upright looking directly at them and then, as she began to walk towards Gabriella and Middlenight, a great movement was heard deep inside the forest. Closer and closer came the sound of wings, beating the night air, until at last they could see, flying directly at them, the hugest owl Gabriella had ever seen.

Its eyes were golden yellow, wings honeyed silver, talons outstretched. The fierceness of it left Gabriella frozen where she stood. Nearer and nearer it flew, swooping so close they felt the cool breeze of the night air stirred by the flapping of its wings. They were broader, it seemed to Gabriella, than she was tall, and her mouth opened in awe of the majestic bird. As it came within an arm's length from the Mother's head, it withdrew its sharp talons and rasped its spine-chilling call once more. Although the Mother immediately fell to the ground, as though struck, Gabriella oddly no longer felt any fear. She felt, rather, as though the great owl had something to give her, something to say to her.

Gabriella ran to her Mother's side and held her tenderly. Middlenight came alongside and there the three remained. The owl passed directly overhead and then rose to a great height in the sky. Higher and higher it flew, its form silhouetted by the golden disc of moon. The bird looked down upon them as it circled above the cottage seven times, before alighting on a branch, nearly at the top of a tree, just at the edge of the forest.

From here it gazed at the little girl and did not avert its eyes. It was as though it knew her somehow. Gabriella, hand upon her Mother's brow, Middlenight just at her side, looked up at the beautiful creature and the four remained motionless in this way until cloud cover grew so thick they could no longer see.

The Mother was the first to speak, 'The owl has returned. It is a sign. We are not abandoned.' Her speech was barely a whisper, her tone, slightly broken, quivering with emotion. 'It was as the night you were born, the day of the Midwife's death and again on the day I could not find the courage to cross the bridge; the owl has returned, to restore our hope. I am awakened in its presence.' Looking at her child, eyes filled with tears, she said, 'Forgive me, sweet, sweet Gabriella. I love you so,' and wrapped her frail arms around her daughter.

'Oh, Mama,' Gabriella said, tears pouring down her cheeks as well.

Their crying unsettled Middlenight, who, without a proper introduction, responded to the distress by licking the salty wetness from both their cheeks with such persistence, they found their sobs giving way to bubbling laughter.

By the time the three made their way indoors, both Gabriella and the Mother were exhausted. Every part of Gabriella ached, especially her left side, which felt particularly tender. The Mother tucked her child into bed, for the first time in many, many nights and then she gently stroked Middlenights's ears until he, too, fell fast asleep.

Sometime in the early hours, Gabriella sat bolt upright, suddenly remembering words her Mother had spoken to her about her birth and her eyes grew wide with wonder as she mused over all that had been said. *Could it have been true that an owl appeared when I was born?* she thought.

Middlenight opened his eyes. Gabriella looked over towards the wall and seeing that her Mother had not stirred at all asked, 'Middlenight, what does it mean, this visitation of the great owl?' He did not reply but inclined his head to the right as if to imply that he, too, was curious and then, the two of them returned to sleep.

THE CHRYSALIS

Gabriella woke to pouring rain and a dull gnawing ache from deep within her body. Middlenight came close, but even he was no tonic for her discomfort. Gabriella held her tummy with her arm and gentle rocked herself in an effort to ease the pains. Middlenight took to lying directly behind her, supporting her spine, and this helped just enough so that she could get to sleep. She dozed as the rain pounded upon the cottage roof until a feeling of dampness awakened her.

At first she thought the roof had leaked, but when she looked at her skirt, where she felt the moistness, she saw that it was red. It was blood. She examined her legs to see where she had cut herself, but there was nothing there, there were no cuts or scrapes. It was dark red and sticky and it was coming from inside her. *What is happening?* 'Mama, Mama,' she cried out and ran to her Mother on the bed. She shook and shook her until the Mother rolled over and looked at her with tired eyes. 'Mama. Mama I am bleeding. My tummy aches and now my blood is everywhere. I think am dying.'

'You are not dying my beautiful Gabriella. This is the sign of your womanhood. Some, especially the priests of the Law, would have you believe it is a curse and, to be sure, every month the pain will remind you of your lot. But it is no curse, it is a blessing, for without it you would not be able to bear a child.' And with a great deal of effort, she rose from her bed, gathered a length of clean muslin, folded it into a rectangular shape, and handed it to Gabriella with a gentle kiss, saying, 'This will help.' She began to walk towards the bed once more, but her knees began to buckle beneath her, her feet could not carry her another step. Gabriella ran to her side and together they eased her back to the heather bed, where she collapsed, exhausted, once more.

Mama said it is not a curse, but it must be a curse to hurt me so badly, Gabriella repeated to herself. *Maybe Mama is wrong, maybe it is a curse.* Her tormenting thoughts ran wild in the darkness of the night. She wanted to ask her Mother to reassure her again, but she had seen how tired she was and knew that she was still very sick and in need of the power of sleep to fully heal. So, for the rest of the week, the flow of her blood seemed matched by the moisture from the skies.

Finally, on the day her blood ceased, so too did the rains and the sun shone brilliantly once more. It had been nearly five days since the owl had come, since the rains had begun, and still her Mother slept.

The fire was by now long extinguished, as Gabriella, in her preoccupation, had forgotten to tend it. *Now there can be no food cooked, no tea and no warmth,* she thought. *What will become of me?* She looked to her Mother, 'Mama, Mama,' she called. *If only I could rouse her, perhaps she could build another fire for us,* she thought, but the Mother was far far away and unable to be roused. Middlenight, sensing Gabriella's fear, urged her out of doors and the two of them emerged from the dim interior of the cottage to sunlight so bright it was nearly blinding.

The warm rain had soaked the earth. The hardened soil, so terribly parched and barren, had responded to the moistness with new life. Gabriella could see that all was renewed as she walked towards the well and when she arrived alongside it, she saw that the once empty bucket was filled with rainwater. Helping herself with a ladle she offered a drink to Middlenight, which he lapped at gratefully. Taking off her skirt and blouse she scooped up handful after handful of the clear water to wash all of herself. *It is a gift from the sky,* she thought. Running back inside the cottage, she put on a clean skirt, blouse and apron. Now she, too, was fresh for the new season.

Returning to the well with a cup to fill with water for her Mother, something caught her attention. It was nothing grand, nothing as spectacular as the owl had been, but it stopped her in her tracks all the same. On the lowest branch of a young plant, which was tucked up against the side of the cottage, glistening in the morning sun, was a small milky sac suspended beneath a half-eaten leaf. At first, Gabriella thought it was the work of a spider. Then, on closer inspection she could see that it was like nothing she had ever seen before. The milky sac had a host of distant colours within it and Gabriella wondered what it could possibly be. She filled the cup and carried it inside the cottage, full of curiosity.

The cool water seemed to be just what the Mother needed most, its moistness refreshed her lips and her spirit and she came fully back to Gabriella that day. As she woke, she realized how hungry she was and, therefore, how hungry Gabriella and Middlenight must also be. Knowing she was too weak to do much of anything, she asked Gabriella to go into the woods and gather, once again, bulrushes, fiddlehead ferns and other spring greens.

'You know the way, simply follow the stream until you see the brown heads of the bulrushes. Take care to step only on the raised mounds of grasses, as the earth near the marsh is likely to be waterlogged, following those mighty rains. While you and Middlenight do this,' she said with a smile, 'I shall tidy up and light a fire, for it feels damp and cold inside.'

Gabriella, seeing that her Mother had returned to her, felt nearly overwhelmed with joy. She and Middlenight spent the next few days happily exploring the woods, finding what they could to eat and, more often than not, returned each day with baskets filled with edible delights, bulrushes, berries, leeks and wild garlic, all the edibles the Mother and Gabriella had first partaken of, were sustaining them once more.

Each day, on her way to and from the woods, Gabriella would visit the milky sac and found, on the morning of the third day, it was milky no more. The whole bag had grown translucent and shimmered with all shades of colours.

It was so wonderful Gabriella gasped when she saw it. 'Look Middlenight,' she cried out, 'it has changed completely. Now it is more beautiful than ever.'

Later that day, after a particularly scrumptious feast, made by the Mother from all the forest bounty, Gabriella went to get fresh water for them all to drink. As she neared the cottage, on her way from the well, she walked to the branch to see what wondrous colours the sac would have on display now. When she looked, Gabriella could not believe her eyes, for there, hanging beneath the half-eaten leaf, was something else entirely. What was there, in the same position as the sac had been, was far from inanimate.

She sat down, staring at all that was happening, wondering what she was watching. As the setting sun warmed her back, it also warmed what had been the stagnant sac and the shape began to unfold. Slowly and deliberately it started each movement from its centre, opening to something greater than itself. 'Why, it has wings,' Gabriella cried and Middlenight bounded over to see.

The creature had a centre body and from it, two wings were gradually emerging. They were covered in a clear, sticky film. At first Gabriella wanted to help free it from the gluey substance, but as she observed, she could see that the wings, although working very hard to free themselves, were quite capable of doing so without her assistance.

Her Mother had once told her that butterflies began as caterpillars, but she had not believed her. As she looked upon this little creature, slowly opening itself to a new form, she could see the shape of a caterpillar in the middle of the two wings and thought, this must be it. *Can it be true?* she wondered. *Could I be seeing the very moment a caterpillar becomes a butterfly?* She could not believe her good fortune and raced inside to invite her Mother to the glorious occasion as well.

And as the three of them watched, for what seemed an age, at last all seemed complete. 'Oh, it really is a butterfly,' she whispered to Middlenight and her Mother. As the stunning creature stretched its wings in the sunshine, the light upon them was dazzling. Each time they opened wide, Gabriella could see new shades of lilac and pink, a little green, then dapples of gold and even splashes of red. She was mesmerized as the light began to dance even more magnificently upon the wings of the butterfly, warming it, urging it to take flight. So brightly did the sun shine, the butterfly simply had to comply, and with one great expansive stretch, it flew. Up it fluttered, off the leaf and into the sky.

Gabriella jumped up to follow. She was enraptured, joyous in the discovery of it all and had no eye or thought for anything other. The newborn creature fairly danced in the clearing, flitting from wall, to grass, to windowsill, and back again, before alighting on its original branch.

As the sun began to descend in the west, the butterfly turned, as if to face Gabriella, and very slowly fluttered its wings at her as if to invite her to come closer. Gabriella did so and as she took two small steps in the direction of the branch where it sat, she held out her hand towards the creature. In that instant, it flew towards her and landed on her first finger causing her to gasp with glee. It hovered there for a few moments, slowing opening and closing its wings, before flying off once more. The look of absolute delight upon Gabriella's face prompted the Mother and Middlenight to smile as each gave her a kiss. And so ended a nearly perfect day.

The next morning Gabriella ran outside to see if the butterfly was still there, but it was nowhere to be seen. 'Mama, my beautiful new friend is no longer with me,' she called out, tears trickling down her cheeks.

'Do not be sad little one, maybe it is simply looking for breakfast. Look for the flowering plants, for they contain the nectar the butterflies thirst for. But before you run off, you and Middlenight must have some nourishment of your own,' said the Mother as she set down two bowls, one on the table and one on the floor.

Middlenight bounded over to his and without even a sniff gobbled all of it. Quite the opposite of him, Gabriella reluctantly sat down to her breakfast of bulrushes and berries, but she was only disgruntled on the outside. Secretly, she was delighted to have the loving care of her Mother restored to her once more. *What a long winter it was,* she thought. *And how very far away it all seems this sunny morning.*

When they finished, Gabriella asked if they might play in the woods. 'Perhaps my butterfly is there after all,' she said, unable to contain herself indoors any longer.

'Yes, of course you may go in search of it,' said the Mother. 'Do you think you could gather food for us as you go?'

'Of course, Mama.' Gabriella kissed her Mother briskly and she and Middlenight ran off quickly towards the woods, past the well and the garden and alongside the now rapidly flowing stream. But by the time they had arrived as far as the marsh with the bulrushes there was still no sign of the butterfly and Gabriella, determined to find it, chose to travel more deeply into the forest and, in her excitement, forgot all about gathering food.

Minding her footing on the soggy soil, Gabriella picked her way through the vast clumps of bulrushes and arrived at a place she had never been before. On this side of the marsh, the trees were different; hemlock, oak and pine were replaced by beech, hazel and birch. Through the branches of the first stand of hazel trees twined an ancient honeysuckle, its perfume scenting the air with sweetness. Gabriella paused to take a deep breath and it was then that she found it. Her butterfly. It seemed to see her as well, flew near and landed right upon her head, which made her giggle. Then it was off once more, flitting and fluttering in all of its iridescent glory.

Determined not to lose sight of it, Gabriella followed, with Middlenight fast on her heels. In and out of the new forest they skipped and jumped in the dappled light of the springtime. So fully engaged in play was Gabriella that she did not notice the sun rising or lowering in the sky. Suddenly, she felt too tired to take another step and so she lay down on a soft cushion of moss and closed her eyes. When she awoke, the sun was setting and she knew that the whole day had passed.

'Oh, Middlenight,' she exclaimed. 'We must go back, Mama will be so worried about us.' He seemed to agree and stood alongside her, ready to head for home. But Gabriella did not know which way home was. She had followed the butterfly so deeply into the unfamiliar woods that she could no longer see the bulrushes and they, and the basket that she had left at its edge, were her only landmarks.

She tried very hard to be grown-up and decided to walk twenty steps in each direction to see if something familiar would appear, but it did not help. Then she decided to climb up a tree for a better perspective. She found a hazel tree with a branch low enough that she could grab it with her hand. This she did, but with only one arm, she found she did not have the strength to hoist her legs over the branch to pull herself up. *What do we do?* she wondered.

With the sun now nearing the horizon, she was not only scared, but growing hungry and cold as well. She sat down on the ground and prayed, 'Dear Guiding Lights, please help me to find the way back home.' As she spoke the words, the butterfly flew to them once more; and for a moment, she was less frightened. This time, rather than flit about, the butterfly came and sat still directly before her and it seemed to be looking into her eyes. 'What do you want me to do?' Gabriella asked it. And the butterfly responded by taking to flight, in a very direct manner. 'Shall I follow you?' she asked and the butterfly seemed to nod yes in response to her question. So, follow they did.

A FIRE IN THE WOODS

In the glimmering light of the sunset the butterfly sparkled, making it not difficult to follow at all. Then, as they entered a dark glade, it was no longer visible. Nothing was visible; Gabriella could scarcely see anything at all, as the moon was just a sliver. She reached out for Middlenight, who was always at her side and he, as always, helped her to feel less afraid. The land beneath her feet was growing steeper and she could tell she was climbing a hill. Part of her thought she should stop, but another part felt inclined to continue and so she did. When she arrived at the highest point, she saw a glistening in the distance and slowly walked towards it. As she came closer she saw and smelled that it was a fire.

She knew a fire meant another person. The thought of something warm compelled her towards it, but she remembered her Mother's words about being special and how people who were special were often misunderstood. She stood very still and wondered what to do. *Maybe Mama is wrong; maybe not everyone is mean and afraid of things they do not understand.* She did not want to be disobedient, but she did yearn to warm herself by the roaring blaze of the fire. So, even though she had no means of disguising her disfigured body, she made her way, very gingerly, down the slope and towards the light.

As she came closer she stepped on a large stick. Snap! It sounded through the night air. From behind a large tree leapt a very hairy man, waving a stick, shouting in a booming voice.

'Who is there?'

Gabriella let out a yelp, followed immediately by, 'It is only me.'

When the man asked her to come towards him, she did so. Her heart was beating so quickly she could hardly breathe and her knees felt wildly unsteady. She moved, along with Middlenight, tentatively closer to the fire's edge.

'Come into the light!' the voice thundered in the night air. Feeling anxious and afraid, she obeyed his command, lowering her head and inching her way forward until she could feel the heat of the flames upon her hair.

'Now, let me see you. Look at me,' he demanded. Ever so slowly she lifted her chin and looked in the direction of his voice.

Before her stood a huge man with grey matted hair, which not only covered his head, but grew thickly from his cheeks and chin, tumbling halfway down his chest. It all seemed on fire with the reflected light from the flames, and his eyes were wild with some sort of pain.

'Come closer still, I can hardly see you!' he insisted.

Gabriella, wide-eyed, made her way around the fire so that he might better see her face and as she drew near, she saw his expression soften and his eyes fill with tears. Dropping his menacing stick he fell to his knees, and he cried out in a cracked and broken voice.

'It is you! At last I have found you.' And then he began to weep.

It was a sound like nothing Gabriella had ever heard before. It was as though some part of him would never cease crying and, feeling overwhelmed with loving care, she drew near to him, knelt alongside his body and placed her hand, ever so softly, upon his head.

Feeling her gentle touch, the man grew still, turning to look deeply into her eyes.

'Gabriella,' he began.

She gasped. 'How do you know my name?'

'It is all I know,' he replied.

'Dear one,' he continued, 'you and your dog must be hungry. Let me prepare you a meal.'

'His name is Middlenight, and we would both be very grateful for your kindness,' she replied.

Within moments the man had prepared some welcome food for them all and the three of them basked in the warmth of the bonfire in a strange silence.

But unbeknownst to them, their every movement was being observed from within the shadows.

After they had eaten, Gabriella felt overcome with exhaustion and longed to rest her head and sleep, but she knew she had to find her way back to her Mother who must have become very worried for her by now.

'I can sense that you are anxious,' the man said as if he could read her thoughts. 'But it is far too late to travel now. I promise I will help you find your way home when the sun returns.'

With a few quick movements he prepared a place for her to sleep, near enough to the fire to keep her warm, yet far enough away from any sparks that might harm her in the night.

As Middlenight settled in alongside her, Gabriella silently asked her Guiding Lights to give her Mother a sense of peace. And, feeling calmed by her thoughts, she fell quickly asleep.

Gabriella awoke to the intoxicating smell of honey. The man had prepared her a bowl of oatmeal covered with clear sweet honey, which she hadn't tasted in years and, in her enjoyment, Gabriella nearly forgot that she needed to find her way back home. By the time she had finished, the man had extinguished the fire and packed his belongings into a small satchel. He then covered the remnants of the fire with leaves and sticks, disguising the fact that they had been there at all.

'We must go then,' he said. And the three set off into the forest.

Gabriella remembered climbing a hill to get a better view the evening before. 'This way,' she said, pointing a finger and running ahead of him. Up they climbed the little knoll and down once more into the stands of hazel overrun with honeysuckle.

'This is where I followed my friend the butterfly,' she told him with a smile. 'That is how I ended up being at your fire to begin with.'

'I am indebted to your winged friend,' he said with a little bow. Gabriella did not know what indebted meant, but she could tell from the tone of his voice that it was something good.

'Now, this is where I get confused,' she said after a few moments of wandering through the hazel trees. 'We came past the marsh with the bulrushes, which is the farthest I have ever been from home and now I do not recognize anything at all.'

'Have no fear. I know this marsh of which you speak,' he said. And with sure steps he guided them to it. As they drew closer Gabriella saw the basket, exactly where she had left it, and ran to retrieve it.

'Now, you must have a meal with Mama, Middlenight and me,' she said as she began to pick enough bulrushes for them all. 'Come on, hurry.' She fairly ran along the stream, gathering berries, leeks and wild garlic until, at last, with a basket full to overflowing, the three arrived at the cottage.

'Perhaps you should go in first,' said the man.

Gabriella nodded and called out, 'Mama, Mama we are home.'

'Gabriella!' came a hoarse voice from within the walls.

'Yes, Mama I am here.' She ran indoors.

There she found her Mother lying on the heather bed, pale as snow. Her eyes had dark rings beneath them and she looked as though she had been crying.

'Where have you been? Where did you go, my beautiful child? I searched for you all the night, until the cold and the darkness made it impossible to continue.'

'Oh. Mama, I am so sorry. I got lost in the woods and could not find my way home again. And then, when I went to the top of a little hill to try and get a better view, I saw a blazing fire. I knew I should not go near, as it meant a person was there, but I was so cold. I walked down the little hill towards the fire and a man jumped out from behind a tree.

'He asked me to come closer and even though I was afraid, I did. And then, when I was close enough for him to see me, he called me by my name.'

115

At this the Mother turned paler still and repeated her daughter's words, 'He called you by name?'

'Yes, Mama and then he fed Middlenight and me, twice, before he helped us find our way home.'

'Did he follow you here?' she asked in a near whisper.

'Yes, I told him it was our turn to cook him a feast,' she said with a big smile.

The Mother sat upright on the bed of heather, swung her legs around until her feet touched the ground and with some effort she stood up. After straightening her blouse and skirt she took a deep breath and asked, 'Where is he now?'

'I left him sitting by the well.'

'Well, go and get him then,' she said.

When Gabriella had left the cottage, the Mother rushed to the kitchen and grabbed a stool. This she held high over her head as she stood waiting for whoever was outside. The man called to her from the front garden.

'Please forgive me,' said the man.

'What do you want?' cried the Mother. 'I know your voice,' she shouted with as much strength as she could muster.

'Your forgiveness. I need your forgiveness,' came the response. 'I have not rested since those two days, so long ago. I have searched my heart for answers and a peace which will not come.'

'Why have you sought to find us now, after all this time?' she called back.

'I was awakened by an owl on the night of the roundest moon, just passed. And in its call I hoped that perhaps, against all odds, you were still alive. For I had not heard its voice since the day following her Naming Day.'

Hearing these words, the Mother's fears diminished, for the owl had come also to her that night. She lowered the stool on to the floor and walked out of her cottage. There before her was the High Priest, but she was shocked by the sight of him. He was dishevelled, his hair was knotted and filthy, his fingernails brown with the dirt caked beneath them and he stank. This was not the pristinely dressed man of the Law who had dropped her child from his raised arms and then handed down a sentence of death to the Midwife.

'Since the day you whispered, "Her name is Gabriella" in my ear, since the moment I set eyes upon this child, something has stirred within my breast,' he said, in a voice that was fragile with awe. 'All I had believed to be true was suddenly made false as I gazed at the light within her. So fierce, so brilliant was that light on her Naming Day, I felt as though my very eyes were on fire.'

He paused, looking deeply into the Mother's eyes. 'The burning pain I experienced in gazing upon her was overwhelming. It was an exquisite agony. As I looked upon her, tears poured down my cheeks and I was powerless to stop them. I had to force myself to turn away from her. I was blinded. And yet for the first time in my life I could see.

'In tearing her rainbow garment from her body, it was clear to all that she was grotesquely disfigured, obviously misshapen, and yet, in having looked upon the staggeringly beautiful essence of her creation, that which existed simply by her being alive, her nakedness exposed only the deformed nature of my own spirit.

'But, even knowing this, my pride and fear of retribution clouded my judgment that day, and I chose not to speak of this truth. I chose to remain silent, a decision that has haunted me ever since.'

When it was clear he had finished speaking, Gabriella turned to look at her Mother, frail and weak with exhaustion; her once shining golden hair, now faded to grey, her face drawn and pale, old before its time, and saw past all of this to the depths of her strength and her devotion. Her heart felt warm with the knowledge of how well she was loved. Gabriella put her arm around her Mother's tiny waist and held her close.

'I love you, Mama,' she whispered.

'And I love you,' the Mother whispered in response.

After the two held one another for a long while, the Mother turned towards the broken figure of a man in her front garden and said, 'I forgive you and I thank you for your courage in finding us. Your words have brought healing and strength to us. You are welcome here.'

And with that, the three of them, closely followed by Middlenight, went into the cottage and drew near the fire. The talk between them continued throughout the day as the High Priest told of his sorrow on the day the basket of ash was given to him as proof of their deaths following the Mother's flight from the village.

He was genuinely shocked to hear of the vandalism and the attempted stoning that had taken place, precipitating her early morning exodus. And he did not know that his son had been one of those who had discovered the basket, until the Mother told him she had heard his voice, very clearly, along with the voices of one of his guards and the Father.

He went on to say that he had fallen into a dark world of self-loathing and hatred, knowing that he had remained silent when presented with an opportunity to speak of love and, instead, had chosen to continue leading the people on a path born of fear.

'And so, from the moment the basket was presented to me, until this day, I have resigned myself from the priesthood. I no longer believe the Mountain of Remembrance has dark powers, that the River of Dreams holds a horrible secret; I no longer need to judge those things, which I do not fully understand, as evil. I choose, instead, to hold fast to the hope that my life might be of service in some other way. I have found I can no longer serve a Law that sees such light, the light that I saw then, and still see this day, in both of you, as worthless, simply because of a difference in shape or form.

'On the day of her naming, all such differences were lost to me. I knew then from my depths that we are all part of a greater whole and we all are uniquely given to one another as gifts of uncommon value. Please, call me Brother, and know that your forgiveness and grace have healed the aching within this old man's heart.'

'My Brother,' said the Mother, giving him a hug. 'How joyful I am to have this time with you.' She smiled at him and then, looking to Gabriella, she said, 'Oh, Gabriella, you were right to have gathered such bounty for us, for there will be three for meals as long as our Brother would like to stay.'

As she spoke the words, it was as though an unbearable weight was being lifted from her. For so long she had been alone, isolated, with all the worry of protecting Gabriella and providing for them both. She had carried the knowledge of her daughter's deformity and the horrible consequence of having kept the truth of it from the authorities on her own shoulders and now, in this reunion, she, at last, found relief.

The talking continued as the meal was prepared, but the focus shifted from the distant past and became more about the present. The Mother was praised for her remarkable cooking and the stories of her finding the cottage, of planting the garden, the bounty and the gift of the market days were recounted and then they spoke of getting to work in the earth once more, now that the rains had come and restored the moisture.

There was a lilt in the Mother's voice that Gabriella had rarely heard and she was grateful that all had happened as it had happened. As she lay on the floor, stroking Middlenight, not really hearing the words of the grown-ups as more than a hum, she thought of her butterfly. She had not seen it all day. *Hmmm, what a gift it was. If I had not seen it transformed from a caterpillar, I may not have been so interested in it. But as I had watched it become its new self, I simply had to dance and celebrate with it. And if I had not gone in search of it, I would never have happened upon the Brother's bonfire. Things have a special way of fitting together if you listen and observe* she thought.

The warmth of the fire and the comfort in stroking Middlenight's silky coat soon made her eyes grow heavy and she fell fast asleep. The Mother, seeing this, knew it was time to put her in bed and walked over to where she slept, stooping to lift her on to the softer heather bed. The Brother said, 'Allow me', and lifted her little body with ease on to the fragrant mattress. The Mother watched him with gratitude and, again, a feeling of her load being lessened swept over her.

'You, too, must get some rest for we have much to do on the morrow,' he said. And with a slight inclining of his head he wished her a good night and walked out of the cottage, explaining that he would be most comfortable beneath the stars.

Patchy clouds reflecting the sliver of moon cast a silvery glow on the cottage as the Brother unrolled his blankets and climbed between them. His body was tired, his journey to this day had taken eleven years and he knew, this night, he would rest at last. As he drifted to sleep he gazed at the sky, the light breeze shifting the clouds ever so slightly to reveal different patterns of starry sky, which twinkled merrily down upon him. He felt his legs and his arms grow heavy and then to sleep.

Crack! Footsteps! Silence. He found himself sitting bolt upright, straining to hear more but he heard nothing. He gathered his blankets and slowly crept inside the cottage, hoping he had not been seen. He stealthily made his way to the bed where the Mother and Gabriella were fast asleep. Middlenight woke, but made not a sound. The Mother was closest to the door and he placed his hand gently over her mouth, which startled her.

Quickly he placed the finger of his other hand to his lips, removed his hand from her mouth and whispered, 'Shhh, I heard noises, footsteps outside the cottage. Has anyone ever come this way before?'

'No,' she replied. 'Not a soul in all the while we have lived here.'

'I fear I may have placed you in grave danger,' he said, his eyes wide with worry.

'Whatever it is, whoever they may be, we shall face them together. For I know you would not have brought any harm upon us knowingly,' the Mother said.

'Wake Gabriella,' the Brother whispered.

This the Mother did silently, and with great tenderness.

The three sat, not sure of what to do and then a voice cut through the night air.

'Father, I know you are in there with the woman and her demon child. Come out,' shouted a disdainful, mocking voice.

It was as a knife to the Brother's heart.

'You are the High Priest of the Land of Never Forgetting. Have you abandoned your vow to uphold the Law of the Almighty? Since the birth of this child, an evil has plagued our Land and it is your Holy Duty to put an end to this abomination. You failed in this when her deformity was first discovered, allowing the two of them to live. This weakness shall end this night. For, I, as your eldest son, the rightful heir to the throne of High Priest, will assume this responsibility, even if you do not. I shall reclaim the power of the Law, which you so carelessly discarded. Your weakness disgusts me, old man. I am humiliated in it. This night, it is finished.'

The Brother looked out the window and saw a group of men, with torches, standing at the end of the gate, his son directly in the middle of them.

'My son, there is no need for violence. There is no evil here. Merely a woman and her child.'

'Do not attempt to instruct me on what is evil and what is not. Your spirit has been enchanted in this and my ears have grown deaf to your voice. This child's form is sin. She is imperfect, nothing of the Almighty's making. We all bore witness to this on her Naming Day. You, too, were there. Have you no memory of this, you wretched man?'

'I have thought only of this. While it is true she is not as others, I have been given new eyes to see her creation as simply different than my own, nothing to fear, nothing to revile. In her birth I have found a new life.'

'Blasphemer! Did you hear him?' he cried out to those around him. 'He credits this hideous creature with new life. This is a gift only bestowed on us by the Almighty. You shall not diminish His authority in my presence. Enough. Silence yourself.'

The son gave a signal and suddenly there were arrows of flame being fired at the cottage. A few fell short of their mark, but many more lodged within the thatch. The roof began to smoke, the rains having left a residue of damp within the heather, as the Mother and Gabriella clung to each other, eyes wide with terror.

'Take me and leave them be,' pleaded the Brother to his son.

'No. They shall not escape the punishment they have so long avoided. This time, without your simpering protection, they will meet their deaths. It will be, as it should be, according to the Law,' he bellowed back.

The thatch was now crackling with fire, and smoke began to fill their little home. The Brother took strips of muslin, soaked them in the bucket of water and showed them how to breathe into them. Gabriella made one for Middlenight as well, hoping to help ease his panic.

'Now we shall wait for you to crawl out on your bellies, like the serpents you are,' came the voice of the son over the roaring flames.

Pieces of the roof fell on to the heather bed, setting it alight as well, and they soon realized they would all perish if they remained inside.

The Brother turned to the Mother and said in hushed tones, 'Could you find your way to the River of Dreams, even in the dark?'

'I think so. I know these woods well, and once through them, the River is not far.'

'Good. Then this is my plan. You, Gabriella and Middlenight will follow me. I will walk through the door, directly towards the men and then cross in front of the cottage, in the direction of the well. As soon as we are clear of the cottage wall, run for the River as fast as you are able. No matter what happens, do not stop; do not look back. Do you promise? The River is your only hope of safety. For, in their ignorance, their fear of it and the Mountain beyond will be too great for them to pursue you past its border with the Land.'

The Mother knew the depths of what he was offering and her eyes filled with tears. 'I cannot receive this gift from you,' she cried.

'You must,' he said wiping away her tears. 'You must.'

Then he turned to Gabriella, took her face in his hands and said, 'Shine, beautiful child, shine.'

'Now come, we have not a moment to waste.'

The Mother told Gabriella to hold her hand and run, as fast as she had ever run. Then, hugging the Brother, she said, 'We are ready.'

The Brother took a deep breath and expanded his chest to what seemed an enormous size, then held between his hands his blanket, which he hoped would shield the precious lives entrusted to him. The Mother took her place behind him, gripping Gabriella's hand tightly and Middlenight stood behind them. Not wanting to delay any longer, the Brother slowly walked out the door, directly towards his son.

'Foolish old man, do not make me kill you as well. Stop. Stop and save yourself,' came the command.

But, as the voice of the son was not heeded, rocks began to be thrown at him. Thuds of stone meeting tender flesh and skull nauseated the Mother and frightened Gabriella. But the Brother made no sound and continued on fearlessly. He walked; arms open wide, until he was standing just before the well.

And when the Mother was sure they were completely hidden from view, and the path behind the cottage was wide open to them, she began to run. As she fled, daughter in hand, dog by their side, she heard the first cries of pain as the ancient man was brutally silenced for his part in their lives.

He had told her to run and so she ran. She ran faster than she knew she could, her chest was heaving, gasping for air. At times Gabriella fell and the Mother dragged her by her arm until her feet were beneath her once more.

'Run, my darling. Run. It will not be long before they are upon us.'

They arrived at the wider path that led to the village and for a moment the Mother wondered if they ought to try and find help there. But behind them, in the distance, she could hear the shouts of the men following them; there was no time to pause. She garnered her strength once more and off they ran through the woods towards the River. The Mother had never been this way, but knew the River could not be far, as the summit of the Mountain was growing more visible. The trees soon thinned and the way became easier for them.

Still running, the land grew steadily steeper and she realized she must be nearing the cliff she had nearly fallen off of so long ago, when Gabriella was still a baby. They reached the end of the earth beneath their feet and saw, far below them, the quickly flowing River, nearly flooded by the heavy rains. They were trapped, there was no way they could survive the drop from this height into the depths below them. In the dim of night, the River seemed ominous and horribly threatening. The Mother felt weak-kneed, her mouth grew parched and she began to feel dizzy at the edge of the cliff. She turned to see if there was another way down and saw only the specks of light, the torches, drawing near.

'We have you now, witch,' came the cry from the son. 'There will be no escape this time.'

The Mother stood paralyzed, unable to move.

'Mama, what shall we do?' cried Gabriella.

'There is nothing to do. It is finished,' she replied.

And then, in a flash, Middlenight leapt off the cliff edge and into the River below.

'Middlenight!' screamed Gabriella and she jumped in after him, leaving the Mother alone on the cliff staring as her child struggled to keep her head above the surface of the torrential waters. And then, all fear left her body as she dived in to save her daughter.

The current was so strong and Gabriella was gasping for breath. She flailed about trying to grab something, anything, on the bank that could anchor her. 'Help,' she cried out, 'Help'. Within moments she found she was in the middle of the huge River; there was no bank, no branch to clutch, there was nothing but muddy, brown, icy water. Her fight to stay afloat seemed doomed until she felt a fierce tug at her sleeve. It was Middlenight.

Grabbing hold of her with his teeth he began to swim towards the closest shore, pushing her in front of his body as he struggled. He swam with great strength, guiding her towards the land ahead of them. Gabriella's teeth began to chatter and she felt her muscles growing weak with the shock of the cold as Middlenight strained in the torrent of the River until he, at last, pushed her body safely on to a sloping bank.

Then she heard the voice of her Mother calling, 'Gabriella. Gabriella.'

'Here, Mama, I am here.'

The Mother tried to swim towards the sound of her daughter's cries, but the current was too fierce for her. She was being taken under, into the swirling cold, and almost felt a relief in the letting go. Just when she had nearly given up, she sensed a tugging at her blouse. She was scared and confused until she recognized the form of Middlenight swimming alongside her, pushing her, shoving with all of his might, working to free her from the watery vice. When he managed to bring her to safety alongside Gabriella, he could barely move. The cold and the exertion had exhausted him.

Seeing this, Gabriella and her Mother reached out to help him just as a great surge of water threw them on to higher ground and hurled Middlenight further into its depths and away from the shore. They ran alongside him for as long as they could. Trying to find a stick, a root, something to help him hold fast and stop him being washed further down the River. But they found nothing. When the rocks on the shore grew so large and they could follow him no more, they watched as he was dragged back into the violence of the flooded waters.

'Middlenight, Middlenight,' Gabriella screamed.

But her words did little to help him fight the power of the raging current. His head was just above the surface as he disappeared around a distant bend in the River. 'Middlenight, Middlenight,' they called until they grew hoarse, until clouds had completely covered the moon. But for the first time ever, he did not come.

When they finally stopped calling his name, the Mother and Gabriella stood soaking wet, shivering in the dark cold, clinging to one another and they saw, in the distance, the torches moving away from the edge of the cliff.

'Oh, we have crossed the River of Dreams, sweet Gabriella. We have crossed the River of Dreams. I need to rest now,' the Mother whispered. 'I am so cold, so tired.'

Gabriella felt her Mother's hands and they were like ice. She tried to rub her Mother's body to warm it, but it did little good. Soon her Mother's teeth were chattering and she began to shake from head to toe in an alarming manner. Gabriella tried to hold her Mother in her arm, cradling her head upon her lap as best she could.

'Mama, would it would be better if we kept moving? Would that help to warm you?' But the Mother did not answer and her silence frightened Gabriella.

'Mama? Mama? Are you awake?' She shook her gently in an effort to get a response. This helped, at least for a moment.

'Yes, I am here, my lovely Gabriella. I am here and you are safe beside me. We have crossed the River of Dreams; we are safe from them. Now you are truly safe from them.'

She said these things while gasping for breath, but still continued to speak.

'No matter what happens, know that you are precious and special. Know that you have a gift to give this world and never ever forget that you are, and have always been, my greatest joy.' Again her breathing grew shallow and her chest heaved with the struggle to draw another breath.

'Mama. Mama. You must rest now,' said Gabriella, holding her closer still.

'Gabriella, find your gift. Find the gift you have been given. And when you find it, give it back to the Creator.'

With these words, the clouds moved away from the moon and in its gentle glow the Mother saw the light of her daughter's eyes once more. She took her final breath.

And she felt nothing but love.

PART TWO
THE CHILD

THE FAR SHORE

Mama. Mama,' Gabriella whispered, but there was no response. Her eyes were still looking directly at Gabriella, but there was no longer any life within them, only a glassy stare.

Gabriella sat beside her Mother's dead body, gazing at the bend in the River of Dreams, where she had last seen Middlenight, and began to weep. Through her tears, she could see that the River was no longer violent and fast moving, as it had been when they first fell into its icy grasp. In the moonlight, it seemed to be transforming, somehow, into something more akin to a great lake, calm and mysterious, its waters now rising at an alarming rate, drawing closer and closer to where she sat alongside her Mother.

Gabriella was transfixed, unable to stop staring at the water and in hardly any time at all, the River had risen to where she was seated, its cold wet fingers nearly enveloping her. Realizing that the floods were worsening, she jumped up and struggled to climb further up the bank. Not wanting to leave her Mother behind, she wrapped her arm around the dead woman and attempted to lift her as well.

She quickly lost footing and slipped down the bank, into knee-deep, freezing water. Scrambling to regain her position, she held fast to her Mother and tried again; but it was no use, she did not have the strength to push herself and the body up the slope of the riverbank.

Gabriella grabbed hold of a protruding root and held her Mother's body between the earth and the advancing water, as though trying to protect her. The current quickened and Gabriella found holding on nearly impossible.

She tried to wrap her legs around her Mother's waist, but nothing she did could stop the advancing waters; she could not hold on to her Mother much longer. Again the River rose and Gabriella struggled to keep her head above the water. She had to let go, had to climb for safety. If she did not, she would be swept back into the current of the River once more. 'I do not want to let go of you. I do not want to let go of you, Mama,' she cried out.

She remembered her Mother's last words to her, encouraging her to find her gift, and in remembering, she knew from her depths that she had to let go of all that had been and choose, instead, to hold fast to life, to hold fast to that which was yet to be. With tears pouring down her cheeks, her body poised precariously between safety and danger, she loosened the grip of her legs from around her Mother's waist and in that simple action, the Mother's body was released, set afloat on the River of Dreams.

Gabriella pulled on the root with all of her might, and aided by what strength she had left in her legs, she clambered up the rocky edge of bank until she was out of harm's way and looked back just in time to see her Mother's body gliding, gently, along the River. Her face, an oval of pale luminous reflection, radiant in the moonlight and Gabriella thought that she looked very beautiful, so peaceful, so still.

She stood on tiptoe to see the silvery form of her Mother drifting away from her for as long as she was able. She watched until the Mother's body rounded the bend where Middlenight had last been seen. She strained to see beyond, struggling against the rocky terrain, until she could go no further, she could see no more. Soaking wet, very cold and terribly hungry, with not a tear left to cry, her knees gave way and she sank into a heap upon the ground.

Gabriella, shivering, teeth chattering, lay on her side and curled into a ball. Her knees were drawn up to her chest, her head tucked down, as she attempted, with her body, to comfort the aching within her heart, to ease the horrible pain. She tried to rock herself, tried to calm her mind, but her thoughts were haunted by memories of the flaming arrows, the sounds of the stones hitting the Brother's flesh, the vacant, final look in her Mama's eyes.

Gabriella's clothes were drenched and she could not find a way to warm herself. She ran on the spot, cupped her hand over her mouth to feel the warmth of her breath, she rubbed her legs, she tried everything she could think of to warm up, but none of it helped. After all her efforts, she found she was still bitterly cold and growing weaker and weaker. 'Guiding Lights, I am so cold and so tired and so hungry. I need your help,' she barely whispered, before exhaustion closed her eyes.

She lay, as if in a trance, as though suspended in a cloud. And there, on that solemn night, on the bank of the River of Dreams, at the foot of the Mountain of Remembrance, her voice was heard.

She was awakened not by sunshine, but by the sound of dry wood crackling in a brightly burning fire. She sat up and drew alongside its warmth, amazed at how such a thing could have happened. She looked around her and in the light of the nearly new day, she saw only water and land and sky. There was no other person or animal in sight.

How did this fire come to be lit? Who has done this? Her mind was filled with questions she had no answers for. She stood up, prepared to go searching for the person who had built the fire when she saw, to her further amazement, on the far side of the flames, arranged on a white handkerchief, a breakfast seemingly prepared just for her. There on the square of white linen were freshly-baked biscuits with honey, hot tea and ripe berries in clotted cream. Again, there was no one there to thank for her feast, no one present to share in its bounty. 'How is this?' she asked aloud, pinching herself to see if she was still asleep, but when it hurt, she knew she was awake.

I am not dreaming, but surely none of this is real. In an effort to prove it was an illusion, she walked towards the food, picked up a biscuit and took an enormous bite. The still warm biscuit melted on her tongue, its moist sweetness filling her empty stomach. She ate and ate and ate some more, washing all the biscuits down with honey-sweetened tea and finished her feast by eating the berries and cream.

'I want to say thank you to whoever has given me these gifts,' she said aloud.

And as soon as she had uttered the words a great movement of wings sounded in the towering oak above her head. It was the owl she had seen only days before. It was a wonderful feeling to see something she recognized. *Why is she here at daylight?* Gabriella wondered, knowing that owls preferred the night.

As if she had heard Gabriella's thought, the owl hooted loudly in response.

'Why, it is as though you understand what I am saying. I think you are a very intelligent owl. I shall name you the Owl of Knowing.'

The Owl blinked at her, hooted once more, in apparent response to being named, and then, with some insistence, in the form of prodding wings and scolding tones, she encouraged Gabriella to begin walking up a path, which began at the base of the scree-covered Mountain of Remembrance.

Gabriella, unwilling to leave the warmth of the fire and overjoyed at the presence of another living thing, began to tell Owl all that had happened since the night of the roundest moon, the night when they had first met. 'Owl, so much has happened since then. A man with long white hair came from the Land of Never Forgetting to find us. He told us that he had been the High Priest on my Naming Day and that you visited him on the same night you visited Mama and Middlenight and me at the cottage.

'He had food with us, he helped me find my way out of the forest, but his son followed him and tried to hurt my Mother and me. He protected us against the bad men and told us to run to the River of Dreams. We did, all of us, run and run, but both Middlenight and Mama have been carried away in the flooded water. I cannot go up the path Owl, I cannot leave this place, for it is closest to those I love best.'

The Owl looked at Gabriella intently as she spoke, again, as though she understood everything the child was saying, but this did not change anything. In fact, she grew more insistent the longer Gabriella remained unmoved, even adding a few gentle pecks for emphasis. 'Up,' Owl seemed to say, 'up the path.' Gabriella looked in the direction Owl was gesturing, unable to see the top of the path, and the thought of climbing something so huge and steep seemed utterly terrifying.

Even a normal person would find that difficult, she thought. *But for me, with only one arm, it would be impossible.* She decided to ignore Owl's bidding and said, loudly, as if to bolster her courage, 'I think I'll wait here until the flood waters recede, then I can cross back to the Land and return to the cottage and plant my Mother's garden once more. I am sure the bad men think we have all perished. It will be safe there once more and I can carry on with my Mother's work.'

She leaned against the biggest rock at the base of the path, ignoring the bird's increasingly emphatic efforts to get her moving up the path and waited for the flooding to diminish so that she could make her way back across the River. But as she watched, the waters once more seemed to grow even stronger, rising higher on the shores of both sides. She sat until the sun reached its highest and brightest point and she continued to sit, all alone, until the shadows lengthened. Owl, perhaps tired of being awake in the day, perhaps tired of Gabriella's stubbornness and finding her urgings rejected by the girl, had long since departed.

The fire had by now consumed itself, it was fast growing dark and the stone supporting Gabriella began to feel icy cold against the thin fabric of her dress and apron. She wished she had not eaten all of the food and drink, for the familiar feelings of cold, hunger and thirst returned with the sun's setting. It was odd to be on the opposite side of the shore and to see the Land from another perspective. Odder still that no one seemed to be looking for her, or perhaps that was not so odd. Deep down, it confirmed what she had always known, no one really cared, except for her Mother, if she lived or died. No one even really knew she existed any more. She knew that she had been a burden, her flesh considered an outward sign of sin by those who did not understand, living proof of the presence of evil. *If only I hadn't followed the butterfly into the woods and invited the Brother for a meal, none of this would have happened. Oh, why am I still here? Why has the River not taken me instead of Mama and Middlenight?*

Her left side began to ache but it seemed a deeper, sharper pain than ever before. This time it ached right through her back and into her chest, sending searing hot flashes of pain up and down the whole of her left side. 'Why me? I didn't ask to be born this way,' she cried. 'Why has my life caused so much pain for everyone who has loved me?'

As the air grew cold, so did Gabriella's heart. The wind strengthened and as it coursed down the Mountain it began to howl. She felt oddly comforted by its woeful song, which seemed to echo her own feelings. Feeling a drop of moisture on her arm she thought for a brief moment that it had begun to rain; but looking at the half moon and the indigo sky surrounding it, she saw there were no clouds at all. With the tip of her tongue, she tasted the moist place on her arm and its saltiness told her that the ocean inside of her had begun to overflow once more. And so she joined with the sound of the wind, crying to the moon, begging the darkness to become light, begging the reflection of the sun to lead her home once more.

In a twinkling, her loneliness was lessened by the sudden appearance of Owl, whose now familiar form, silhouetted in moonlight, brought relief to the child. While the beautiful bird, as much mother in this moment as any she had ever known, descended to her side, Gabriella made the decision that she would hearken to the wisdom of this new and faithful friend. And all fear at the prospect of climbing the Mountain, vanished. The great bird flew to Gabriella's side, settled on the ground and nestled behind her, wrapping its huge wings around her in a protective embrace, fending off both cold and sorrow and Gabriella knew, without a doubt, that she was no longer alone. There, in the soft comfort of Owl's wings, she rested.

A Remarkable Dream

Her sleep was deeper than any she had ever known and filled with images and sounds: hooded men holding torches, throwing stones, pointing at her, taunting her, dismissing her very form as something to be reviled. She saw Middlenight being swept away in the waves, she heard the screech of Owl, heard the voice of the Brother telling her to shine brightly. Quick pulsating images of all she had ever known began to travel more and more quickly through the land of her sleep, until all was a blur, a dizzying manifestation of all she had experienced until now. And then, it all burst into flames, like a great bonfire. One giant ball of flame containing all of the faces, all of the words, all of the memories of being bound and gagged, all of the sadness, all of the fear. Then, slowly in her dream, from this great ball of fire came a wisp of smoke, spiralling, from the flames of memory, towards the sky above.

This spiral was not the grey of ordinary smoke. It was red, then orange, yellow, green, blue, violet and white. All the scenes, all the hurts, all the images were lifted one by one in this smoke, ascending skywards from the earth, until they were all finished, until there were no more painful memories. It seemed there was nothing left within her mind's eye at all, just clarity and a feeling of buoyancy, and even though she knew somehow that this was a dream, Gabriella felt as though this fire and its rainbow plume had become the actual story of her life.

Gradually, the smoky helix began to take the form of a ladder and she could see it coiled from the path at the base of the Mountain of Remembrance, all the way to its summit. There, at the very top, the glistening white part of the smoke ladder entered a cave, carved within the side of the stone. In her dream, Gabriella began to climb, slowly inching her way higher and higher alongside the slate-coloured slopes, she felt no fear, only excitement. Her hand moved, with ease, from rung of colour to rung of colour, and she noticed that the higher she climbed, the more delicate the texture of the smoke plume became. When she arrived at the very edge of the violet-turning-white she found, to her delight, that she could actually see inside the cave.

'Come, my beautiful child, come inside,' a voice called to her from within.

'Mama! Where are you?'

'Come beloved Gabriella. Come. Come to the cave at the top of the Mountain of Remembrance, here you shall find your great gift,' the Mother said.

Gabriella tried to step off of the ladder, but found it impossible to do so. She could only gaze into the cave. She did not see her Mama, no matter how hard she tried, but it was almost enough. For the cave was utterly beautiful: ornate rugs of deep blue and violet covered the earthen floors; crystal lamps with coloured oil burned brightly; the mouth-watering scent of delicious food, warming on a stove wafted in a gentle breeze; flowers of unearthly beauty filled vases made of silver, and there on the wall was an elegant mirror in a golden frame. Even though she had not entered the cave, she could somehow see the mirror quite clearly. As she gazed into it, Gabriella caught a glimpse of long silver hair, glistening in the moonlight, alongside her own face. And then in a whispered glance, another face, next to hers in the mirror, seemed to see her, truly see her, looking directly into her eyes and to the depths of her heart. So fierce was the gaze it caused her to gasp aloud.

Now wide-awake at the foot of the Mountain, with Owl's wings still embracing her, Gabriella wondered at the dream. It had all felt so very real to her. Lost in her thoughts, still dreaming, though awake, she could think only of the cave and her Mother, whose voice had beckoned to her from inside it.

Owl, aware that she was not paying any attention, gave her a gentle nudge with a wing. This was enough to rouse her from her reverie and when she opened her eyes, to truly see, she found there, laid out before them, another sumptuous feast, another roaring fire. This time there were nuts and fruits; more hot tea with honey and a loaf of bread with cinnamon and sweet brown sugar, swirled through the middle. Gabriella gave thanks for the mysterious gifts of food, drink and fire, offered some of the feast to Owl, which was refused, and then ate just enough to feel satiated, wrapped the remaining bread, fruit and nuts in her handkerchief, tucked the parcel of goodies into her apron pocket and looked up towards the peak of the Mountain.

She saw that it seemed no less daunting in size than it had the day before and although nothing in her wanted to leave the River's edge, for it was here she felt closest to the Mother and Middlenight, somehow, the gift of her dream created a deep desire within her to reach the summit. She had heard her Mama's voice tell her to come inside, that she would find her gift inside the cave. With a final glance at the still swollen waters of the River of Dreams, knowing she had to find her way to the cave, she closed her eyes and said, 'Goodbye Middlenight. Goodbye Mama. I shall love you always and always.'

Her left side ached. It was not the piercing pain of yesterday, but the pulsing, throbbing ache, which had grown more constant as she had grown older. She gave it a rub, thanked her Guiding Lights for her safety and said a prayer that her feet would find safe footing.

Taking a very deep breath she turned away from all that was familiar, from all that she knew, and began to walk up the Mountain. On her fifth step, she noticed something sparkling brightly on the ground beside the path. Pausing, she stooped down to take a closer look; it was a dark red stone, clear and deep. And then she heard a voice inside, which said:

Garnet, stone of red, for you,
Will help you know just what to do.

Hold it now within your hand.
And turn your back upon the Land.

Commit your Self to your new goal.
Release the past. Be still. Be whole.

Who is that? she wondered. It had sounded like an old woman's voice. 'Who is that?' she asked aloud, but there was no answer. So, she picked up the beautiful stone, placed it with reverential care in the pocket of her apron and began to walk.

The Reflecting Pool

With Owl as her guide she found herself nimble-footed and much more agile than she could have imagined. Owl would fly ahead, find the best path and then return to Gabriella's side to guide her in safety and in this manner, step by step, the two made their way. The mountainside about them was covered with a variety of plants and flowers, which looked especially beautiful in the morning air, all dewy and fresh, awaiting the warmth of the sun.

From far away the Mountain had looked like a great mass of stone and pebble but once embarked on the pathway up, Gabriella could see that it was filled with all sorts of life. She did not see any animals or hear any songbirds, but the mountainside was covered with wild orchids, lichen and moss which grew wherever they could between the stones, and there were waterfalls, waterfalls, everywhere. Graceful arcs of cascading water falling to clear still pools in which Gabriella could catch glimpses of her own image.

As the sun drew high in the sky, to a point directly overhead, she began to feel tired and decided to find a pleasant spot to rest. She found herself by a gentle waterfall, which began quite high above her head and ended its tumble down the slope in a small pool of the clearest water Gabriella had ever seen. The sun was brightly shining on the surface of the water and all of the beauty surrounding it was reflected in its depths.

Gabriella could see the purples and pinks of the wild orchids and the iris which lined its banks; the yellow of the buttercups and gorse; she saw the clouds which floated high in the sky and then beyond the reflections; she found she could look straight down to the bottom of the pool. It seemed very deep, indeed. Gabriella felt that it went as far down as the Mountain went up and, in some way, she thought she was looking into a watery reflection of all that was.

Feeling drawn to gaze into it more deeply, in hopes of seeing more and more, she began to walk around the edges of the pool, with purposeful steps, searching for exactly the right spot to begin her study. About halfway round, just opposite the point where the waterfall entered the pool, Gabriella found a perfect circle of greenest clover, surrounded by orange-coloured wildflowers. 'Here it is. This is the just the place!' Gabriella exclaimed to Owl.

I will eat a bite of food first in order to be able to concentrate more, she thought and reached into her apron pocket for the remainder of the morning's feast, but when she pulled at the handkerchief wrapped round it, her hand felt something else. *What is this?* she wondered, reaching back into her pocket to feel the cool rounded shape of the stone.

'Of course, it is the stone of red,' she said to Owl, turning it from side to side, admiring it once more, thinking of the strange words that had accompanied its discovery.

Then, very carefully, she placed it back into her deep pocket. Gabriella felt quite grown-up for having rationed some of her feast as she unwrapped the food in the handkerchief. She ate half of all she had, offered a portion to Owl, which was, once more, refused, and then turned to the clear water for refreshment. As her cupped hand slid through the shimmering surface in order to draw water towards her lips, she saw her face fully for the first time. Here in this moment she almost believed there was someone quite beautiful returning her gaze.

How remarkable it is to look deeply into my own eyes, she thought.

Gabriella cupped the water three times in all: twice to drink and once to feel its refreshing coolness on her eyes, her cheeks and her throat. After she did this, she again looked within the water. She saw all she had seen before: flowers, clouds, the mountainside; but suddenly she, too, was contained within the watery image. She could see herself and all of the beauty around her at the same moment. She was in it and it was in her. In amazement, she stared and stared and it was as though the water grew more and more settled in response to Gabriella's increasing stillness.

Then, the ripples on the water's surface ceased and the only sounds were those of the gentle waterfall and Gabriella's breath, moving deeper and deeper, quieter and quieter.

As her eyes adjusted even more, Gabriella could see the deep descent of the banks of the pool, but she could not see the bottom, its depths seemed almost endless. *It is truly wondrous,* she thought, *this seeing-me-see-the-world.* The more she saw its beauty, the uniqueness of each cloud, each flower and each pebble, the more she began to realize the uniqueness of her own Self. As this incredible thought flickered brightly in her mind, Gabriella suddenly saw the butterfly.

'Oh, hello again,' she said, quickly breaking her gaze into the water, to see the whereabouts of the winged creature in the air behind her. To her astonishment there was no butterfly at all. *It is probably near one of these flowers gathering nectar,* she thought, waiting for it to reappear. But it did not.

Thinking this odd, Gabriella looked back into the water and there it was once more! Determined to see it flying near her, she quickly looked up from the pool, but, again, it was nowhere to be found. *How silly. Butterflies cannot swim. It simply must be here on the dry ground with me,* she thought.

After waiting what seemed ages, Gabriella looked back into the water one last time, and there, remarkably, was the beautiful creature. It appeared to be hovering very close by and in no hurry to move away from her at all. It was as though it was trying to tell her something, something very important. In the water its wings were fairly iridescent, purple red, shades of orange and green, blue and yellow all sparkling like some sort of diamond as the sun shone upon it. *Such glorious colour and grace,* she mused, feeling very blessed to be in the company of such a special creature once again.

As the butterfly's wings beat a gentle rhythm in the shining water, a circle of ripples began to pulsate, creating a spiralling shape. Gabriella found herself intently watching the butterfly and the circle, which had started to appear around its form. Her eyes moved from the body of the butterfly to its wings and then to the tip of its antennae, which seemed to be the centre point for the spiral. Gabriella traced the shape with her eyes, moving slowly to the right, then down, to the left and up, very slowly, very deliberately. With each completed circle she felt as though something within her was unwinding, easing. When her eyes reached the very edge of the spiralling circle, which seemed endless, they grew heavy and she felt the need to rest her chin upon her arm.

She lay in this way for a long while, without any thought, without any outward movement. And then, she began to race through time and place, as one only does in one's dreams. The once clear pool now seemed cloudy and she could no longer see her butterfly. But just as she was about to call its name, it reappeared before her.

'Are you here to help me climb the Mountain? It is such a long way and I could so use another friend,' Gabriella asked.

But the butterfly shook its head, answering, 'Dear one, I cannot help to remove this weight from you. Remember the day you first met me? You wanted to help me free myself from the sticky fibres that enfolded me, but had you done so, I would never have had the stamina for my journey. Thank you for enabling me to find my own way. For it is in this very act, of struggling with that which binds us, that we find our courage and increase our strength. And this allows each of us to be our truest selves. So, dear one, although I would like to help, you must do this by and for yourself.' Its voice sounded like the soft breeze of a summer morning and there was just the tiniest scent of honey and lavender upon its breath.

'Do not be afraid; wait for the truth and it will be revealed to you. Remember, the caterpillar becomes the butterfly. Remember, the girl becomes the woman. Rest in the mystery. Be open to possibility.' With those words, the butterfly disappeared as suddenly as it had come.

Gabriella woke with a start and found she was looking into the pool of water. There was no butterfly. Gently shaking her head to force herself fully awake, she saw a flash of light glittering out of the corner of her eye. Upon closer inspection she saw, at the shallow water's edge, a brilliant, flame-coloured rock she had not seen before. Reaching her hand into the water, she took hold of a stone the colour of sunset. It was oddly warm. Holding it closely in her palm, she heard the voice inside her once more, *Add this to the one in your pocket and hold fast to these words,* it said.

Carnelian, orange-gift for you
Will help you know just what to do.

Transformation, strength to grow,
All you need to know, you know.

The outward journey starts within.
From this truth you now begin.

She placed the nearly transparent orange stone in her pocket and thought of all that had just happened. The dream, the butterfly's words and the new lessons learned, filled Gabriella with the sense of being quite special indeed. She grew more and more confident as she wound her way back across the mountainside from the reflecting pool, paying little attention to Owl, who seemed, to her, to be quite annoying, repeatedly demanding that she follow a certain pathway.

'No,' she said. 'I am not going to do as you say. You are very kind and good, but I must do this on my own. It is the only way for me to grow strong. I know this now and, while I am sure you are only trying to help, I am afraid I must refuse. I think this is the quickest way up to the summit. It may be much steeper, but it will be much quicker in the long run and I must get to the cave as soon as possible.'

And with that, she turned her back on Owl and continued her determined climb up the Mountain.

She hopped from flower to flower, tree to tree, criss-crossing her way up the side of the Mountain, ignoring all the accompanying fuss from Owl. She carried on, forging her way, making her own path, even where there was none, certain that her way was the very best. She was growing up now and she was much more clever than she had ever imagined.

FALLING WATER

With her newfound confidence, she moved along at quite a speed, and eventually needed to pause for a moment, to catch her breath. As she did, she noticed the rocks directly above her head had grown alarmingly large, the spring flowers had vanished and the footing was far more difficult. Perhaps it had been this way for a while; but Gabriella had been oblivious to the gradual changes that had occurred along the way. Sure of her own prowess, in absolute determination, she had ceased to be mindful of her surroundings.

Rather than climbing up the gentler eastern slope, she could tell from the position of the sun that she had moved round to the steep and foreboding north face of the Mountain, its jutting rocks cutting into the air above the sea like sharp and angry teeth. Closer now than ever before to the rugged stones, she began, for the first time, to question her judgment in climbing this way, knowing that if she had stayed with Owl, she would probably have been guided up the eastern slope. It was then she heard a sound above her head.

Rocks.

Rocks were beginning to tumble down about her, close to where she stood. She would have to move quickly and to hug the side of the Mountain in order to avoid them. Pressing her back against the wall of stone, she tried to grasp the crevasses with her fingers as she carefully placed her feet on the narrow path. She had taken a number of difficult side steps when a roaring sound met her ears. *More stones tumbling down?* she wondered, listening carefully to the growing noise. *No, this was different, more like a blazing fire.* She edged along until she felt a mist upon her face. She looked to her left and saw a gigantic tumult of water, hurtling down the side of the Mountain. Here, nearly halfway up the steep slope, she found herself confronted with a truly enormous waterfall. The sound of the water pounding on the rocks terrified her and she tried to retrace her path, but with every step she took away from the gushing water, the shingled mountainside gave way, sending bits of stone careering down the steeply sloped north face to the dark waters below.

She called out to Owl, but the din of the crashing water against the rocks drowned out her voice. *Why did I not follow Owl? Who am I to think I could find my way up the side of a mountain? I am barely a woman. How ignorant I am. Foolish. Foolish. Foolish.* The thoughts came upon her like a dark cloud, snuffing out all of the joyous expression that had brought her safe thus far.

It was not long before the voice of criticism and doubt grew louder than the roaring waters. She was gripped by a coldness in her heart, drawing her closer to the edge of the narrow path, forcing her to look down at the base of the waterfall; to peer into the blackest of black, into a pool within which there was no light at all. It seemed like another world away, and yet this blackness felt familiar, almost comforting, like a long-lost friend, inviting her to become reunited.

Quickly averting her gaze from the pitch-black pool, Gabriella raised her eyes and saw before her the sky coming alive with the coloured rays of the setting sun and she sought refuge in its beauty. The longer she remained there, her back pressed against the wall of stone, the more confused she became about what to do, the desire to propel herself downwards, off the Mountain, was so enormous, it shocked her.

She closed her eyes, holding fast to the stone behind her and in her mind's eye there appeared a vibrant picture of the rainbow pillar of smoke and she was suddenly filled with the memory of her dream and the beautiful cave. She heard her Mother's voice and a bright light stirred deeply within her, extinguishing her fears. Forcing the critical voices inside her mind to be silent, Gabriella willed herself to continue onward and vowed to retrace her steps down the Mountain, back to the reflecting pool, where she could begin anew.

Slowly opening her eyes, she began to sidestep gingerly back to her right. She had managed only a few when she felt an obstacle on the path. She paused and looked down to see a rather large rock that could not possibly have been there before. Stepping over it, she continued on, around a slight curve and there before her, she saw that the path she had originally followed was now completely obstructed with pebbles and large rocks. There was no way she could return from whence she had come, for an avalanche had fallen while she had been standing on the ledge, frozen in fear.

Forcing her eyes away from the now stone-covered path she gazed to the north and saw the clouds reflecting the light of the setting sun. They were quite exquisite. And then, with hesitance, she looked to her left, towards the crashing waters and took a few halting steps back towards them, careful to avoid the stones that littered the way. The ominous sound of the falling water crushed her spirits like a weight, yet a voice inside of her encouraged her to *Look again. Look more closely.*

Inexplicably, Gabriella found herself compelled to walk closer to the waterfall, all the while forcing herself to stare at its awesome force. Transfixed by the spectacle, she began to see past it, almost through it, and gradually, rather than seeing one enormous sheet of water before her, she became aware that she was actually witnessing a multitude of tiny prisms of light. The rays of setting sun, reflecting upon the individual drops of water, seemed to her like a collection of miniature rainbows, each dancing madly as if to confound the impending darkness.

When she had first seen them, the drops of water had seemed nondescript, appearing be a huge and raging flood, crashing, uncontrollably, down the sides of the rocks; but now, seen as individual points of light, they were almost inviting. The longer she gazed at them, the less frightened she felt and the deeper became her need to study the mysterious veil of water.

As her eyes continued adjusting to the force of the water and the ever-diminishing daylight, there appeared, right before her, a path of stone, directly behind the waterfall, which seemed to lead to the other side. *Surely I am imagining this,* she counselled herself, but the longer she stared, the more she knew it was not an illusion. *This must have always been here,* she thought, but the more she studied the path behind the falls, the more she realized that it would be impossible for her follow it. The stony path approaching the edge of the falling water was terribly narrow and as the falls were on her left side, she would have to sidestep, inch by inch, without the benefit of her arm for balance.

She forced herself to look back at the stones piled to her right, then at the abyss of black at the base of the falls and then back towards the dazzling wet colours. *Yes,* she decided. *The only way forward is through my fear.* Taking a deep breath, she asked her Guiding Lights for strength and then focused, with all her might, on the stone nearest to her left.

In the setting sun, the rock behind the veil of flowing water had assumed a reddish glow. It was a beautiful ruby colour; very like the Garnet she had found when she first began her journey. *What had the voice of the old woman told her? Commit yourself to your new goal. Release the past. Be still. Be whole.* Reaching into her apron pocket she felt for its shape. It seemed warm and the touch of it gave her renewed confidence as the words of the woman flooded her mind and her heart with purpose. Looking once more at the glowing red rock behind the falls, she gently moved her left foot towards it but quickly pulled it back, heart pounding.

A loud noise startled her. More rocks were falling to her right and they seemed to be getting closer and closer to where she was. At any moment, she might be hit by one of them, and then the decision to try and cross behind the waterfall would not be hers to make any more. She took a deep breath and then, with eyes and spirit focused, she stepped off the path.

In that very instant a cloud covered the glorious rays of the sun. She could no longer see at all. Her weight was totally suspended between the ledge she had been standing on and the red rock she thought she had seen. It seemed she had stepped into a void. In the ageless seconds that followed, Gabriella did not know if she was plunging to her death or if her inner vision had, indeed, been true to her. She was falling. *So it was an illusion after all,* she thought, but as quickly as the words crossed her mind, she found herself landing heavily on a large slab of rock. It was there, it was really there, and she was standing safely upon it.

Just as quickly as the cloud had covered the sun, it moved away once more and, in the final moments of the day, Gabriella saw with greater and greater clarity the stones that would become her steps to safety. As she made her way across them, she realized that each new stone was bigger than the one that had preceded it and each was a different colour. The second was orange, the third yellow, the fourth green, the fifth sea-blue, the sixth the colour of twilight and the last whitest white, like the first of the snows that blanket the earth in winter.

Beyond the great white stone was a path leading to an open plateau and there, awaiting her arrival, as though someone had known she would be coming, was a crackling fire, a blanket warming beside it, a pot of tea, hot rolls with butter, more sweet honey and the biggest piece of cheese she had ever seen. In the twilight, before allowing herself a single bite of food, she said seven prayers of thanks for the seven steps that had brought her here, to safety.

From a place deeper and stronger than her fear and despairing, a voice had urged her to look past what she first had seen. And in listening to that voice she saw the solution to her problem. Rather than judge or dismiss the voice, she had paid attention and followed its counsel. *Whose is this voice that keeps speaking to me?* she wondered.

It was and is your deepest Self, whispered the voice of the old woman, in answer to her silent questioning. Here, poised on the side of the Mountain, she knew that not only had she heard, she had listened.

The joy and relief in this truth brought tears to her eyes. They were proud and gentle tears, which rolled down her cheeks to soak the solid earth where she was seated, like the first rains of spring after a long harsh winter. Gradually, in the glowing firelight, she saw something sparkling amongst the white-coloured stones, which formed a ring around the blaze. It was another glistening stone, this one with a golden yellow hue and nearly the size of an acorn. Picking it up she gave thanks and placed it in her pocket, where the red and orange ones were held. She waited for a while, knowing the words would come:

This yellow Citrine stone for you
Will help you know just what to do.

Within its depths you'll be amazed
By golden focus-past the haze.

Rest in judgments you have made.
You listen well. Let Self be stayed.

That night Gabriella fell asleep holding her three stones and never felt her shoulder ache, not even once.

THE STORM

Gabriella woke to charcoal-grey skies and howling winds. The once blazing fire was now extinguished and the crisp morning air chilled her to the bone. Hugging the blanket close to herself, she felt very much confused about her next step. Gazing into the distance she could see only a vast expanse of water stretching out before her, covered with galloping white horses that gleamed against a murky green.

Her spirits began to shrink under the sooty gloom of the darkening sky, leaving her feeling quite isolated and frightened. It was as if yesterday's courage and confidence had been met not by light and beauty, but impending storms.

The clouds thickened and an ominous light filtered through them on to the crashing surf far below. In the distance, on the horizon, a bolt of lightning slashed at the surface of the water. The winds picked up even more, scattering small pebbles and ash into the air. All that lay in the path of the oncoming turbulence became like seed, tossed about as if sown by some gigantic gardener.

This is a big storm, she thought. *Here I am, alone, on the side of the Mountain, fully exposed. What can I do?* She forced herself to examine her situation and when she had done so, rather than waste another moment, she gathered the bread and cheese which she had saved, tucked them into her pocket, touched her stones and rolled her blanket into a small bundle, which she could easily hold beneath her right arm. She knew she had to search for some sort of protection.

With the waterfall behind her, she continued across the plateau, the spring grasses all around her, bending as if in deference to the force of the wind. She was walking with the Mountain on her left and the choppy waters below her on the right.

Her steps were lightly hampered by the softer surface of the earth on the grassy col. The rain which had so drenched the Land and flooded the River of Dreams had also collected here, on the other side of the Mountain of Remembrance.

Stepping as quickly as she could, in an effort to avoid the softer moss, she looked for rounded tussocks of heather, which were much less boggy and supported her weight with ease. But after a while, the number of these diminished and she was unable to avoid the waterlogged earth. Every step plunged her into cold muddy earth, making her legs feel unbearably heavy. The force of the winds and each arduous footfall pressed heavily upon her spirit. She had come so far now. She simply could not stop.

Gabriella looked around anxiously for any large rocks that might offer her the sort of sanctuary she was seeking. 'There. There they are,' she exclaimed when at last she spotted, slightly below her, an outcropping of large boulders, which might afford her comfort. Keeping her eyes on her goal, she forced her leaden feet to keep moving towards them. As the distance to the outcrop lessened, so did the amount time between lightning flash and thunder clap. The rains, which had been threatening, began to fall, lightly at first, then heavier. In an effort to keep the blanket dry, she tucked it further under her arm, and dared herself to push past her discomfort and increasing exhaustion.

Slowly she slogged across the muddied earth, near gale force winds creating a wall of opposition to her forward momentum. *Get to the boulders. Get to the boulders,* echoed the refrain in her mind as she made painstakingly slow progress. And then, for a moment, all was still as could be, as the rain and wind ceased entirely. With a window of calm, Gabriella picked up her pace and half-ran, half-tumbled the rest of the way to the rocky shelter. As she got closer to them, she could see clearly that the great slabs of stone could, indeed, offer her a temporary hideaway. There were two large stones placed nearly twice the length of her body apart from one another and, perched on the top, like some sort of rocky roof, was a third. Together they formed a makeshift house, perfect for someone in need of shelter. She was flooded with a sense of gratitude as she clambered down to them and arrived to find the floor of the outcrop was completely dry.

The moment she sat down all traces of the momentary calm vanished. Bolts of lightning ripped through the skies, punctuated by earth shuddering thunderclaps, which resounded and echoed across the face of the Mountain. Wave after wave of blindingly bright flashes illuminated the craggy rock faces and the stormy waters below. This was a storm like none Gabriella had ever seen. Round white pebbles hurtled down from the sky, bouncing on the stone roof above her, creating a percussive din. So loud was the sound, so overwhelming the power of the storm, Gabriella wondered if it was the hand of the Almighty casting His judgement upon her.

Is this the end of the world? Have I broken all the Laws, is this the beginning of my punishment? she thought. She knew that in the Land she had been born in, the River of Dreams and the Mountain of Remembrance were considered evil, as was she. Yet, here she was, alive, poised on the side of one, having crossed the other. *Mama and Middlenight did not survive the crossing. Maybe I have only been spared the vengeance of the Almighty until now. Maybe the Law is true.*

She unfolded the blanket, which had miraculously remained dry in all of the fury, and placed it about her body in an attempt to warm a chill, which seemed to penetrate deeper than her flesh and bones. Huddled against the darkening storm, Gabriella heard voices deep inside, telling her that this was all her fault. If she had never been born, never existed, none of this would be happening, the voices said. It truly felt as if the heavens were sending their wrath down upon her.

As she drew the blanket even closer to her body, she remembered the three stones in her pocket and reached inside to touch them for comfort. She took them out and placed them on the earth before her and with the sense of calm they brought, she found herself questioning all that the voices were saying.

Firstly, she was safe. She was harboured here, within this earth, with these beautiful gifts. There was no monster reaching for her, intent on dashing her to pieces, in the raging fury of itself. No. She was safe and, somehow, in the midst of the chaos and fierceness of it all, she was unscathed. As her thoughts grew clear, she sensed a change of spirit come upon her. The booming voice of the thunder, which had, only moments before, been associated with the wrath of the implacable Almighty, became in her mind, less a condemnation and more a display of magnificent strength.

Forcing herself to breathe deeply and slowly, she kept her eyes open and chose to hide them no more from the power of the storm. This unbridled force, which made her so totally aware of her insignificance and weakness, was the same force that had flooded the River of Dreams. It, like the butterfly, was somehow part of her being on this journey. It was connected. They were connected. She had not done anything to make it occur. It simply was. And as she realised this, gradually, she felt her fears assuaged. Instead of being overwhelmed by terror and shame, a sense of wonder and reverence came upon her and she spoke this prayer aloud:

What storm has brought such sense of peace?
What thundering voice has called,
Across the crashing waves of doubt
Into my heart, once walled?

I hear you in this thunderous din,
I see you in the dark.
Your light illumines everything,
The dismal and the stark.

I saw my life as set in stone,
My story at its end.
But here, today, I see the truth,
That world was just pretend.

Stretched out beyond this stormy sky,
Above this sea of green;
Is life, unfolding, everywhere,
A mystery to be seen.

The storms, the calm, the waterfalls,
The rocks that blocked the way,
These all were gifts to help me know
I am alive this day.

When she had spoken, she moved towards the left hand wall of the great protective rocks surrounding her and, turning to face them, she pressed her form fully against the shelter, as if to know it better; as if to allow it to know her better. And then, once more, Gabriella looked at her three small stones and remembered the words spoken by the ancient voice when she had been given them:

Commit yourself to your new goal
Release the past. Be still. Be whole.

The outward journey starts within
From this truth you now begin.

Rest in judgments you have made.
You listen well. Let Self be stayed.

As quickly as it had come, the storm passed, leaving a brilliant, brightly shining sun in its wake. In the distance, to her left, Gabriella could see the rain was continuing to fall, but at the point where the sun met the path of the storm the two forces created a full arc of rainbow that touched the horizon at both ends and seemed to reach high into heaven at its apex; every band of colour, like shining raiment, against the gloom of the sky. It was a reminder, once more, of the dream that had preceded her first step up the Mountain.

She longed to rest and think on all these things, but by now much time had already passed and Gabriella knew she needed to keep going; partly to get the warmth of the sun's rays upon her skin and damp clothes before the cold of nightfall came upon her, but more than that, she felt an inner urging to heed the words her Mother had spoken to her in her dream. 'Come to the cave at the top of the Mountain, come to the cave and find your gift.' There was simply no time for delay.

Stepping out of her sanctuary she looked back in the direction from whence she had come. It was all much steeper than she recalled and she wondered how it could have been possible to keep her footing on such a precarious slope. And she saw that, once again, she could not retrace her steps, for the rain had gouged huge channels into the soft earth of the Mountain and these had been transformed into a host of small waterfalls. In order to make progress, she would need to continue circling in the same direction, but now, she would have to walk down, rather than up. *How can this be?* she thought, for her dream had clearly shown spirals of rainbow smoke travelling up to the summit from the base of the Mountain.

The correct path cannot possibly be one that leads me down instead of up, she brooded, wishing Owl was with her. But Owl was nowhere to be seen. 'Oh well,' she said, her voice filled with frustration, 'I have to press on. I will simply have to go down for now and see where it leads me.'

It seemed a totally illogical move for one who was becoming quite wise. Yet she chose to trust her instinct, even though it appeared to contradict her ultimate plan. And so, she walked back into her temporary shelter, picked up her three stones, returned them to her pocket, put the blanket under her arm, and emerged to continue her journey.

A Three Fold Path

She proceeded to travel down and to the left, careful to avoid the numerous waterfalls and crevasses that had been created in the unleashing of the storm's power. With no immediate goal in sight, she felt wild, almost free, a strange new world stretching out before her as far as her eyes could see. Here was a landscape rapidly become green with spring grasses, highlighted by the bold yellow of gorse in full bloom. Tucked in between the rocky slabs were slips of pink thrift, which danced in the breeze. They, in particular, gave Gabriella joy and she secretly hoped she might be like them, a touch of beauty in an unlikely place.

'I wonder where I am going?' Gabriella whispered, almost afraid to hear any answer that might come.

Home, came the response from the now familiar voice of the old woman.

'Home? Oh, I can't go home, there is nothing left for me there. I need to get to the top of the Mountain. Even though I have felt alone and frightened, I know I still have much to learn and so very much to see. Please do not send me back. Not yet.'

Be still, came the soothing voice. *The home I speak of is nowhere you have ever known. It is a place within; where you are young and old, restless and peaceful; alone and in the company of those you love. It is a place where what is seen, truly is.*

That certainly is nowhere I have ever known, Gabriella thought, agreeing with the old woman's words.

As she wondered about the meaning of being young and old, alone and not alone, she lost all track of time. The sun seemed to linger much longer and held itself much higher in the sky than usual this day. And as she ate her last portion of food and quenched her thirst with freshly-fallen rainwater, a breeze stirred. On the wings of it came the sweetest of smells.

What is that? It is so familiar, she thought, sniffing the air. She smiled as she at last identified the scent. It was the perfume given by the blossom of the bluebells as they matured into delicate periwinkle-coloured blooms, suspended, ever so gracefully, from pale green stems. These were the heralds of spring and their bouquet was intoxicating.

Deciding to follow this glorious scent, she continued on down the Mountain towards a small patch of earth, tucked under some large green trees. *Well, that makes sense,* she thought, for the bluebell is a flower that needs less light than most to produce its magnificent blossom. She felt pleased at such a comforting discovery and, emboldened, continued on.

By now, the mountainside had changed immeasurably, becoming thickly wooded with a host of different trees. It was indeed a large forest and she found it amazing that, up until now, she had never known it had existed, for, from the other side of the River of Dreams it had been hidden. Then, as she continued walking, a curious thing happened, for the path, which until this point had been singular, became not one, but three, all of which led ever deeper into the forest.

With her back towards the summit, she wondered what to do. On her right was a path lined with primroses: great golden bits of light. She loved these flowers; often they were the first hope of warmth after winter's harshness. Directly before her was a field of bluebells, like an exquisite carpet with a path meandering through its middle and, lastly, to her left, there grew a huge collection of fiddlehead ferns, clustered on either side of the third path, all bright yellow-green, just waiting to expand and grow.

'Which way? Oh, I know. I smelled the bluebells first, that must be the way,' she announced, but then felt immediately unsure of herself. *Or, was their scent merely to get my attention so I would arrive here at these three paths?* she wondered. Standing before all three, she felt very confused indeed. 'Wait. My stones!' she said. Reaching into her pocket, she found the stone of Citrine and pulled it out.

Within its depths you'll be amazed,
By golden focus - past the haze.

She gazed into the stone for a number of moments, delighted that she could remember the words and then she placed it on her tummy, in the uppermost part of the soft flesh between her ribs. After taking a deep inward breath, she exhaled slowly into the cooling air. She did it again, and then once more. On the third exhalation an idea came to her. *Why not set foot on each path and see what you hear?* It made good enough sense to her, so that is just what she did.

She began with the primroses on her right. Having decided to take seven large steps down each path in order to give herself the opportunity to choose with greater clarity, she counted out loud with each step, 'One-two-three-four-five-six-seven.' Closing her eyes, she placed the golden stone on her tummy and waited.

Softest yellow flowers of spring
Gentle to the stone-face cling.

Follow us this merry day
We will laugh and we will play.

'Well, that sounds pleasing enough,' she said aloud. 'Yes. I think it is time for me to laugh and play. What a lovely path this is.' She was about to continue on, when suddenly the stone in her hand grew cold. 'What?' she asked.

What do the others have to say? came the old woman's voice.

'I don't much care,' grumbled Gabriella.

I heard you, scolded the ancient one.

Reluctantly, she turned back from the primrose path and walked towards the bluebells. Their beautiful perfume brought a smile to her lips. *Perhaps this is a better path for me after all.* 'Let's see. Seven steps. One, two, three, four, five, six, seven; eyes closed, stone in hand, hand on tummy.'

Purple carpet, lovely bloom,
Fill your life with sweet perfume.

Come along this path and see
All the beauty there can be.

'Oh my, a path which leads to beauty.' As she said these words, Gabriella thought of all the sad and ugly things she had known, not the least of which being her own body, and as she began to run down the path lined with the lovely-scented flowers, the stone in her hand turned icy cold once more. 'What?' she demanded.

The voice inside gently reminded her, *There are three paths to be tried,* it said. It seemed a very long time before Gabriella could bring herself to retrace her eager footsteps and head towards the fiddlehead ferns.

Entering the third path, somewhat reluctantly, and, feeling slightly annoyed, she counted her steps out loud, 'One, two, three, four, five, six, seven.' The smell here brought to mind damp earth and things beneath the ground that had not yet seen the light or felt the warmth of sun upon them. *This cannot be the path for me,* she thought. Closing her eyes, in a somewhat dramatic manner, she placed the stone once last time upon her tummy.

Fiddlehead ferns at every turn
Bring you lessons - time to learn.

Spirals waiting to unfurl,
More a woman, less a girl.

The stone, which she held fast to herself, began to grow warmer and warmer, and much to her surprise, Gabriella became quite sure, from somewhere deep inside, that this was, indeed, the path. But this was not what she wanted at all. She could barely see the primroses or smell the bluebells from here but could remember them both.

The messages from the others had been much more inviting: 'We will laugh and we will play,' had said the bright and cheery primroses; 'Fill your life with sweet perfume,' had chimed the periwinkle bluebells. Here with the newly emerging fiddlehead ferns, the stone had become warm, but she did not care for the thought that there would be lessons to learn.

'Why should I follow this path?' she asked aloud, to no one in particular, with an emphatic tone on the word *should* and a foot stamp, for added effect.

'Because we need you,' came the response from a voice she had never before heard. It was rather breathy and quick in its speech. 'Who said that?' Gabriella queried.

'Why, me of course,' was the hasty reply, this time accompanied by what seemed to be some sort of snort. Gabriella looked up and down the path to find the person addressing her. 'I'm sorry. I cannot see you. Are you hiding?' she asked.

'Well, you must be blind. I am right here before you.'

'Where?' she said, straining her neck first to the right and then to the left and even rising on to tiptoes to see if that would help.

'Not up there, down here. If you truly want to see, don't look in the familiar and predictable ways,' came the rapid response.

Gabriella looked down and there at her feet, just peeking out from a bed of fiddleheads was the most beautiful rabbit she had ever seen. It had a brilliant white coat and pink eyes that were shiny and bright. Gabriella gasped, 'Are you talking to me?'

'Of course I am. Do you see anyone else here at the edge of the path to the Forest of Compassion?' said the rabbit.

'Is this the Forest of Compassion?' asked Gabriella.

'Of course it is. You already know that. What a silly girl asking questions you already know the answers to. Know what you know, and live, always knowing that you will never fully understand any of it. In this way you shall always remain open, kind, and becoming.'

'Becoming? Becoming what?'

'Why, the best you. That's who!' exclaimed the rabbit.

Scratching the earth in a rather precise manner with his left paw, he looked directly at Gabriella and hopped very close to her.

Nose twitching with excitement, he said, a bit more slowly, this time, 'Precious moments are being wasted. Follow me. We have been waiting a very long time for you.'

He looked so intently at her, with such enormous eyes, that Gabriella felt she had gone into a trance and then she said, in a voice that surprised herself, 'Yes, all right, I am here at last. Let us go.'

And off they raced down the winding path of fiddlehead ferns and moss into the Forest of Compassion. As the ground sped by beneath their feet, Gabriella thought how natural it seemed to have had something as unnatural as a conversation with a rabbit. *What a peculiar place, the Mountain of Remembrance is. Why is it I feel so comfortable here and why did the rabbit say I already know this is the Forest of Compassion? I know no such thing.* These thoughts and questions filled her mind and her heart as the two raced on, deeper and deeper into the Forest.

THE FOREST OF COMPASSION

Forever they seemed to run, until, just as Gabriella felt as if she could go no further, the rabbit slowed his pace and, in the most breathless voice yet, he called out, 'She has come! She has come!'

In response to his pronouncement, a host of rabbits emerged from everywhere. All had perfect snowy white fur with pink eyes and twitching noses and they energetically hopped over to her, welcoming her with a chorus of voices saying, 'We are so grateful. We are so pleased. We can hardly believe you have made the long journey.'

Who do they think I am? Gabriella wondered. *I am just a girl who was born in the Land and fell into the River of Dreams.* And yet, the rabbits, which now numbered easily into the hundreds, seemed to know her and celebrate her. The rabbit on the path had said they had waited such a long time for her. *Why?* she asked herself. *What could they possibly want from me?*

Gabriella studied the rabbits as they hopped about around her, fairly dancing with glee. And it occurred to her, that with the exception of Owl, these were the first living creatures she had seen since she began her climb to the summit. As she was pondering this the rabbit who had first met her on the path hopped up on to a large mound of moss-covered earth. Illuminated by the setting sun, his coat of purest white shone golden and his very presence settled the masses.

Clearing his throat, he said, 'We have prepared long for this day. Let us begin.' And at that, every rabbit hopped to what seemed to be its designated place, forming two large circles, which overlapped in the centre. This centre portion looked rather like an almond and there were two pronounced gaps, one on the northern point of the intersecting circles and one on the southern.

The leader rabbit, as Gabriella had begun to call him in her mind, descended from his golden mound, his coat returning to silky white as he did so, and hopped to the northernmost vacant space, his form almost completing the two circles.

Looking up at Gabriella with a steady gaze, he said solemnly, 'We know you have travelled a long way to arrive here. We also know you have had trials from the moment of your first breath upon this earth, even until this very day, when you were offered paths of laughter and play, beauty and gentleness. Instead, you chose an earthy, not-yet-formed path and listened well; in order to speak a language you did not know. We have asked you here for a purpose that I am not at liberty to reveal. If you would but grant us the gifts of your courage, your deepest truth and your wisdom, all shall be made known to you.'

The rabbits gazed at her with pink, unblinking eyes. Each animal was identical to the one next to it and each seemed to hold its breath, awaiting Gabriella's response. It seemed natural for her to take her place in the one remaining gap and so she did. Now standing directly opposite the rabbit leader, she said, from the bottom of her heart, 'Whatever I have is yours.'

Suddenly, Owl swooped down from high amongst the tree branches and descended towards them holding something in her talons. The great bird hovered above Gabriella, staring at her, as if indicating that Gabriella should receive that which was held in her grip. Gabriella extended her hand, palm upwards, into which Owl released a rod of beautifully polished hazel wood. As Gabriella's hand closed around the smooth wooden surface, Owl flew back to the tree from whence she had come.

Feeling hundreds of pairs of eyes upon her, Gabriella wondered what on earth was required of her. Truly having no idea what to do, she reached into her pocket, in a slightly nervous manner, and felt the shapes of her stones for comfort. She paused. The leader had said they needed her courage, her deepest truth and her wisdom.

Well, the red stone came when she chose to climb the Mountain and leave behind her all that she knew. That, certainly, took courage. The orange stone came when the butterfly reminded her about her transformation from girl to young woman and encouraged her to trust that all would be revealed. Surely this was her deepest truth, even if she did not fully realize it, as of yet. And then, of course, her yellow stone had been given to her after she had crossed behind the waterfall and learned to listen to the wisdom of her own voice. And it was this same listening that had brought her to this very moment.

Here they were: courage, deepest truth and wisdom. *Oh, I don't want to give these away,* she thought and in the very moment she thought the thought, she knew she had no other choice. She laid the hazel wood rod on the earth beside her and took a deep breath. Looking deeply into each rabbit's eyes, she felt an aching tenderness in her chest for each and every one of them. It was the same feeling she had sensed when she first met Middlenight.

With her heart pounding, Gabriella took a step into the almond-shaped space where the circles overlapped. Her movement caused an audible gasp from the rabbits on either side of her. When they had quietened, she reached into her pocket and felt the stones, whose shapes she had long-since memorized and, finding her Garnet, she placed it on the earth closest to the leader, saying, 'For Courage.' Then the Carnelian beneath it, with the words, 'For Deepest Truth' and lastly, she set the Citrine down closest to herself saying, 'For Wisdom.'

Stepping out of the interlaced circle of rabbits once more, she picked up the hazel wood rod from the earth beside her and said, 'These gifts, which were given to me, I now give to you, with all of my heart. May they be a blessing.'

The eyes of the rabbits no longer gazed solely on Gabriella, but looked expectantly at the gifts of coloured stone as well. No one moved, until a loud voice from above them, broke the silence. 'Use the wood. Use the wood,' it hooted. Gabriella looked in the direction of the sound and found it had come from high in the trees. She had never heard the voice before. Well, she had sort of heard it, but never understood it so clearly.

She stared at Owl with wonder and Owl returned her gaze, adding a subtle gesture with her wing. Gabriella was not at all sure what she was to make of it. Owl gestured again, and hooted, 'Use the wood,' once more.

'Use the wood? Use the wood, for what?' she asked. The rabbit leader lowered his head in silent reply, his left forepaw gently scratching the earth before him. As she observed him, Gabriella instantly interpreted his actions and the meaning of Owl's words. She was to touch the rabbit on the crown of his head with the hazel wood rod. How she knew was a mysterious thing, but that she knew was all that mattered.

Feeling confident, she began to walk around the circle, towards the leader, holding the rod in her hand. Although she did not need it as a walking stick, it seemed fitting to touch the earth with every step she took. When she arrived alongside him, she realized that she had touched the earth with the hazel wood rod behind only half of the rabbits, and that did not seem correct to her. It seemed very important that the path she walked with the hazel wood rod encircled all of them. So, she continued on, until she arrived at her original starting place. When she had reached it, she held the rod slightly up, off the ground, and walked back to the leader.

One and one half circles had been made around the rabbits by the time Gabriella arrived directly behind him. He remained as he had been, head bowed, ears gently lowered, paw still lightly touching the earth before him. Reaching out towards the crown of his beautiful head with the hazel wood rod, she touched him, ever so carefully, saying, 'Bless you.'

In an instant, he was transformed into a stag of mighty proportion, his huge body fairly towered above her, taking her breath away. He snorted; his front hooves stomped at the earth and his strong neck stretched from side to side as if unwinding. His antlers were wider than any Gabriella had ever seen and she thought he must be ancient indeed. He stopped his display of strength for a moment and lowered his head to look at her. His eyes, no longer pink, had become huge and green, but it was no ordinary green. It seemed as if all the shades of green on earth were contained within it; the colour of new spring leaves, the spicy green of ancient pine trees, the soft green of moss under the oak trees and even the green of the first daffodil leaves after the snows. They were all there, deeply held in his eyes somehow.

Feeling humbled and completely amazed, Gabriella continued to travel the entirety of the rabbit circles touching each creature with the hazel wood rod, in a similar manner. With every 'Bless you', and gentle touch, a new creature of beauty and utter uniqueness emerged.

When she had finally completed the circle of blessings, she was surrounded by every variety of creature she could imagine: snakes, deer, mice, voles, birds of every kind, a bear or two, the odd mole. She could hardly count them all. Every single white rabbit had been transformed by her touch and the Forest of Compassion came alive with the sounds of rediscovered voices and bodies. 'Thank you. Thank you,' resounded the chorus of the newly awakened beings. Even the trees, whose branches fairly embraced them, seemed to wave and cheer in delight.

Gabriella could scarcely believe what she had seen with her own eyes and heard with her own ears, and yet there was no denying any of it. In the last moments of the setting sun she found herself surrounded by miracles. Her heart pounded within her breast as she laughed and smiled and greeted each re-born creature with joy.

For one fleeting instant, she wished someone would take the hazel wood rod and bless her too. *Oh, how lovely to be released from a body not fully expressing itself,* she thought. She wished that she, too, could be different, changed, but she did not dwell long with these thoughts, for the gaiety in the forest was far too enticing. Reminding herself that it had taken her, exactly as she was, in that exact moment, to help release all of them from their white rabbit bodies, she felt a deep sense of contentment and purpose, which she had never before experienced.

After much merriment and celebration, the great stag came towards her and lowered his head with a sideways gesture, as if asking her to follow him. Reaching out her hand towards his muzzle, she touched its velvet softness with delight. He nuzzled back and seemed to be asking her to walk with him to the place where he had first stood as the rabbit leader. So, together they walked to the mound, which was now much bigger than she remembered.

Encouraging her to climb the mound with the gentle nudging of his head, he lowered his entire body to her, inviting her to sit upon him. She found climbing on nearly impossible with both the hazel wood rod and her blanket under her arm. Owl, seeing her struggle, flew down and took both from her, so she could have the full use of her right arm. She reached across the expanse of his beautiful neck, held fast to his mane and then stretched her right leg across his strong and mighty back. With all of her strength, she pulled herself on to the stag and centred herself in the middle of his back, her legs now on either side of him. It was awkward at first, but the longer she sat upon the stag's back, the more familiar it became. Once seated comfortably, the stag stood up to his full height and very carefully began to carry her deeper into the Forest.

It was dark now and Gabriella was acutely aware of being tired and hungry, but the longer they walked, the more the exhaustion began to take hold, easily outweighing the powerful hunger pangs which seemed to fade with every step. She was thankful for the stag's strength, for she felt she had very little herself.

As they slowly made their way deeper into the darkened Forest, her eyelids grew heavier with the cadence of the stag's movements and it became an enormous effort to keep her body upon his back. Feeling unable to support her own weight any longer, she gradually became aware of other presences: they were creatures with wings, on either side of her, holding her fast and keeping her safely upon him. In her half-dreaming state, after what seemed a very long time, the great stag stopped.

Here the air was thick with the smell of pine and hemlock and many of her newly-made friends were there to greet her. They had made a mattress from the fragrant needles of the evergreens which towered above her, their scented branches a canopy for her dreams. The feathered creatures tenderly lowered Gabriella to the ground, laid her down upon the soft and aromatic bed, and tucked her snugly beneath her blanket. She did not notice Owl place the hazel wood rod by her left side, and the tenderly hooted 'Goodnight' fell upon ears already fast asleep.

Her rest was filled with fragmented dreams; flashes of story mixed with snippets of sound. There were familiar faces in unfamiliar settings: odds and ends tumbled about in her mind, forming a kaleidoscope of images, some of which made sense and some not at all. From time to time, Gabriella awoke startled, but the smell of the pine-trees cleared her confusion and settled her spirit, allowing her to return to a deep and delicious sleep.

And throughout the night, in the stillness of the Forest of Compassion, Owl kept watch over Gabriella, the sweet human who had freed them all.

CIRCLES OF GREEN

The most magnificent dawn chorus broke through the early morning air as the birds greeted the sunrise with a cacophony of song, conspiring to awaken their liberator with beautiful melody. Robins, song thrushes, warblers, doves, wrens, blackbirds, all joined in to celebrate the new day, each restored to their truest selves, each singing their own unique song. Gabriella lay on the soft bed with her eyes closed, giving thanks for the warmth she felt in her heart. Even her left side, which almost always felt cold, seemed warm.

Opening her eyes, she saw that the day was clear and the air was just beginning to warm with the rising of the sun. She found herself lying on a bed of pine needles in the centre of a clearing beneath a circle of noble trees. The sky above her was a cloudless blue surrounded by a ring of deepest green. It reminded her of the reflecting pool she had gazed into beneath the first gentle waterfall, except this time she found she was looking up into the depths of the skies.

Not really wanting to sit up quite yet she closed her eyes to listen to the birds more intently. Although she had heard the dawn chorus before and could recognize many of their calls, they had never sounded so sweet to her as they did that morning. *Has it always been so magnificent?* she wondered. *Perhaps I am only now beginning to hear the wonder of each individual song.* She felt at peace; quiet and rested, despite not knowing what to do next. *Perhaps that is part of this new way of listening. Perhaps it is not about doing anything.*

As she mused beneath the warming sun she became aware of a growling hunger. Half-expecting another sumptuous feast, she roused herself and sat up to see if there was anything prepared for her, but saw nothing. *Why am I not being provided for?* And then, as an after-thought, came the words, *Why is there nothing for me, after all I have done for them?*

The words flooded her mind and with them came the memory of her Mother's words to her in the cottage so long ago. The angry words she had spoken when she slapped her, the words that had made her feel as though she was to blame for all her Mother's sorrows. Gabriella's hand went to her heart and she began to sob, truly feeling, for the first time, a portion of what her Mother must have felt during the years of her exile, her loneliness, her hunger, her fears, her struggles. Gabriella felt them all.

At that moment Owl descended to her side, without the slightest sound, startling her. The great bird held Gabriella in its gaze and in the fire of her golden eyes, Gabriella heard these words, *One of the greatest gifts any living creature can know, is to give, expecting nothing in return.*

And with that, a great intake of air filled Gabriella's lungs. Slowly moving her hand away from her heart she reached towards Owl and gently touched the soft grey feathers on the great bird's chest saying, 'Thank you for your love.' They remained like this for a number of moments and then Owl flapped her wings and hooted, 'Bring the wood' and slowly closed her right eye, as if winking.

Gabriella knew Owl was guiding her once more, and, with a smile of her own, she picked up the hazel wood rod, knowing that this time she would follow, without questioning, her friend's wisdom. Keeping her eyes steadfast on Owl, she left the pine needle bed and her blanket behind, her hunger and momentary disappointment, forgotten.

Owl flew towards a path that led even deeper into the Forest. As Gabriella followed, the once bright circle of sky, framed by the top of the evergreens, left her sight. In the dimming light of the thickening forest, Gabriella could barely see Owl perched upon the lowest branch of an oak tree, which marked the entrance into a much denser stand of trees.

The path beneath her feet was overgrown and she was fast being surrounded by a gathering gloom. *This is not nearly as beautiful as I had hoped to encounter,* she thought, but Gabriella trusted Owl to lead her in the way in which she should go. So, on they travelled, her stomach loudly complaining with hunger, but her heart feeling quiet and sure.

After a while, the gloom lifted and Gabriella saw that the trees were increasing in height and girth. Their branches, now much higher in the sky, allowed a different, more intense sunlight to pass through them. Looking down at the earth, Gabriella could see old, tired leaves and the giant shapes of twisted roots, which snaked along the earth like sleeping serpents. Tucked in among them were some reassuring spring flowers; primroses, bluebells, foxgloves; it was like a woodland garden just for her. *Why here they are,* thought Gabriella, *the choices of yesterday returned to me this day. It was not such a loss to have chosen the fiddlehead path after all.* For there before her, as far as her eyes could see, were all of the flowers she so loved and, clustered in the shade, were the fiddleheads as well. *All three paths have become one,* she thought, gliding along with delight and ever increasing wonder.

However, her comfort was momentary, as the path became narrower and narrower. The tall-trunked, ancient trees were replaced with dense stands of holly and closely packed vegetation of all sorts. It became difficult for her to see anything to the right or to the left of her. At times Gabriella had to use the hazel wood rod to balance her footing on the uneven surface of the path, which was now treacherous with moss-covered rocks and slippery roots. Darkness loomed and the birdsong had long since ended. This was no cheery part of the Forest at all.

Instinctively, Gabriella reached into her pocket for reassurance, feeling for her stones. 'Where are they?' she exclaimed as her hand felt only a few stale crumbs from long ago eaten gifts of food. *Oh, I have given my beautiful stones to the animals,* she thought, feeling increasingly lonely and frightened. Owl was no longer visible in the dense thicket of trees and it seemed as if a moonless night had usurped the day in the Forest of Compassion.

See yourself. Be yourself. Free yourself.

Like niggling thoughts at first, the whispered words persisted with her every step.

See yourself. Be yourself. Free yourself.

'I do see myself,' Gabriella yelled aloud, trying to stop the voice in her head. 'And I also see that it is impossible for me to free myself.'

Why? the voice queried.

'Because, I was born like this,' she said, gesturing at her left side. 'I am trapped in this flesh with only one arm, and no one has a hazel wood rod that can help me,' she snapped back, picking up the pace of her steps.

See yourself. Be yourself. Free yourself.

The thought came more quickly than ever.

'Stop it. I do not want to be me. Being me has brought sadness and pain to every single being who has ever touched me. Everyone who has ever loved me, has died because of me.'

But what about the animals of the Forest, what about them? asked the voice.

Gabriella paused, not knowing how to respond for a moment and then she knew the answer. 'They are safe because I touched them, they did not touch me. No one must touch me,' she said and began to run down the overgrown path as fast as she could.

Immediately, the path grew even more densely covered. Bramble, holly, and stinging nettle began to encroach upon her, causing her skin to burn, her clothes to tear and blood to drip from her arm and legs. Every step, upon the now nearly impossible pathway, caused her immense pain and she realized that she was trapped.

With a growing sense of horror, Gabriella felt the brambles progressively tightening about her and with each movement she made, the more constricting they became. She was absolutely and completely trapped. Sensing that any attempt to escape would be futile, she became perfectly still. She closed her eyes and from the darkest corners of her mind came a vision.

It was as though someone had drawn back a curtain, revealing a picture she had never seen before. In a cold and dingy room, a frightened little girl lay on the floor, abandoned, shivering and hungry. At first glance, Gabriella was uncomfortable, her skin crawled and she felt a reluctant kind of pity towards this child and then, from the centre of her palm, where she was grasping the hazel wood rod, she began to feel a circle of heat and realised that it was the only part of her body not in pain.

The rest of her flesh ached. In standing perfectly still, her muscles had begun to cramp and the wounds inflicted by the thorns and sharp-edged leaves seemed to cut deeper and deeper every moment; but she compelled herself to re-enter the vision by focusing upon the circle of heat on her hand. Gabriella found, to her amazement, that in doing this she was able to lessen all her physical pain and increase her concentration.

Closing her eyes, she felt herself surrendering and slowly she began to see the child once more, only this time it was surrounded by a circle of pure green light.

All the pity and disgust she had at first felt for the child before her became something else; something more akin to an inexplicable kindness and compassion. As she allowed herself to draw nearer to the child in the circle of green, she became aware that she was dirty, tattered and unkempt. Her hair was matted, her clothes were in tatters, her legs were bruised and her skin rough from being repeatedly scrubbed and cleaned. The child repulsed Gabriella and, knowing it was more dream than real, she found herself longing to simply run away and abandon the vision that lay before her. But instead of doing so, she stepped closer still. The child's head was bowed low, as if hiding itself, and as Gabriella came closer, the little one cowered, as though she might be struck.

At last, when Gabriella came to within an arm's length she said, 'Hello.' The child started, as though she was unused to being spoken to, and did not reply. Again, Gabriella said, 'Hello.' Slowly, ever so slowly, the child raised her eyes from the dirt floor to see who was speaking. Their eyes met and, with a gasp, Gabriella recognized that the child was really herself. *No, she cannot be me,* she thought. *I was never abandoned. I was never like this.*

Gabriella tried desperately to shift her mind away from the scene in front of her, but a force within demanded she look again and then, when she looked once more, she saw what she most dreaded; there, on the left-hand side of the little girl's back, showing through clumps of torn fabric was an ugly lump of flesh.

This is, truly, some part of me, she recognized. *Some part of me I do not want to see. This little child has not harmed anyone. I have not harmed anyone. Oh, I can no longer leave her here, so frightened, so terribly alone.* With pounding heart and barely a whisper of a voice, Gabriella reached her hand out to the child and said, 'Come with me. I will love you.'

As she stretched out her arm, the dark cloud behind the child's eyes lifted and after what seemed like an age, their hands touched. Together they stepped into the circle of green, that now surrounded them both, and these were the words that came:

The heart's true gift within this life,
Beyond the sorrow, pain and strife,

Is but to rest. Be still and know
The light of all above-below.

Listen, look and understand,
All has meaning, all is planned.

To see the world with loving eyes,
Accepting it, with no disguise,

Is like the purest breath of air,
It fills your lungs with all that's rare.

Within this act of outward grace,
You'll find a deeper tender place.

Beneath the smiles and the tears,
Far past the good deeds, past the years,

A place unguarded, opens wide,
To let the warmth of love abide.

So, giving love is half the test;
Receiving it, is all the rest.

As the words ended, the green circle about them began to spin gently, creating a succession of emerald green ripples, pine-green sparks and streaks of brightest white. The pulsing energy in the bands of colour embraced both younger and older Gabriella, the circle growing stronger and stronger, its force like a storm, swirled around them both like a cyclone. Yet, neither felt any fear when the child's body was swept up into the powerful vortex by an unseen force.

Seven times the younger Gabriella encircled her older Self; and each of the seven times the younger child made a full circle, she changed. Her clothes were no longer tattered; her hair became clean and golden red; her body's bruises healed; her eyes became bright and focused, her voice full of laughter and joy.

It was as though she was flying of her own accord, leaving a trail of scented roses behind her. Then, at last, when the seventh circle had been completed, the child hovered directly in front of her older Self and said simply, 'Thank you. Thank you. Thank you.'

And then, with a great rush of air, the two became one. There was no storm of green; there was no longer a sense of separation, there were no darkened corners to avoid. Gabriella was left with a circle of warmth on the palm of her right hand and a blazing heat deep within her heart.

Clutching the hazel wood rod towards her chest she gently closed her eyes. 'Thank you,' she said to the gloom of the Forest about her. 'Thank you for the miracle.'

With almost unbearable difficulty, she lifted the hazel wood rod, ever so slightly towards the sky and then lowered it slowly to the earth. Suddenly, as if driven forth by the very essence of life, the overgrown path receded in one enormous flourish, as if being blown back by the breath of Creation.

The Sacred Grove

Stunned by all that had happened, Gabriella closed and opened her eyes a number of times. She had to be sure she was not dreaming, for there before her was a magnificent arbour of elder wood in full blossom. All traces of the brambles, holly and stinging nettle had gone. She was intoxicated by its honey-sweet scent and longed to enter into the glade that lay beyond.

Walking under its arching grandeur, Gabriella came upon a very special place indeed, in the centre of which was a carpet of soft green grass, leading to a lake of the bluest water she had ever seen. On either side of this beautiful lake were two clear streams of pure water, one fed the pool with waters from the Mountain of Remembrance, the other flowed away from the lake and poured down the Mountainside, falling freely to the waters below.

On the far side of the lake, growing upon a mound of emerald green grass, were six beautiful trees. They were the most perfect trees Gabriella had ever seen: an ash, a beech, an oak, a pine, a blackthorn and lastly a graceful willow, its leaves gently rippling in the breeze. Beyond the six was another arbour of elder wood, which seemed to beckon to a distant path.

Gabriella turned to look from whence she had come. The path, once completely overgrown, was now as clear of obstacles as when she had begun her walk with Owl this morning. *Did I imagine that?* Gabriella asked herself, lifting her hand to her forehead to wipe her brow. As she did, she noticed her right arm was blotchy with blood, covered with cuts and scrapes and red with the prickly rash left by stinging nettles. She looked more closely at herself and saw that her clothes were torn and her legs and torso badly cut as well.

'It did happen. It did,' she said out loud, over and over. *What sort of place is this, this world of animals that change shape, and brambles that appear and disappear, and light that comes and goes so quickly?* So many questions came to her mind; but, for once, she needed no answers. A simple, yet profound, trust was all that seemed necessary.

Sitting at the edge of the expanse leading to the lake, she removed her shoes from her very tired feet, grateful for the softness of the grass; and after placing the hazel wood rod next to her side, she reclined against a mossy hummock. The earth around her smelled musky and warm and there was a sweet tang of clover in the air. Closing her eyes, she began to listen to all the sounds that surrounded her; the babbling stream, the gentle breeze rustling the leaves, occasional birdsong, and, then, her tummy grumbled loudly.

I am so hungry, she thought. Just thinking about food had increased her appetite and she knew she would need to find something edible soon.

As she began to make a move to do just that, the stream began to tumble more rapidly. In its quickened pace it seemed to flow over the pebbles with a growing sense of urgency. Gabriella sat up, her legs extended before her on the grass, and inclined her ear to listen more closely.

Come within. Come within.
Feel my water on your skin.

Did I make that up? No, I do not think so; but I will ask the water to speak again. If it does, I will know.

She cleared her throat, 'Ummm, excuse me lovely stream, I think you spoke to me. If this is so, could you give me your message again?' The stream burbled in a delighted way and said most clearly:

Come within. Come within.
Feel my water on your skin.

Gabriella looked around her to see if anyone else could have spoken the words. No. She was alone; even Owl was nowhere to be seen. No one else could have done so. She stared at the stream flowing happily into the lake of blue. With the sun's rays dancing across the surface, it seemed incredibly inviting. Standing up, she took the hazelwood rod in her hand and walked towards the lakeside. As she reached out to dip her bare toes into the water, the stream said:

Come within. Come within.
Feel my water on your skin.

Not just feet and hand and face,
All of you must be embraced.

'All of me?' Gabriella asked.

All of you must be embraced
Not just feet and hand and face.

When you enter you will find,
Life you thought you'd left behind.

Journey to the other side
Answers for you there abide.

Naked to this moment come.
Many parts become the sum.

The language of the stream was a complete riddle to Gabriella. *What answers awaited her on the other side of the lake? And what parts would become the sum? The sum? The sum of what?* she asked herself. It all seemed rather cryptic and yet, Owl had led her down the path which had brought her here. As odd as it might seem to her in one way, Gabriella knew there was a resonance to the message, even if she did not fully understand. So, if naked she must enter, naked it must be.

Without hesitation, Gabriella began to remove her tattered, filthy clothes. Her blouse of woven linen was yellowed and dirty, torn and blood-stained from the cuts she had just received; her apron was thoroughly worn, one of its big pockets fraying at the edge; and her skirt, lovingly sewn by her Mother's hand, now damaged, beyond mending.

Still, these were the only clothes she owned. So, as she undressed, each item of clothing was removed with exceeding care, folded gingerly, and piled beside her feet. Placing her shoes at the bottom of the clothes, she wrapped the apron strings around the lot, bundling them together, tucked them under her arm and prepared to enter the lake.

Holding the hazel wood rod firmly in her hand, in case she lost her footing, she walked to the water's edge. She could see the bottom of the lake all the way across, so, clearly, it was not too deep. Gabriella felt relieved, for she could not swim.

Moving closer to the water, Gabriella saw her own naked body for the first time in her life. At first she looked away and then, hesitating, she looked back. *How ugly,* barked a voice inside her head. *Who said that?* she wondered. *Why have I even thought that? It is who I am without my clothes. This is my body.*

She stared at her reflection, more defiantly this time, and as she looked at her long strawberry-blonde hair and her blue eyes she saw herself smile, *Oh, that was nice, I smiled at myself.* She saw her rounded breasts and pink nipples; the curve of her waist; the wisps of curly hair between her legs; her strong thighs; her shins, and then, she lifted each foot to examine them in the reflection. They were quite large. *That is probably good design,* Gabriella thought, with a grin, *I need help balancing sometimes.*

When she had finished studying her profile, she wondered why she had been hidden away all of her life, why people had been frightened of her body. *Why is that?* she wondered. *This is simply the way I was born, nothing more, nothing less.*

And with that, she entered the water. It was both cool and warm simultaneously and there was no need to get used to it, it was as though the water was getting used to her. With the hazel wood rod and her bundle of clothes in hand, Gabriella slowly crossed the glistening lake. The depth of the water increased, but only to the point where Gabriella was covered above the shoulders.

Walking to where she thought she was halfway across, she paused and arched her neck backwards, allowing her hair to become wet with the water's velvety touch. Straightening her head once more, she felt the water trickle down her face and touch her lips. It tasted incomparably sweet. Gabriella wanted to linger as long as she could, for it felt truly blissful, but, just as she began to allow herself to sink further into the lake, the voice of the stream said:

Time to go. Time to go.
All you need to know, you know.

These were not the words Gabriella wanted to hear. In fact, they were not even true. She did not know anywhere near enough yet; there were so many questions which remained unanswered, so many puzzles to be solved. She began to walk again, but deliberately slowed her steps and thought again about melting into the watery embrace, and then:

Time to go. Time to go.
All you need to know. You know.

The lesson that you gain from me
Is only part of what you'll see.

Much more awaits you beneath the oak,
Go on, get out. No time to soak!

The stream picked up its speed and the once welcoming temperature of the lake grew icy cold. The water had a very persuasive manner and Gabriella needed no further encouragement. Hurrying to reach the opposite shore, she lost her footing and, though the hazel wood rod helped maintain her balance, her shoes and her clothes were whisked away by the water. They were moving much too quickly for her to rescue them, and the lake was far too cold to remain in any longer, so out she stepped. As she set foot upon the land, the water calmed and the sun grew in intensity, drying her almost immediately.

She looked down at her skin, unable to believe that she was not feeling chilled. Glancing again at her arm for the telltale chilblains, she was completely taken aback. Every single cut had been healed. She looked at her legs and her torso; they, too, were healed. All the bruises had vanished, and the rough calluses on her feet had been made smooth. All her aches and pains were gone. Gabriella stood staring at herself in disbelief.

As she examined her perfectly restored skin with astonishment, Gabriella gave thanks for all that had happened in the Forest of Compassion and found it was almost too much to hold in her heart. As she remembered all the events, from the rabbits, to the stag, to the circle of sparkling green spirals, she began to feel a deep sense of calm and stillness come upon her. It was not quite sleep; but it was very close to it. She lay back upon the clover and grass and let her gaze settle on the sky. The clouds were puffy and white, the wind, barely present, and the warmth of the sun, gentle and comforting.

It is difficult to say how long Gabriella lay in this manner with her back resting against the knoll of green, that led to the sacred grove, overlooking the lake of bluest blue. Suffice to say, she stayed like this until, once more, she was interrupted by the insistent voice of the stream. At first, Gabriella did not want to stir at all and heard only a quickening in the pace of the water. There were no immediately recognizable words, just a rapidly moving current.

However, with her ever-deepening wisdom, she knew that the stream was trying to tell her something, and that it was time for her to listen. She placed aside her desire for rest. There was something more for her to do, something more that she should know. It seemed the stream was hinting at something very important indeed. Sitting up she asked, 'What is it you want to say to me?'

'Neath the oak tree, something new.
Things of beauty, made for you.

'Something for me?' she asked. Silence. Gabriella wanted it to repeat itself, as it had before. *It would be horrible if I went up to the oak tree and there was nothing there. I may be imagining things,* she thought. She walked closer to the stream, to the place where it poured into the lake, and asked it to speak again, but the stream did not respond. After feeling so joyous, she did not want to be disappointed, but she doubted that the stream would play a cruel trick on her.

And so with hazel wood rod in hand, she started up the hillock towards the six trees. At first she couldn't see the bases of the tree trunks at all but she could just make out their foliage and recognised them: a beech, an ash, an oak, a pine, a blackthorn and a willow. She knew the trees were very old, for they were substantial in girth and had the silent wisdom of living things that have borne witness to much in their lifetimes.

As Gabriella approached the top of the hill she was almost afraid to look at the oak tree. She had learned early in her life not to desire too much; it had been easier not to hope at all, rather than to hope and have her heart broken. The thought of receiving gifts, solely for her, seemed impossible to comprehend. *Still,* she thought, *everything has changed since I crossed the River of Dreams.* Expecting the worst, Gabriella looked down at the base of the oak tree.

The Parchment

There, as though awaiting her arrival, lay the most glorious clothes. On top of a small pile was a crisp white linen blouse that had buttons of carved rowan wood up the front, leading to a softly rounded collar. Its sleeve was long, soft and billowing, gathered at the wrist with a soft linen tie. Below that, spread upon the grass like a treasure chest just opened, was a skirt, woven, as if with threads of rainbow-coloured light. Gabriella ran to the beautiful garments, desperate to touch them.

The skirt was as soft as a baby rabbit and there was a succession of hues that started at the hem; a deep crimson-red, a sunset-orange, a golden-yellow, a green that reminded her of the great stag's eyes, a deep mysterious-blue and then just below the pure white waistband was a shade of purple that looked like woodland violets in summer. There were deep pockets woven from the same fabric and sewn to the front of the skirt. *It is exquisite,* she thought, and just as the stream had said, it was made purely for her.

Without a second thought she slipped the blouse over her head and pulled the skirt on as well. They fitted perfectly and the skirt went nearly to the ground; she had always wanted a skirt that went nearly to the ground.

Wait. There is only one sleeve, it has been made just for me, Gabriella thought. *Who could have made this for me? Who would have known and taken time to create such a wonderful gift for me?* Without really expecting an answer, she raced down the hill towards the lake. She was desperate to see her reflection in the water. As she looked down through the ripples on the surface, the lake became still and she could see that the garments she was wearing fairly glowed in its depths.

She felt a surge of joy well up inside her and, running back to the oak tree, she discovered that there was a gift of slip-on leather boots and a pair of warm socks to protect her feet. Each of these fitted perfectly as well.

She danced among the trees, half skipping, half spinning, until she fell, giggling, against the trunk of the mighty oak.

Unbeknownst to her, Gabriella's ecstatic dance had been observed. On one of the higher boughs of pine, sitting still as a statue, Owl had been a spectator to each of Gabriella's gasps of delight and her newfound joy. When Gabriella finally paused long enough to catch her breath, Owl hooted out 'Hello'. Gabriella looked up to see where her friend was. When she at last saw her high in the pine she called, 'Look, look at my beautiful new clothes!' Gabriella stood up once more and lifted the side of her skirt with her hand, pirouetting in a graceful manner. 'Oh, Owl, who would have given me such a special gift?' she asked.

Owl flew down to Gabriella's side beneath the oak, bearing a large pouch within her talons. Gabriella held out her hand and Owl gently released the pouch into her palm. The bag was as beautiful as the skirt Gabriella was wearing. Its coloured pattern was identical; but seemed to be much older, faded almost. 'What is this? Gabriella asked.

'A clue,' Owl answered.

'A clue for who?'

'Why for you,' came the quick response.

Here was another gift. It seemed truly difficult to comprehend. But here it was, in her hand, and she longed to know what lay inside. Gabriella carefully untied a simple drawstring and from within she pulled a piece of flint, a piece of pyrite and a bit of fungus from a paper white birch tree. Next were the three stones she had given to the rabbits and the sight of them filled her heart with gladness. 'Why, they have not been given away at all, only borrowed,' she said with a smile, whilst placing them in one of the pockets of her new skirt.

And there was one last item contained in the rainbow-coloured pouch. Reaching in for a final time, she found a piece of parchment, tightly wound. As she began to unroll it, the words written upon it spoke out loud to her, saying:

Oh tender child, with heart so pure
Receive these gifts from me.
The weave of rainbow-coloured threads,
A sign of what's to be.

Though all are different, each unique,
They journey side by side.
The blending of their separateness
Is how they each abide.

You, too, were different from the start,
So many years ago.
Your form confused and frightened men.
I was there, I know.

'Twas my hands caught your tender flesh,
When first you came to Earth.
Your Mother asked my help and care
Upon your wint'ry birth.

At first we both were terrified
With what our eyes beheld;
But when we saw with heart, not head,
Our plan began to meld.

We kept you safe within your home,
With tales of harsh travail.
The priests and townsfolk stayed away,
As you were weak and frail.

Of course, you were not weak at all;
But this is what we'd said.
We chose deception, born of love,
And courage over dread.

The eve before your Naming Day
Was fullest moon once more.
'Twas then I gave you your first gift
Of rainbow, which you wore.

Into the deepest woods we went,
Your Mother, you and I,
To pray for your protection,
As your Naming Day grew nigh.

That night I built a ring of fire
From wood of sacred tree.
The ash of each, became the whole,
And then, on bended knee,

The rod of purest hazel wood
Mixed ash with salty tears;
A paste was formed and placed on you,
With prayers, to quell all fears.

I raised my voice, with humble tone,
Petitioning all of life,
To hold you safe within itself,
To keep you free from strife.

A gentle, quiet hush came next,
Deep peace, from far within.
We journeyed home, by light of moon,
Hearts full of what had been.

Your Naming Day dawned clear and bright,
New spring was everywhere.
We brought you clothed in rainbow garb,
Before them in the square.

They gasped each time their eyes met yours,
Such light they'd never known.
And you remained so calm and still,
The seeds of change were sown.

Now listen child, and listen well,
To what I next will say,
'Twas I who chose to end my life
Day past your Naming Day.

Your Mother chose to stay with you,
To guide you as you grew.
And I, I journeyed far beyond-
To life; but all was new.

And from this place beyond, beyond,
Our Spirits join once more,
To celebrate the gift of life,
To end what was before.

Go forth to places deep within,
Hold fast to what is true.
And know that, past all raging doubt,
Pure Love created you.

If you are reading this, my dear,
Your steps have found the way,
Past gossip, hate and treachery,
To this, most precious day.

The items first removed by you
Will give you your next clue.
So pick them up. Create a spark.
Remember what you knew.

A sudden gust of wind snatched the parchment from Gabriella's hand and, as the stream of air lifted it higher and higher into the sky, it began to move quite rhythmically, propelling the parchment upwards. The air beneath began to swirl, causing it to circle above the tops of the trees within the sacred grove.

As it passed over the willow tree, the parchment was transformed into a beautiful white swan, wings outstretched, neck gracefully arched. And as the swan flew round the treetops once more, it seemed to bow its head reverentially at each of the trees one at a time; ash, beech, oak, pine, blackthorn and willow, and then lastly towards the elderwood arch that marked the path which led away from the grove. Gently landing on the water's surface, the swan drifted majestically to the middle of the lake and then, it slowly turned and looked at Gabriella with a tenderness she could hardly receive.

A Spark Becomes a Flame

She found herself looking away from the beauty of the bird, as its gaze left her feeling oddly exposed. *What does all of this mean?* Until this day, she had blamed herself for everything. She was the cause of it all; the death of the Midwife, her Mother, Middlenight and the Brother, all the sadness and grief would never have happened to them if she had not been born.

Here, in the message from the Midwife, there was no blame placed on anyone, simply an explanation of events. *If the Midwife's words are true, I am not guilty of harming those who have drawn near to me. They were drawing nearer to the light within me, all of them.*

Gabriella looked down at the incredible beauty of the colours and weave in her skirt, which shimmered with every detail. The hands that created this had done so with love, it was altogether obvious to her and a weight began to lift from her heart.

She picked up the hazel wood rod, which she had laid beneath the oak tree, and as she did she noticed a distinct sense of heat in her palm where the rod touched her flesh. Snatches of the words from the parchment came back to her:

That night I built a ring of fire
From wood of sacred tree.
The ash of each became the whole,
And then on bended knee,

The rod of purest hazel wood
Mixed ash with salty tear,
A paste was formed and placed on you
With prayers to quell all fear.

Could this be the very hazel wood that was used the night before my Naming Day? Gabriella wondered. *And are these the trees; are these the holy trees, which lent their wood and bark to create a protective shield for my life?* The questions did not really need any answers, other than the great depth of silence and peace that followed the moment it had been thought. In this hush, Gabriella's spirit became calm, and she began to realise the truth about her birth, and thus, the journey of her life.

How long she stood there, beneath the expanse of the great oak pondering these things, is unknown. However, as she returned from a place deep inside her thoughts, her stomach rumbled with hunger and once more she looked for the welcoming fire and glorious feast she had grown accustomed to. But neither was to be seen. Suddenly, the very last words of the parchment popped into her mind:

The items first removed by you
Will give you your next clue.
So pick them up. Create a spark.
Remember what you knew.

Gabriella looked down to the ground and saw the faded rainbow bag, alongside it the flint, the pyrite and the fungus, which had come from beneath the bark of the paper-white birch.

Create a spark, the words had directed. *Why, of course these are the tools necessary to make a fire,* she thought, *but what good will they do me?* Still, the words had instructed her to create a spark, and, as it was quickly becoming colder and darker, she thought it could not hurt to try.

And so, Gabriella leant the hazel wood rod against the oak and began to walk along the border of the sacred grove gathering kindling. Beneath each of the majestic trees in the centre were small pieces of dead wood, which seemed dry enough to ignite, if she could create enough of a spark.

She placed the fungus in the centre of a small amount of dry kindling, well away from the sacred trees, topped the pile of small twigs with dried pine needles, and went about the business of trying to ignite them. At first she sat on the ground, placed the pyrite between her feet and began to strike it with the flint. Every time she made contact, the pyrite slipped from between her boots. She simply could not create enough tension to hold the stone in place. Between the awkwardness of her position and the lack of strength in her arm it all seemed quite hopeless.

She stood up and walked towards the beech tree. 'This is impossible,' she said, sitting on a large flat stone that was resting against its trunk. *How can I keep it more stable? Maybe if I lift it up from the earth it would help,* she thought, trying to imagine a method of raising the pyrite from the earthen floor. She pretended to strike it, in an effort to establish how much height was necessary, when her hand hit something hard. 'Of course! The rock I am sitting on will work perfectly,' she exclaimed with delight.

With a renewed burst of energy and purpose, she half pushed, half rolled the large stone across the ground to the small pile of kindling. When she had reconfigured the fungus and kindling so that they were just below the stone, Gabriella suspended the pyrite so that half of it was hanging off the edge. She tucked one end of her skirt into the waistband and, with her foot now firmly bracing the pyrite, she picked up the flint and began to strike the two together.

Slowly at first, and then with growing strength and confidence, Gabriella pounded the stones. Initially all she produced was debris from the pyrite; but she persisted, clearing away the broken bits from the surface of the fungus to make room for a spark to land. With each strike Gabriella found her sense of helplessness waning.

She had never lit a fire before; no one had taught her; her Mother had never believed her capable. *Well, maybe Mama was right; but still, I am trying,* she thought. On this dark, moonless night Gabriella gave thanks for it all and, just then, a large spark landed on the fungus. Leaning forward quickly, she blew gently, until the pine needles ignited in a blaze, just as she had anticipated; the kindling lit next and then the small twigs from the six trees and the elderflower followed, each of them helping to feed the growing flames.

The fire was burning at last, and Gabriella collapsed, exhausted by her efforts, sweat dripping from her brow. All the fears she had felt about being unable to succeed began to loosen their grip on her as she gazed into the crackling flames, now dancing merrily in the grove. Then a most peculiar thing happened.

In the very centre of the fire was a slowly forming image of the mighty stag, only he was much smaller, like some sort of miniature version of himself. *Oh, I must be really hungry,* thought Gabriella. But the longer she looked, the more she saw. Now she was certain it was the stag, but he was no longer formed of fire, and he was definitely no longer small. As Gabriella continued to observe, his form grew larger and larger and the fire, stronger and stronger.

Suddenly, the stag began galloping towards Gabriella from deep within the flames. She could hear the pounding of his hooves upon the earth as, with each step, his stature loomed. When he seemed nearly life-sized, Gabriella strained her neck to see the tops of his antlers and in that moment, he leapt, in all his glory, from within the blaze. Fast on his hooves followed all the animals Gabriella had blessed the day before. All manner of flying, crawling and running creatures came forth from within the golden circle of fire.

The last creature to join them was Owl. *Wait,* she thought. How had Owl come from within the fire? *She was with me when I arrived in the grove, she gave me the rainbow pouch,* she thought. Owl flew up into the oak tree and perched on one of its highest branches.

From a few small sparks and twigs, Gabriella's fire was now a roaring blaze, illuminating the faces of all the animals, as well as her own, with a warm and embracing light. In the excitement of seeing them all once more, Gabriella was oblivious to what was being prepared beneath the sacred trees. There, between the trunks of the six were five tables laden with a bounty of delicacies beyond imagining: fruits and nuts, vegetables, grains, honey, tea, scones with cream, all the things that could delight and satiate each of them. When she saw it, Gabriella giggled with glee and ran towards the feast.

There, Gabriella and her newfound friends ate and drank and filled the crisp night air with laughter and conversation as they spoke, in turn, of all the wondrous events that had so recently occurred. The food and drink seemed unending and, indeed, when all were satisfied, they were surprised to see that the tables were still fully laden and the fire had taken care of itself.

With totally contented bellies, the warmth of the fire beckoned. A few at first, then more and more of the gathering of new friends came side by side, encircling the flames. When each had found a place, they looked upon one another with loving eyes. The night air grew quiet as the sounds of chatter and merriment gave way to stillness and a sense of devotion, the crackling blaze drawing the gaze of them all. Suddenly, a nightingale burst forth into song, accompanied by a chirping of crickets so sweet that even the frogs conspired to add their voices to the reverie.

The stag cleared his throat and all eyes turned to the mighty beast; his antlers reflecting the light of the fire; his shape casting a huge shadow on to the leaves of the oak tree behind him. 'Gabriella,' he said. 'We honour you this night and give thanks to Creator for your courage, your deepest truth and your wisdom. The three were great assets, in and of themselves, but powerless without the greatest gift of all. The gift above all others, that which brings thought to action, healing to the broken, light to darkness, the gift of love. Without this, none of what we have seen, and know to be true, would have been possible.

'It was love that urged you to follow me when I appeared to you as a white rabbit; love which allowed you to give your precious stones to all of us; love which guided your steps and gave you the prayer of blessing you prayed as you touched us. Love helped you see your Mother in a different light, and love opened your heart to a part of yourself you had long since scorned and rejected.

'And finally, love's last great test was that of receiving it when it came to you. And here you are, dressed in rainbow finery, wearing new boots and a new blouse and with the Garnet, Carnelian and Citrine stones returned to you. Gifts of fire, truth of story and an unending feast, these, you welcomed

194

with joy and abandon, open hand, open heart, open spirit. In that same spirit, I would like to tell you the story which began long ago and ended with your arrival in the Forest of Compassion.'

He paused for a moment as a log collapsed on the fire, sending a shower of sparks up into the night.

'Many years ago the men of the Land of Never Forgetting abused not only their earth, but the animals of the fields, the fish of the sea, the creatures which crawled upon their bellies as well. They lost respect for the balance of things and began to kill for pleasure and sport, to torture and maim for amusement. When they had depleted their own Land, they sailed across the River of Dreams in search of new prey.

'It was a dark season for us, as many of the creatures on the Mountain were slaughtered. Where once we wandered freely, we were soon forced into hiding. The bigger the animal, the greater the reward for the men, who vied with each other for prizes. Many of us were on the verge of extinction.

'It was then that a friend appeared to us,' he said, looking at the circle of animals surrounding him, and at Gabriella, who was enthralled.

'In the middle of the night, on the eve of a fullest moon, a woman came to this very grove. She had long silver hair and piercing green eyes, she was dressed in a hooded robe woven of fine wool in beautiful colours, and she walked with a stick of hazel. Knowing there would be no men from the Land of Never Forgetting hunting on the night of the roundest moon, she began to speak to us freely. Slowly, at first, came her words, then with greater rapidity. She did not speak human, however. Instead, she spoke the language of creatures, saying:

Come, she called us. Come to me.
I will help to set you free.

Dressed in rainbow garment bright
She called to us one winter's night.

I am friend. I am not foe.
My heart is heavy, filled with woe.

The calloused hearts of men cause grief.
They come in darkness, like a thief.

They rob you of your life, your peace.
Until they change, it will not cease.

I fear your land will know, like ours,
A widening loss as hate devours

All the good and noble things,
All that is different, all that sings.

'Tis not an easy plan I give,
I want to help you thrive and live.

If you would trust me, listen well
And I would tell you of my spell.

I have devised a clever plan
To save you all, and confound man.

You each will, from the waters, drink,
And in so doing, men will think

That all the game has disappeared,
They will be troubled, think it weird.

And in their boats, their trip in vain,
They'll have no pride in what they've slain

And you, dear ones, will not be dead.
You will be small and white instead.

For in the waters you will find
A spell to hide you from mankind.

The spell transforms you, for a while,
To little ones who have no guile.

As all of you will be the same,
In killing you, they'd feel but shame.

A small white rabbit, bright pink eyes
Will be life-saving as disguise.

All food and water will be yours.
Look underground, not out of doors.

You will remain in altered state,
Until the one whose soul is great,

Arrives upon these earthen shores
To end all sorrows, stop all wars.

She will arrive as human child,
And by her own, she'll be reviled.

Her flesh will not be as the rest,
In this, will lie her earthly test.

The stars have shown her path to me.
And it is clear, yes, I can see

That she can choose to light the way,
To turn the darkness into day.

So, look for her each new-born Spring,
For deep within the gifts she'll bring,

Will be the key to set you free.
And now, dear ones, will you agree?

The time is short, the day is near.
You need to trust, you need not fear.

Within this child, your lives are safe.
She too, lies hidden, not a waif;

But rather all the powers of Life
Are hid within her earthly strife.

And when her path leads her to you,
She'll know exactly what to do.

Yes, she will know, from deep within,
That who she is, she's always been.

Her eyes will guide her, from her heart,
Where seeing, is a loving art.

Be at peace now. Come, partake.
Save yourselves, for Heaven's sake.

The stag continued his tale, 'She was so beautiful and kind. We knew, instinctively that she would do nothing to harm us. And so it was that she stirred the waters with her hazel wood rod and each of us drank from it. Then, one by one, in a painless transition, all traces of our former selves were gone and we became the small white rabbits you first met.

'The woman then led us to a small hole in the earth, which opened to a series of underground tunnels, where there was room for all of us. As she had promised, there was food and drink in plenty. We never had to risk leaving the warren, save for the newest days of spring, when it was my job to come and find you, if you should happen to be upon the path.

'I knew I would recognize you, as she said you would have bright clear vision and blue eyes that could truly see. We have awaited your coming, year after year, and now you are here, just as she said you would be. We honour all that is the miracle of your life and the gift you have been to us.'

When he finished speaking, the animals turned to look at Gabriella, but she could scarcely see them, for her eyes were filled with tears. If all of her life had been necessary to bring her to this moment, then every second of sorrow and pain was worth it.

Wiping away her tears, she took a deep breath and then slowly looked at each of the incredible animals surrounding the fire, how beautiful, how unique each was in its creation.

Gabriella's heart was pounding when, at last, her eyes met those of the stag. She looked at him, but only for a moment, feeling she needed to embrace him. She walked closer to him and reaching up with her arm, she wrapped it around his neck and rested her head upon his shoulder. In turn, he inclined his head to hers, and thus the two exchanged their version of a hug.

As is the way with all tender moments, they have a beginning and an end. The stag seemed to sense that it was his responsibility to ease them all towards that which was yet to come. He gently moved away from Gabriella, backing from the blaze of the fire, up the little knoll, until he arrived at the base of the huge pine tree. Stomping at the earth with his front left hoof he pawed and crushed the pine needles beneath it, releasing a scent into the air that was at once spicy and pungent. It was as if he was digging in search of something quite specific. All eyes awaited the stag's next move.

When at last he stopped digging, he invited Gabriella, with a toss of his head, to join him beneath the great tree. As she walked towards him, the circle of animals opened, allowing the light of the fire's glow to illuminate the earth beneath him.

There, nestled within the soil was another stone, this one, green. It was not a solid colour, but seemed to have a dark green background with spirals of a lighter emerald hue ringing its periphery. It reminded Gabriella of the spiral shapes within the trunks of trees. 'Oh, how beautiful,' Gabriella exclaimed, picking it up.

'Thank you. Thank you so very much for showing it to me.' And she held it up to the stag, as if to return it to him.

'It is yours, dear one,' said the stag. 'It is yours.'

'Thank you,' was all Gabriella could muster, looking into his enormous green eyes. She wanted to say so much more, but simply found no words. Nodding his head, it was clear he understood completely and, easing towards her tenderly once more, for one last nuzzle, he rose from the earth to the fullness of his height. Balancing only upon his hind legs, he bellowed out the haunting call of the stag, sending echoes out deeply into the night, and then, with his coat glowing golden in the light of the fire he galloped directly towards it and leapt into the heart of the flames.

One by one, all the other animals followed him and disappeared from sight. As the last creature, a spectacular eagle, flew into the blaze the fire sent up a huge spray of sparks and heat into the night air. When the flames settled down again, Gabriella felt a terrible loneliness overcome her. Being in the company of the animals had created in her a wondrous sense of belonging and fellowship, but it had come to an abrupt ending, all too soon.

The Mystery of the Owl

She was alone, once more, in the sacred grove, standing before the fire she had begun, dressed in a rainbow-coloured skirt made just for her and holding her newest stone as the now familiar voice of the old woman came to her ears:

Malachite, green gift for you
Will help you know just what to do.

In its spirals learn to see
What is truly meant to be.

Use your heart, and not your eyes,
To seek with love, past earthly guise.

From within her deep pocket, Gabriella gently drew out the other three stones, Garnet, Carnelian, Citrine and held them together with the newest emerald-green of the Malachite. Each had come as she had learnt a lesson; Garnet as she followed her new path; Carnelian as she celebrated her passage from child to woman and the power of transformation; Citrine when she had trusted her own voice to overcome her inner doubts; and, lastly, Malachite which marked the many ways to greater love and deeper understanding.

She placed the four in the depths of her pocket and within moments Gabriella was fast asleep, her spirit at peace as she rested alongside the still burning fire. The earth beneath the sacred trees felt soft as eiderdown and the flames blanketed her with warmth. Although it seemed as if she hardly moved that night, she dreamt and dreamt, for, as is the way of darkness, strange illuminations are often revealed within it.

It was as though she was experiencing all that had happened, anew, as flashes of memory came to her in dreams; messages from long ago, the talking stream, the fire which birthed a host of leaping animals and birds, the gift of exquisite clothes, the parchment that became a swan. Then gradually, as though stuck like leaves in an autumn brook, each image began to repeat itself. Over and over the events replayed themselves and each time the images increased in speed, faster and faster. The leaping of the animals from within the fire became more like a stampede, and the moment of the rabbits' transformation began to spin like a dervish, as the two conjoined circles formed by them spun wildly in her mind's eye.

The pace of the images was so frantic, the energy so tightly wound, that Gabriella found herself falling backwards, further and further, until she plummeted into an abyss; she could not even voice a cry for help. Every muscle was frozen, unable to respond to her inner demands. She could not see, could not hear, could not feel. All around her was total blackness.

Disoriented, and now almost awake enough to realize she was dreaming, she tried to stem the flood of fear she felt inside her. Summoning every last bit of strength, she forced herself to peer into the inky void once more and it was then that she saw a huge dark shape before her. Oddly, it did not frighten her; even though it was no ordinary shape, for, as the beating of wings grew closer and the shape became clearer, she could see a mottled grey form. It was a huge face staring at her with piercing yellow eyes. Gabriella knew these eyes. They belonged to the Owl of Knowing. Suddenly the bird screeched loudly and Gabriella sat bolt upright, shivering, wide-awake.

She looked for Owl, but did not see her. The dream had seemed so vivid she was certain Owl would be in the grove with her; but she was nowhere to be seen. Overhead, the stars were beginning to fade into a gathering blue as a gentle pink dawn appeared above the horizon. All the earth felt as though it was waiting, anticipating something new, a beginning as never before.

Trying to restore the fire, Gabriella blew upon the embers and shifted some bigger, unburned pieces of wood on top of them and when she was certain it had taken hold she sat down to think. *I must remember this dream,* she thought. *It is very important, for I am sure there is a message in it.* She was grateful that it had reminded her of her journey. *But it was not only the places and things I have experienced,* she thought. *There was that dark black part at the end, too, which frightened me.* Not able to get back to sleep, she found herself pondering the meaning of the dreams.

What are they trying to tell me? All the animals are in the first part of the dream and then I receive the gifts of clothes and hear the Midwife's story, I fall backwards, then it becomes terribly black and then Owl appears in the darkness.

Owl.

All of the sudden, like a bolt of lightning, it came to her, 'Owl was separate. She was with the animals; but she was not really one of them. Owl carried the hazel wood rod to the Forest of Compassion and gave it to me. It was Owl who guided me down the path to the sacred grove and then delivered the rainbow-coloured pouch to me at the base of the oak tree.'

Where was the Owl of Knowing when all the others drank the water? Why did she not disguise and hide herself from the men in the Land of Never Forgetting? How did she stay safe during all those years? The questions fairly flooded Gabriella's mind.

'Where did she go? How did she survive?' Gabriella spoke the questions out loud, as if the very act of doing so would bring an answer. Surely asking the question of Owl's whereabouts was not the singular purpose of the dream. *No,* she thought, *it is not enough, I am to find the answer to this question of Owl's survival.*

Why not ask Owl, she thought, feeling foolish. It was such an obvious thing to do. 'Owl, Owl, if you can hear me, please come.' Her voice rang out through the silence of the early morning, but there was no response. After a number of unsuccessful attempts, she sat down and tried to rearrange her thoughts.

Gabriella was determined to find out the truth and, as she sat, gazing at the red-hot embers of the fire, her inner Self willed Owl to reveal the answer to her.

By the time Gabriella looked up from the flames, the sun was high in the sky and her stomach was complaining bitterly of hunger. Walking over to the tables beneath the trees, she helped herself to an oatcake, some fresh strawberries and a handful of figs. She found herself wondering why Owl had not responded. It was daylight of course, but that had not always proved a deterrent. 'Oh, Owl, I really need to know. I don't know why I need to know; but I know I must know,' she called up into the boughs of the trees above her.

If you know, that you must know,
It is nearly time to go.

'Who said that?' Gabriella asked, looking about to see who had spoken.

Listen sweet one, listen here.
'Tis my voice that meets your ear.

I can help you find the way.
Not today, though, not today.

'Oh, it's the stream.' Gabriella giggled in recognition and ran down the hillock to the bank that bordered it. 'Can you really help me answer my question about the Owl of Knowing?'

Yes, oh yes, oh yes I can;
But you must wait. There is a plan.

Gather strength within this grove.
Dressed in rainbow that She wove.

Food and drink will nurture you.
This you'll need, for what you'll do.

After seven days are done,
Past the setting of the sun,

When the moon is full and round,
You will hear a haunting sound.

It will draw you to my shore.
Make you want, for less, and more.

Step within a boat of birch,
At last, begin your holy search.

No human soul will steer or guide.
Will you embark? You must decide.

The way is dark, the night is long,
You will forget your childlike song.

Your deepest depths contain the light
To free your shadowed, earthly sight.

You must decide, twixt now and then,
Can you go past what's safe, again?

Do not begin if you give pause,
Still linked to man-made rules and Laws;

But if you dare past absolute,
The journey brings you 'naught but fruit.

Go on, sweet girl, away with you.
Your heart will point the way that's true.

And with that, the stream ceased to burble and Gabriella walked slowly back up the hill towards the oak tree, contemplating all that she had been told.

Following her conversation with the stream, Gabriella spent seven days peacefully resting in the shade of the six trees of her sacred grove. The tables beneath the trees were magically replenished with food and drink and the fire renewed itself whenever needed. In the ease of it all, Gabriella found her mind wandering away from the perplexing questions about Owl, which had so preoccupied her. The more comfortable she felt, the easier it became to push aside all thoughts of finding the truth. Here, in the sacred grove, she wanted for nothing, and quite honestly, she felt that staying here forever might just suit her; except that was, for one thing, each night she had a dream.

The first night she saw a light in her dream, not quite a lantern, something larger and brighter. It was coming from the path, which led from the Forest of Compassion to the sacred grove. It was a most exquisite light, with a luminescent quality that seemed to draw her towards it. In her dream, Gabriella began to move in its direction; but after only three steps the light extinguished. She felt saddened and, try though she might, she was unable to re-enter the dream that night.

On the second, third, fourth and fifth nights, Gabriella was visited by the same glorious light in her dreaming, only, with each consecutive night, the light came closer to where she stood within the sacred grove. Gabriella had tried to run more quickly towards the light on the second night; but again, as on the first evening, her very movement extinguished the glowing presence.

Having learned from her first two experiences, Gabriella consciously willed herself to remain still on the third night. This time, the light glowed in the Forest once more, but Gabriella did not move and the light grew larger and brighter than ever. The stiller Gabriella became, the closer the light came to her, until, by the sixth night, the light had moved from the path, across the green grass and settled beneath the arbour of elderflower. It seemed to have flecks of light dancing from it. No longer a distant, non-distinctive shape, the whole thing now resembled a great column of light, moving purposefully, and directly, towards her.

It steadily made its way from the path in the woods to the arbour, where it stopped abruptly, just beneath the white-flowered arch, as if unable to enter the sacred grove. The light remained poised, as if waiting, and then a most wondrous thing occurred. The light began to sing in a language Gabriella had never heard. She could not hear distinct words but only a melody; deep-throated, calming, like the healing hand on a temple brushing away a fever. It was captivating and Gabriella wanted to hear more. In her excitement, she forgot her commitment to stillness and took a step towards the light. In a breath it was gone. No light. No melody. Nothing.

Gabriella awoke, angry with herself for having moved. She tried to remember the music she had heard, but the notes would not come to her. It was as though she had no reference for them at all. Lying beneath the trees she looked up at the moon, which was nearly fully round. The stream had told her that a boat of birch would come for her to help her solve her questions about Owl.

But why does it always speak in riddles? she thought. *Why would I ever want to leave this place with such plentiful food and drink? I am safe and contented. No, I think I will choose to let the boat go on without me. I will choose to stay. I have done enough. It does not matter where Owl hid herself away, it only matters that she did. In so doing, she helped to bring about the transformation of the animals and she delivered the precious gifts to me. Yes. It is enough.* Closing her eyes, she slept, dreamlessly, until the warmth of the seventh day's sun awakened her.

The thought of staying in the sacred grove filled her with joy. Gabriella had never known such peaceful delight. *At last,* she thought, *I have found a place where I am at home. I have been given a great reward for my generosity and courage. It is right that this should be the place I spend my remaining days, all comfort and ease, no more darkness for me. I deserve this.* Gabriella's chest puffed as she continued her litany of self-congratulations, *Now I will suffer no longer. The season of ease and comfort has come at last,* she thought, popping fat, juicy blueberries into her mouth.

Even my dreams tell me to stay here, she realized. *Every time I step away from the grove, the light is extinguished and last night the song stopped altogether, the moment I made a move. Clearly these are all signs that I am to remain here in this grove for all of time. In many ways, it is the only choice I have.* 'And I will have it!' she proclaimed. She stood poised beneath the noble trees, hazel wood rod in hand, like a queen with her sceptre.

And with her decree, there was a tremendous clap of deafening thunder. The blue skies became fast covered with great grey clouds, which piled higher and higher above her head. The breeze, calm only moments before, began to swirl and increase in speed. Gabriella looked for a place to seek shelter. She would have to rely on one of the trees and decided to make for the oak. Running to its huge trunk, clutching her hazel wood rod, she huddled down against the power of the oncoming storm.

Within minutes, the wind grew to gale force and Gabriella tucked her body on the lee side as best she could for shelter. In one great gust the banquet tables were upended, scattering food and drink to the ground. The fire was snuffed out and branches snapped off the boughs of the ancient stand of trees as if they were kindling. Ferocious in its might, the storm left Gabriella drenched with rain and trembling with fear.

After what seemed an age, the storm passed, leaving utter destruction in its wake. The six once beautiful trees were now ravaged; the feast destroyed; all sense of peace and sanctuary now only a memory of what had been. Gabriella's knees felt weak and, sinking to the ground, she began to sob.

'Why has this happened to so beautiful a place? Why was it not protected from the storm?' but her questions went unanswered. For, spreading out before her to the west was a most spectacular sunset. The reflected light of setting sun cast a golden glow upon the lake; the first shades of amber gradually giving way to a deepening orange until, eventually, shades of plum and violet washed the evening sky for as far as she could see.

Exhausted, she clutched the stones within her pocket, wrapped her body around the base of the oak tree trunk and fell asleep. Fast and deep her slumber came. Her limp, aching body, needing little coaxing towards the welcome release of sleep and, as she rested her head on the earth, once more, her dream returned.

The Woman of the Wood

On the far shore of the lake she saw a light flickering on the path that led from the Forest of Compassion. Closer and closer it came and it seemed to be moving directly towards her. Rising to her feet she tried to see more clearly, only this time, her movement did not halt the progress of the light. With every step the light elongated, becoming taller and taller, and then, when it arrived beneath the arbour, Gabriella heard its song once more. The soothing balm of its tone washed over her, easing her pain and lessening the sorrow of her heart, but she reminded herself to stay still, just in case any movement would bring the dream to an end.

And then, the light moved again. It passed beneath the arbour, ducking slightly as it did so, and continued to walk slowly, towards the stream. The glowing column reached higher than ever, up towards the roundest moon. It walked directly to the edge of the water, singing its beautiful song. It was glorious. Gabriella's gaze was transfixed and then to her amazement and delight, the column turned around, completely, to reveal a face and two arms that were crossed over its chest.

The face was white as sun on snow, with eyes of palest blue-green, the arms seemed to glow from within, and they shone as brightly as the moon. When the two saw each other, the column of light smiled at Gabriella, uncrossed it arms and removed a hood of whitest white. The hood was attached to a cloak and the raiment beneath was the colour of its eyes. The fabric of both had long, frayed and curling edges that glittered with every movement the column made. Moonbeams played upon long golden hair, which was now fully visible without the hood to cover it.

The entire creature seemed to shimmer and twinkle in a gentle, sighing breeze. The glorious figure kept its eyes fixed upon Gabriella and then it gestured with its right hand. As it extended it in front of its body, the first finger pointed at Gabriella and beckoned her to come down the hill towards the lake. Still afraid that the dream might end; but almost more afraid that it might not, Gabriella picked up her hazel wood rod and took one step.

'*Gabriella. Gabriella,*' came the sound of her name as the beautiful being sung to her in a voice that reached directly to her heart. By now, the vision before her was truly enormous and even though Gabriella was still high upon the hill, the two were looking eye to eye across the water.

I am the Woman of the Wood,
Please listen to my voice.
Tonight I come to guide the way;
But, you must make a choice.

Remain on ground you think you know;
But is it really truth?
Or, travel on, to unknown lands,
Far past the land of youth.

Each soul must make this choice in time,
It is one's greatest task;
To seek the answers deep within,
To do far more than ask.

You know that Owl was not transformed,
Instead, she hid away.
This place of hiding, this I know;
But not by light of day.

Within the Mountain's tender grasp,
A shelter there she found.
Her cave is entered not by foot,
And exited with sound.

If you set sail upon this night,
Of this you can be sure.
The water knows the truth of things,
The way to make things pure.

So, when a boat arrives for you,
Look deep, and deeper still.
And know that love is sometimes rough;
Its birth, oft' born of will.

If it is time to take this step,
From solid earth to sea,
Let go of why, and where, and how,
For all that is, must be.

Release, into the vast domain,
Where human strength grows weak,
Where heart and Spirit light the way,
And all will find, who seek.

As she sang these words, the Woman of the Wood grew taller yet and the play of light dazzled even more brightly upon her aquamarine-coloured gown. Her arms now extended high into the sky, creating an enormous v-shape in the heavens. As her glorious song ended, the fullest moon was perfectly centred above her head and it appeared as though the Woman of the Wood was actually holding the shining orb of light within her hands. Mercurial, silvery-golden beams danced their way around her until she was like a tapestry, woven of light.

Her sea-green eyes pierced Gabriella's as they gazed upon her. All was hushed and, with the fingers of her left hand still high above her head, the woman made an almost imperceptible gesture, encouraging Gabriella to come further down the hill. *No*, Gabriella said to herself, *the dream will end!* And she remained perfectly still. Again, came the gesture, more obviously this time, but Gabriella remained unmoved.

Gabriella. Gabriella.
I am not a dream.
Come closer now, if you would like,
Come nearer to the stream.

As though in some hazy trance, Gabriella realised that she was feeling in her pocket for her four beautiful stones. After she touched each of them, she picked up the hazel wood rod and, gripping it firmly, walked down the hill towards the Woman of the Wood. Half-expecting the dream to vanish at any moment, Gabriella found herself nearly tip-toeing to the water's edge. When she arrived, she found the size of the white and aqua adorned Woman before her quite overwhelming and she could do little else but gape at the sheer strength and size of the magnificent being.

Gabriella. Gabriella.

Never had her name sounded so beautiful. Never had it been so tenderly sung. A lump came to Gabriella's throat as tears welled within her eyes and she smiled at the sheer brilliance of the moment in which she found herself. Again, came the gentle silver-toned words:

Gabriella. Gabriella.

I said, before, I knew the way,
To Owl of Knowing's nest.
Please come aboard; trust but in me.
And I shall do the rest.

Remember this, and only this,
As we go on our way,
What looks like death, is often birth,
And night, leads but to day.

With that, the Woman of the Wood turned her back to Gabriella and began to slowly shrink from sight. *Oh, please do not leave,* thought Gabriella, for she hoped beyond hope that the beautiful Woman might stay just a little longer.

And then, as though the Woman had heard her unvoiced plea, she lowered herself, backwards, into the waters of the stream. Her torso, arms and legs began to form the body of a canoe; the fabric of her robe transformed into a birch bark outer hull; her lovely aquamarine dress became a bundle of silken cushions, which padded the base of the canoe in a most inviting manner. The Woman of the Wood's long golden hair floated upon the water, as her upper back and neck lifted gracefully from the surface to form the bow. From here, she could gaze at anyone who would be a passenger within.

After navigating across the lake, she pulled alongside Gabriella, gently bobbing on the surface of the current and looked directly at her. Gabriella, shaking her head in disbelief, reached out to touch the canoe and found it really was birch bark. Tapping it with her hazel wood rod, she felt it was solid. Knowing now that this was no dream, Gabriella turned to look, rather wistfully, one last time at her sacred grove, now devastated by the storm. It would no longer provide a place of rest and sanctuary for her. *It is time to move on,* she thought. The words the Woman had spoken about death looking like life and of night becoming day were both perplexing and not completely enticing to her; but the voice which had sung them was entirely so.

Gingerly, Gabriella stepped one foot into the boat and, using the hazel wood rod for balance, she lifted her other foot into it as well. The cushions of silk seemed perfectly placed for her as she settled back against them in the stern. *So it truly is no dream,* Gabriella thought to herself as the face of light directly opposite her, smiled, as though she had heard her thoughts.

The two set off, away from the lake, into new waters. Great towering willows lined the embankments just beyond the second elderflower arbour that bordered the sacred grove. Its graceful foliage burnished in the glowing moonlight's silvery beam, creating a wonderland of shimmering radiance everywhere Gabriella looked.

It is odd that none of this was harmed in the storm, she thought.

The Woman of the Wood sang once more, her wordless melody seeming to propel them through the rippling waters.

After what seemed a long while, Gabriella found she was drifting to sleep, mesmerized by the song and by the magical surroundings all about her. Her head grew heavy, her eyelids heavier still, and to sleep she drifted within the Woman of the Wood, to a place where dreams are truth, and what is thought to be true is often exposed as no more than folly.

So deep was her slumber that she was unaware of the many pairs of nocturnal eyes observing her progress along the meandering stream; mice, bats, possums, owls and a host of smaller creatures all beheld the human, whose courage and wisdom had freed the animals of the Forest of Compassion from their altered states.

Each seemed to bow their heads in acknowledgement as the vessel passed by, the Woman of the Wood keeping constant vigil over her precious charge.

The morning was glorious, sunshine basked the white boat with warmth and a golden glow. Gabriella opened her eyes and beheld, once more, a spread of food prepared for her. There was a muffin topped with great clumps of cinnamon and sugar, a bowl of ripe raspberries, the largest she had ever seen, and a flask of milky tea. She munched small bites of her muffin, which melted on her tongue, sipped her tea and delighted in a handful of raspberries, savouring each berry, one by one.

'Thank you,' said Gabriella to the Woman of the Wood, 'Thank you for bringing me here.'

Quite where here was, Gabriella could not say. Looking at her surroundings, she could see that the once narrow stream had grown wide and still, becoming almost a vast and mirrored lake, much bigger than the one in the sacred grove.

Willow trees, once close enough to touch, were now a great distance away and alongside the shore were hundreds of birch trees; the paper-white bark of their trunks, like molten gold in the sunshine.

From this great expanse of water, the shape of the Mountain was recognizable again. Gabriella had nearly forgotten that she had been, all along, on the Mountain of Remembrance, for the trees of the Forest of Compassion had obscured its form from her sight. Here, held safely in the embrace of the Woman of the Wood, she could see the mighty peak glistening majestically in the light and it looked almost jewel-like.

In a flash, she was reminded of her first dream, when she climbed the ladder to the summit and saw inside the cave, heard her Mother's voice calling her, beckoning her to come in and find her gift. It seemed such a long while since she had thought of the dream, and she felt a renewed sense of urgency in her desire to climb the Mountain once more. But she had no idea where to begin.

By the time she had finished her breakfast, the sunlight was so strong it created a blinding reflection on the surfaces of land and water. Using her hand to shade her sight, she made one last attempt to see the summit, hoping to catch a glimpse of the cave she had seen in her dream. She squinted and strained, but the light was painful, like a dagger piercing her eyes.

Having little choice in the matter, she closed them to protect against the glare, and soon became lulled to sleep once more, as the canoe continued on across the wide and glistening waters. And all the while, the Woman of the Wood gazed at her with loving eyes.

Sometime later, Gabriella woke with a chill. The once bright sun was nowhere to be seen and although the skies above were still clear and blue, the boat had come upon a river that was passing through a tall canyon, the sides of which had obscured the sun. Steep, jagged cliffs towered above them and as the wide waters narrowed, their once unhurried progress became quicker and quicker, as the smooth, unruffled surface became turbulent and the current much stronger.

Rocks threatened the craft from all about them and, although the Woman of the Wood was skilful at avoiding them, Gabriella found herself often dashed against the hull and soon she began to feel very unsafe. Her heart began to beat wildly as the river took on a chaotic energy. Soon the Woman of the Wood was also being thrown about at its mercy, seemingly unable to guide the boat in such tumultuous currents. The water hurtling over stone and rushing through the canyon brought back the memory of the waterfall.

Recognizing the danger, Gabriella cried out, 'We are heading for a waterfall. We are heading for a waterfall!' The Woman of the Wood only blinked at her. *She cannot hear me,* Gabriella thought. Lifting herself off the cushions, gripping her hazel wood rod in terror, she began to crawl towards the Woman of the Wood, in an effort to make her voice heard. Suddenly, Gabriella was slammed to the floor of the canoe, but now, with her head up against the bow, she heard these calm and reassuring words sung to her:

Trust that I will hold you close,
Safely to my breast.
Darkness will give way to light.
Your soul shall find its rest.

Over and over came the refrain of the Woman of the Wood as the waters grew more and more menacing. Then, as if tugged by an unseen force beneath the surface, the stern of the canoe dipped awkwardly into the river. The force pulled stronger and stronger, until, like a hooked trout, the boat sunk deeper and deeper. With one final jerk, the birch bark canoe became completely vertical, standing on end, poised on top of the water. The sides of the boat melted away and the Woman of the Wood appeared as herself once more.

True to the words of her final song, she wrapped her arms around Gabriella and held her tightly to her chest. The two began to spin, slowly at first, and then with great velocity, as the water beneath them rose like a funnel.

All the spectacular colours of their clothes began to meld into a dizzying spiral; aquamarine, white, rainbow-coloured skirt, all seemed to fuse into one.

Faster and faster they spun, until it was no longer possible to discern one from the other. And then the giant force from beneath, which had begun it all, tugged one last time and the two disappeared from sight. Down into the depths of the water they plunged. All breath left Gabriella's lungs and a great weight pressed down on her. On and on they plummeted, spinning and spinning, but Gabriella could see nothing and heard only the sound of her own terrified screams.

ONLY AN ECHO

G abriella was hurled from the water into the air, where she hovered, suspended for a few moments before crashing down on to a hard, unforgiving surface. 'Oh my back,' she cried, convinced she had broken something, but feeling relieved that she could move a little. Whatever she had landed on was very, very hard and, as her mind began to comprehend what had happened, she became aware that she was completely surrounded by darkness. She had fallen on her upper left back, which was always sensitive anyway and she tried to rub the place where it throbbed; but the pain seemed just out of her reach.

'Where am I?' she called out.

'Where am I?' answered a voice from what seemed like far away.

'What?'

'What?' came the distant reply.

'Hello?'

'Hello?'

An echo, she thought. *It is only an echo. I am alone in this place.* Drenched, and feeling badly bruised, she wondered what to do next and not being able to see, made her much less able to think. The weight of the darkness seemed to pin her down, both in body and spirit, and she sat, shivering in the darkness with her knees bent up and drawn close to her chest, trying in vain to keep warm.

She called out once more, shouting for the Woman of the Wood, but the only response was that of her own voice coming back to her, faintly, from the distance. She was truly alone.

In an effort to fend off a growing sense of panic, Gabriella reminded herself of what the Woman of the Wood had said, '*Darkness will give way to light. Darkness will give way to light.*'

I am alone, but this is alright, I have been on my own before, she thought feeling buoyed a little. 'I can manage this. I can survive this, she whispered as she stood up. Despite the darkness all around her, she decided to explore. Using her hazel wood rod as a sort of guiding stick, she began to tap the floor before her, listening carefully as she did so. If the surface she tapped felt flat and sounded solid, Gabriella would take a step.

Tap, tap step. Tap, tap, step, and on she went. *Yes, this is working*, she thought excitedly. *I will find my way out of here and arrive at Owl's hiding place, as this cannot possibly be it. I had better hurry. The Woman of the Wood may need me and I may find her, or she me, if I just keep moving.*

Tap, tap, step. Each attempt brought Gabriella to a solid wall of rock, she was going in circles. *One more try*, she thought. Tap, tap, splash. *Water, this must be how I arrived here.* Taking the utmost care she took a step back and knelt down, edging herself carefully towards where she had heard the splash.

There was no sound of running water, just an eerie silence. Gabriella had definitely heard a splash. In an effort to stabilize herself, she lowered her entire body to the stone surface she was kneeling on, until she was prostrate. *There, that feels more secure.*

Now, touch the water, she thought. Reaching out her right hand into the void, she began to pat the surface, touching rock, rock, and then moist.

'Oh, how warm,' she said.

'Oh, how warm,' came the echo.

Trying to ignore the echo, she felt herself longing to plunge into the water, but knew this would be a very foolish thing to do, as everything around her was inky blackness. How could she, with only one arm, risk getting into an unseen body of water without knowing if she could climb out again? She felt comforted by the thought of the warm seductive water.

One hand cannot possibly warm my whole body, she thought. *And yet, I am nearly soothed in this simple act.* Inching closer to what she assumed to be the edge of a rocky ledge, she allowed her entire arm to swing down freely into the depths. 'Oh, this is bliss,' she whispered, too softly for her echo to answer.

After some time like this, Gabriella became aware that she was shivering. Her entire body, save her right arm, was covered in gooseflesh. She had not been warmed at all. It was simply that the temperature of the pool was so inviting it had overridden all the other sensations. So, there she remained, her right hand and arm feeling luxuriously warm and the rest of her, in a very bad way.

This is no solution, Gabriella reasoned, as she carefully moved back away from the water to reassess her situation. She positioned herself where she thought she was fairly safe and reviewed her facts. *There is definitely some water there in front of me, even though I cannot see it and I am sure there is a rocky ledge beneath me,* but none of this seemed encouraging at all. *Wait!* she thought. *This must be a cave. If it is, surely there must be cracks or fissures or something.*

Picking up the hazel wood she started to tap in front of her until she felt what seemed like a solid wall of stone completely blocking her way. She cautiously explored the wall with the back of her hand, searching for a break somewhere, anywhere. And, after a little while, just as she had hoped she would, she felt a small break in the rock beneath her fingers. Trying as best she could, she struggled to make out what was beyond the fissure, but, after feeling up and down its entire length, she concluded that it was nothing more than a crack in a wall of stone. And, with a deep sigh, she began to tap again.

When she heard a splash of water, she realized she was back where she had begun. By now she had begun to picture the space around her in her mind's eye and it seemed alarmingly small, despite the echoes which teased from a faraway place. And before long, she felt completely disorientated.

'Help!' she cried out.

'Help,' echoed her voice once more, but this time she could hear how frightened she sounded.

'What else can I do?' she cried.

'What else can I do?'

I know I am clever. I am sure there is a way. I know I will find my way out of here, she thought, gritting her teeth; but again, nothing new appeared as she tapped and stepped, over and over again. It seemed there was no way out. Feeling very cold, hungry and thirsty, Gabriella found herself quite dispirited. *Perhaps the best thing for now is to rest and try again tomorrow,* she thought in an effort to console herself, and then, with a sudden pang of fear, she wondered how she could recognize tomorrow when all around her was so very dark.

'*Darkness will give way to light.*' The words of the Women of the Wood popped into her mind as if prompted, and, clinging to them like a scrap of hope, Gabriella slumped, exhausted, to the ground, her back to the wall, which was as far from the water as she could be.

Her sleep that night was fitful and uneasy as she tried to find a comfortable position on the floor of hard stone. Each time she moved a wincing pain surged through her entire being. She found no peace at all, nothing seemed able to rest, not body, not mind, not spirit.

It was as though something within her was churning everything into a great vat of immense pain and with growing exhaustion she felt an insidious sense of panic begin to grip her very heart. *Darkness will give way to light. Darkness will give way to light,* she thought, repeating the words over and over again, as if they were a spark that, if held tightly enough by her, might fend off the overwhelming blackness.

D rifting to a brief, but fitful sleep, after what had seemed an eternity, Gabriella came gradually awake with a sense of warmth upon her face. Instinctively she touched her cheek and to her amazement her hand felt warmed as well. Gabriella opened her eyes and saw the source of such welcome sensation. Passing her hand back and forth, slowly in the air, she appeared to have found a beam of sunshine.

Light! If there is light, there is a way out of this darkness, she thought and leapt up to find a glorious shaft of brilliance piercing the darkness like a beacon.

After taking time for her eyes to adjust, she saw that the light was coming from the wall that had seemed so impenetrable, streaming through what must have been the fissure she had found in the dark. *This is so much bigger than I thought it was,* she thought, stooping down to take a closer look. And there she beheld, to her delight, a large opening, which looked like a huge light-filled space.

Maybe I can squeeze through, she thought with a rising sense of hope. *How amazing, this was here all along and I never saw it.*

Without wasting a single moment, she set about trying to crawl through the fissure towards the sunlight. At first she tried to make her way by crawling on her stomach, headfirst, but her progress was soon stopped, as the breadth of her shoulders could not fit through the gap in the stone.

Wriggling back out, she gathered her wits about her. *Perhaps, if I lay on my right side I will have more mobility.* Manoeuvring herself in this manner, she was able to go a little further than before, but to her dismay she found that because she was unable to use her arm, she had almost become completely stuck. Determined to succeed, she backed out once more and decided to lie on her left side, which proved to be agonizingly painful, but might allow her another chance.

Pushing with her feet, gripping the hazel wood rod in her hand, she squeezed her body into the light-filled tunnel and began to make her way, inch by painful inch. The tunnel was quite narrow, and Gabriella could see little, as the light was almost blinding.

Keep going. Keep going, she coaxed herself as she pushed slowly into the narrowing space about her. By now all she had left to push with was her feet.

Push, came her inner voice, *Push.*

Suddenly she felt a searing pain. 'Ouch,' she cried out, and her head began to throb. Unable to see where she was going, she had not realised that the narrow tunnel had become narrower still, and now threatened to trap her completely.

What do I do? she asked herself with a growing sense of panic.

She was stuck between light and dark, unable to move any further forward. *It was difficult enough to shift my weight forward with the strength of my legs, how will I ever go backwards?*

Not really knowing if she would be strong enough, or that it would work, Gabriella summoned her strength and courage and came up with a plan. She found that the toe of her new boot was strong enough to allow her to kick the wall of the passageway, thus creating a small hole. Then, holding her foot in place, she pulled her body towards the opening with her right leg.

Each time she reversed, her skirt lifted higher, completely exposing her left leg to the rock beneath, her tender flesh soon bloodied by the rough surface. Her right foot began to feel as if it might shatter kicking the stone, and the sweat poured from her, until she was drenched, and yet she continued.

I simply cannot stop. I must not give in.

With all her might, she kicked the wall again and felt a wincing pain on her shin, but then realized, to her utter relief, as her foot had met no resistance, she had made it back to the opening.

I am nearly free.

With brute force and determination she wriggled the rest of the way, until at last, she was out.

Gasping for air, Gabriella looked about her in wonder. The shaft of light from the gap created a beauty she could not have imagined, the centre of the water becoming illuminated, like some sort of iridescent pathway. Peering into it, she could see no bottom within its depths; but the surface, now lit, was the very colour of the dress worn by the Woman of the Wood, only here it seemed to shimmer even more seductively.

Shadows in the Dark

Gazing at the glimmering water, Gabriella became aware of her thirst. She walked to the edge of the pool, bent down to her knees, and, careful not to block the light, she cupped her hand and dipped into the waters.

'Oh, it is so warm,' she said, and tasting it she knew it was the sweetest she had ever known. The waters of the pool quenched not only her parched throat, but satisfied the growling demands of her stomach as well.

When she had drunk her fill, Gabriella began to play with the light, making shapes with her hand in the path of the bright beam, causing shadows to be cast on the opposite wall, on the far side of the water. But her fun soon gave way to sorrow when she inadvertently positioned the whole of her body within the rays of glorious light.

Gabriella turned towards the wall and gazed at the shadow of her own figure. At first, she had stood facing the opposite wall with her back to the source of light. In this position, her missing arm was not noticeable. But when she turned her right side to the light, her misshapen flesh became very evident. Quickly turning away she made her shadow change once more, causing the shape created by the lump on her left shoulder to disappear.

She shifted back again, so that her deformity could cast its shadow once more. And then, Gabriella stared at her shadow-self, hating her. There was nothing of beauty there. When the light shone upon her, it revealed ugliness.

Here in the dark, in the shadow of a mere shaft of light, her hideousness brought the memory of the burden she had been to her Mother flooding back. She was soon overwhelmed by feelings of loss and profound sadness, everyone and everything she had ever loved was gone; Mama, Middlenight, the Brother, the butterfly, the animals in the Forest of Compassion, the sacred grove, the glorious Woman of the Wood and now, even Owl, was nowhere to be found.

Gabriella began to think that her life was exactly like the cave, mostly dark with a few bright moments. *There is a way to greater light; but not one that I can fit through. A normal life is not possible for me. I am trapped in a body that will always keep me in my place. There will never be real freedom or love for me in this world.*

As she thought these words, Gabriella slowly lowered herself to the ground, reaching for neither hazel wood, nor stones for comfort. She sat leaning against the wall of stone, to the right of the crevasse, until the last of the light was extinguished.

When the sun rose again, it flooded the cave in splendour, but Gabriella could not see its beauty. Her eyes were open, but glazed over, vacant of expression. As the light grew stronger, Gabriella, still glassy-eyed, got up and began to pace, back and forth, back and forth.

Occasionally, she would stop to slam her left shoulder into the wall of stone crying out, 'I hate you', and the echo would come back 'I hate you', like some sort of dark affirmation. Like an animal, caged, she circled her tiny cell of stone.

And as the days passed, the water seemed to draw her attention with greater frequency. 'I cannot see the bottom,' she would say over and over. She found herself becoming preoccupied with the thought of simply becoming the water, of falling in, of sinking to the very depths she could not see.

With each passing day the moments of sunshine seemed to lessen and the bright light that had once lasted a goodly time, now seemed progressively dimmer. *It must be the shifting of the sun in the sky,* Gabriella thought, not really caring. *Soon, even the light will go and there will be nothing but the dark.* Each day, she forced herself to stand before the weakening light beam, casting her shadow upon the opposite wall for as long as the light permitted. And every day her self-loathing and despondency increased.

'This seems a fitting end for a life worth not too much. I am so tired of struggling with being deformed and different. I know I helped the animals, for that I am very grateful, but why could I not remain in the sacred grove for the rest of my days?' she said in a bitter and angry tone. 'As soon as I had wished it, the storm destroyed it all. There is an evil in me that ruins all the good I come into contact with; the Midwife was put to death, my Mother was cast out and then driven to despair, the Brother sacrificed his life for us to escape, Middlenight drowned saving my life from the flooded River, Mama died trying to save me and Middlenight and the Woman of the Wood, who tried to help me find the answer to my question, is probably dead as well.'

She began to feel an uncontrollable flood of tears begin behind her eyes. 'What a wretched thing my life is,' she said, clutching her left side as she collapsed in a heap and curled into a tiny ball.

'I want to die,' she said in a timid voice.

'I want to die,' she heard the weak response come back.

Over and over she said the words until at last, rising to her knees, fist clenched, she bellowed them out, 'I want to die!'

'I want to die!' the echo came quickly back, and the starkness of its tone took her breath away.

Feeling something lumpy under her right knee she realized she was kneeling on the pocket that contained her stones. *Stupid stones, stupid Gabriella for taking comfort in them. They are nothing more that misshapen lumps of earth, just like me. They are not blessed or powerful and neither am I.*

Standing up, she reached into her pocket and, one by one hurled the stones into the water: Garnet, Carnelian, Citrine and then Malachite. Each entered the water with a louder sound than she had anticipated. For a brief moment she felt sad; but then, even that emotion left her. She picked up the hazel wood rod next and walked to water's edge, where she threw it, too, into the bottomless pool.

Devoid of all she had carried on her journey, Gabriella returned to the shaft of light. She looked through to the illuminated space, which she could not reach, and turned towards the opposite wall, upon which her shadow was projected. 'There,' she said to her shadow. 'I can do no more. I have no more ideas or thoughts or plans. I am ready to die. I am tired of this struggle and I am tired of pretending that I am contented when I am not. If I am to leave this place it will be a power greater than mine that delivers me.'

A Song without Words

In response to her last words came a beautiful voice singing a melody without words. Gabriella held her breath. *What was that? Is it the Woman of the Wood?* she wondered. Again came the sweet sound. *No, it is not her, yet it seems so familiar,* thought Gabriella. She waited and the sound continued to fill the cave. There was no echo, which seemed strange. Relief washed over Gabriella; someone must have heard her. Yet, she could see no one.

'Hello!' she cried.

'Hello,' came the echo of her voice.

She looked into the lit passageway and the space beyond; but there was no one there and then she looked back, once more, to the water. What she beheld caused her to gasp. Her shadow was no longer upon the wall, but walking towards her across the path of light, upon the water's surface. Midway, the shadow suddenly dived into the depths as Gabriella watched, unable to utter a word.

Moments later, her shadow-self reappeared holding the hazel wood rod within her hand and, drenched with sparkling aquamarine-coloured beads of water, she continued walking towards the now trembling Gabriella.

The shadow walked to the edge of the pool, stepped out from the water and on to the stone where Gabriella stood, her back flat against the wall behind her. Although they looked at one another eye to eye, the depths of the shadow made it seem gigantic.

And then, the shadow of blackest black sang her wordless melody once more. As her voice caressed the cavern with sound, the hazel wood rod, dripping wet with the warm waters of the pool, was extended towards Gabriella and she accepted it with her outstretched hand. Lastly, the shadow-self reached into the pocket of her own apron and produced from within, the four stones which had been so angrily cast into the waters. These, too, Gabriella received with wonder and thanks.

Without a word being spoken, and singing its glorious melody, the shadow continued walking towards Gabriella, closer and closer it came, until there was no air between them. Then, with a mighty gust of wind, and a heavy weight, the shadow pressed flush against Gabriella with a great force. Heavier and heavier the shadow bore down upon her, until Gabriella felt her very life was being crushed. All air was forced out of her lungs and the light grew dimmer and dimmer, until, at last, she could see nothing at all.

And then, her body, in its great wisdom, remembered to breath. It inhaled, a deep rasping breath and, in that moment, the blackness that was her shadow, vanished.

All was silent and Gabriella, heart pounding, facing the wall opposite, now saw nothing but light before her. She closed her eyes and reopened them. *It remains the same*, she thought. *But I can see only light. Why am I am casting no shadow?* Placing the hazel wood on the ground, she reached into her pocket to feel her smooth pebbles once more.

'There are five!' she said with surprise.

'Five,' came the echo.

Garnet, Carnelian, Citrine and Malachite and to them had been added a sea-mist green stone, with a mysterious luminescence deep within it. Gabriella held it to the light and then came the ancient voice, which she had not heard since the sacred grove:

Aquamarine, a gift for you,
Will help you know just what to do.

From shadow-self, receive this day,
The opening to another way.

Awaken what is pure and strong.
Lift up your voice and sing your song.

My song, what could that be she wondered. *I do not think I have a song.* She paused and remembered that the shadow had sung a melody. *If the shadow is now a part of me, could its beautiful song also be part of me?* But she only half believed that such singular glory could live within her.

Trusting beyond her doubt, Gabriella placed the first four stones she had been given back into her pocket, balanced the hazel wood rod against her chest and then, with her arm extended, the aquamarine stone held on her upturned palm, she faced the now dimly lit passageway and began to sing the melody she had been given. Softly at first, and then with growing confidence, Gabriella's voice filled the cave. Moreover, it filled her soul. For the first time in her life, something vast and incomprehensible was opening deep inside.

She took in a great breath, closed her eyes, and with abandon she broke forth in song. With each note of the melody, the walls of the cave responded to her voice and slowly began to quiver. Each time she drew a breath, her voice grew stronger, her desire to sing, greater, and the quaking of the rocky walls increased.

Gradually the melody began to take on an older, richer sound and the very floor of the cave beneath her began to tremble, the surface of the water rippled and great pieces of rock began to fall all about her. Still, she could not stop her voice. Gabriella moved not a muscle, oblivious to the shattering of stone around her, feeling only the great movement within.

When at last she stopped her song and opened her eyes, she saw that the walls around her had fallen down and the space she had seen, through the fissure too small for her to crawl, was actually a huge cavern, filled with light. Stalagmites and stalactites caught the sunshine and scattered miniature rainbows before her as she gazed into the magical space.

Purples and pinks, yellows, greens and blues, the entire spectrum of colour, dazzling and beautiful, stretched out before her. Aquamarine and hazel wood rod in hand, she walked from one crystal to the next, amazed at the wonder of their creation.

Hidden from her sight by the shadows and the walls of stone, she had never known they existed; but they had been here all along. *Treasures within the shadows,* thought Gabriella, taking one final look at her Aquamarine stone before placing it safely alongside the others in her pocket.

Like a world of dripping rainbows, the cave delighted and amused her. Gabriella hummed and skipped and danced, finding willing partners in the brightly coloured conical shapes all about her. In and out, around and around, she circled them with glee, giggling, laughing, humming, singing. Oh, she could not keep from singing.

As she studied her spectacular new surroundings, she half-expected to find Owl. It seemed a perfect place for her to have hidden herself away. Thinking this again, she called out, 'Owl, are you here?' At first, there was no answer, but then Gabriella heard a familiar rustle of wings in the air above her. 'Who invited you?' came the winged question.

'Oh, Owl, it is you,' Gabriella cried. 'I came to find where you had hidden yourself away. I had a dream and in it I realized that all the animals, except you, had become rabbits. Suddenly, I had to know where you had gone.' Gabriella's voice rushed on, telling the still unseen Owl all about her dreams; the Woman of the Wood; the birch canoe; the whirlpool; the darkest dark which had been just on the other side of the wall of stone; and finally about her shadow and the gift of song and Aquamarine stone.

'Owl, I sang my song and the barrier came down. Now I am here. I am in your hiding place; I have found you.'

'You found who?' asked Owl.

'You. I found you,' she answered. 'Only I cannot see you. I can only hear you.'

'Ooh, that is true; but I can see you,' came the reply.

'Where are you then?' There was no answer.

'Where are you Owl?' Gabriella ran around the cavern searching for her friend, but to no avail. It seemed an unfair game to her. 'I can't find you. Please, give me a clue.'

'Look to the blue. Look to the blue,' said Owl at last.

Gabriella looked at the blue-tinted pieces of stone, which surrounded her, but saw nothing, until she looked up. She had been concentrating on the cavern so intently she had not so much as glanced at the source of light above it. There at the very top was a tiny speck, silhouetted by the sky. It was, indeed, the familiar shape of Owl, and when Gabriella saw her, Owl waved a wing and said, 'You are the first to find your way through...now, what do you do?' and off she flew.

Owl's new tone with her was slightly annoying. She had never riddled before. *Why is she not coming down to greet me?* Gabriella gazed upward until her neck began to ache. Clearly Owl was challenging her to come up to her perch; but that was more than a bit tricky as it was not exactly within her reach.

As the light diminished, the atmosphere in the cavern began to alter. The stalagmites and stalactites, which had once seemed so inviting, became ominous in shape, almost threatening, in the lengthening shadows. *I am grateful I saw these in full daylight first,* thought Gabriella. Then, tucked against a wall, in the furthest recess of the cavern from where she stood, she saw something she had not yet seen, perhaps the sun had been too bright. Walking towards the spot, she discovered that there were steps circling up and up and up. They seemed to spiral exactly to the place where Owl had appeared. *This is the way,* thought Gabriella. *Tomorrow morning I will start afresh and these stairs will guide me.*

Delighted, she raced back to the pool of water, which was less aquamarine-coloured now, more a deep twilight blue, and drank her fill, finding its moistness as warm and nourishing as before. She walked back into the great open space, lay down at the foot of the stairs and sang herself to sleep, awaiting the next day's light.

The Spiral Staircase

With the first rays of pink, Gabriella arose, had one last drink of water to sustain herself, and then took a final look at the crystals surrounding her. They were luminescent wonders, each of them, how joyful they made her feel.

Singing softly to herself, she started up the stairs. In the excitement of finding them the night before, Gabriella had not noticed that they travelled in a manner that would leave her left side on the outside. Her right hand, carrying the hazel wood rod, would be closest to the centre. This, of course, filled her with dread, as it was her least favourite way to climb. She simply did not feel secure with her left side exposed. 'Well, there is no other way,' Gabriella said out loud, 'the stairs cannot be rebuilt just for me,' and with that she began her ascent.

At first it was easy. It was so much better than being in the dark cave; around and around she went. When the stairs faced the cavern she looked at all the rainbow-coloured formations and each time around the spiral she had a different view; but the higher she climbed, the thought of looking down became less and less appealing.

Just one step at a time, she said to herself. *'You can do this. Have no fear,* she would say and then she would sing her song. Occasionally, she would stop to catch her breath and regain her sense of balance. It was dizzying, this going round and round, and it was growing increasingly difficult, for, the higher she climbed, the steeper and narrower the steps were becoming. She had begun to count the rotations as she ascended and noted that, while once twenty steps were needed to complete the whole circumference, now only ten were necessary.

As the sun grew brighter, the stairs began to glimmer, nearly blinding her. Gabriella's early enthusiasm gave way to momentary bouts of fear; but still she pressed on. If a cloud covered the sun for a moment, she moved more quickly, as she could see without hindrance. Looking up towards the opening in the roof of the cavern, the spiral appeared endless above her.

Oh, what have I done? she thought. *I have followed my heart and listened to my own voice,* she answered. *Neither will betray me.* And so the inner voice of doubt was silenced as ever upward she climbed, pausing with her back against the core of the spiral every once in a while to pray for the strength to continue.

As the day wore on, every muscle began to ache, and still there seemed no end in sight. Gabriella began to wonder why she had come to find Owl's cave at all. *What difference does it make for me to know this?* she asked herself. *What meaning can it possibly bring? Besides, now that I have found it, it seems Owl is playing some sort of curious game.*

As soon as she thought the thought, she knew it was not true. *Owl would never tempt me in order to harm me.* Gabriella knew that for certain.

'There is no one to blame here. There is a reason; but I cannot see it yet,' she said, aloud this time.

With a deep conviction, and the still ever-present song within her heart, she continued her climb. Glaring sun, now mixed with a brisk wind, gave Gabriella a renewed sense of purpose and the belief that she was nearing the top.

I must be within the Mountain of Remembrance, she suddenly thought, wondering if the stairs might be leading her to the summit, to the cave, and the possibility of it gave her a surge of energy. Bracing herself against a growing cold, and pausing now at every step, profoundly exhausted, Gabriella found herself progressing at no more than a snail's pace.

Her mouth had become too dry to sing and she was breathing much too quickly, it was as though no breath could reach her lungs. She forced herself to focus on the step directly before her, as looking down from the heights had become terrifying.

The wind was now almost gusting and it seemed fully capable of lifting her up at any moment and dashing her on to the rocks below. Willing herself to continue, though gripped with a growing fear, Gabriella was suddenly confronted with what seemed an impossible task. The step before her was the steepest she had encountered, it was so large that, as she stood on the stone stair beneath it, it touched her waistband.

Simply stepping on to it would be impossible; to climb higher would require crawling up on hand and knees. In order to accomplish this, Gabriella would have to swing her left leg out, over the edge of the stairs, and bring it to land on the step above. Then, she would somehow have to hoist the rest of her body on to the step, using her right leg and the hazel wood rod for balance.

As it was growing dark and cold, she knew there was no time to pause. *There is no going back,* she thought, as she hoisted her skirt, tucking it into her waistband. Holding the hazel wood rod firmly in her right hand she swung her left leg out into the open air and jumped. The jump shifted her centre of balance, causing her to lean precariously towards the edge, but she lurched with all her strength back to the right, somehow shifting her weight and regaining her balance. 'Well, that was terrifying,' she announced, in hopes that the sound of her own voice would help her to recover.

'All right, do not overcompensate. Do only that which is needed for the task,' she said, trying to bolster her inner strength.

She took as deep a breath as possible, and this time leant into the vertical stone with her right shoulder. Rather than hurl her body into the air, she used the stone as support, and with her right shoulder she pressed against its solidity, her hand holding fast to the hazel wood rod, which was firm on the stair she was standing on.

Gabriella slowly lifted her left leg, knee bent, to the step above. She simultaneously braced herself against the stone while pushing the weight of her body into the hazel wood rod. In so doing, she was able to resist against the step below, until all of her had arrived on the higher stair. This being accomplished she gave a giggle of delight and collapsed in a heap, leaning against the curved wall of stone and gave thanks. She had succeeded, but she was still not at the top of the stairs.

Gabriella slowly walked around the curve, certain that she would be unable to climb any further, when, to her utter amazement, she found on the other side of the spiral, a vast expanse of land and sky and sea stretched out before her. And she knew she had reached the summit of the Mountain of Remembrance.

The way to the heights had come from within the depths.

It was breath-giving in its splendour. She could see everything. The Land of Never Forgetting seemed small and tiny and the River of Dreams was only a narrow portion of a much larger body of water. From here, Gabriella saw that it was all connected; that the bodies of water given separate names were all one. Looking in another direction, she saw countless other islands she had never seen, surrounded by more of the sea. Each of the islands seemed more similar than different and she wondered at the vastness of it all. She drank in the splendour until her eyes could bear no more.

How limited we are on our tiny plots of earth, she thought. *We see so little past ourselves.* Here, even her deformity seemed insignificant; she was tiny, dwarfed in the magnitude of her new surroundings, which spanned an immeasurable horizon.

Awestruck, she stood at the top the Mountain of Remembrance. The terror at being so far above the sea left her, as she realized she was a part of it all, and it was a part of her.

The Golden Mirror

She spent the night on a ledge, no bigger than twice her size, with absolutely no fear at all. Stars above her twinkled so closely to her, she felt she could pluck them from the sky and craft a lacy necklace from their shimmering light. Behind their flickering diamond beauty, the midnight-blue sky held hints of golden-light.

And then, as if she could hold another ounce of pleasure, the stars began to dance. They swirled above her, leaving trails of glimmering light. Swishing and spiralling, they lit up the sky. This was like no display of light she had ever seen, no shooting star; no, this was some other language of light for her heart's knowing.

What? she wanted to call out. *What do you want me to know?*

In reply to her unspoken question, she heard them urging her to hold out her hand. Opening it wide, she held it up to the radiance of light and her palm tickled as fragments of starry sky came to rest upon it. Gabriella held her breath. She heard the lights urging her to close her fingers around the sparkling dust, and so, she did. The warmth of her hand mingled with the fragments of light and when she opened it at last, a lustrous stone had taken its place.

Lapis, bluest blue for you
Will help you know just what to do.

In its radiance you will find,
Your eyes, before this day, were blind.

Sea and earth and breath meet here,
Within this love, there is no fear.

The familiar voice spoke gently, almost in a whisper. Gabriella looked up from the Lapis to the heavens; but the swirling messengers had gone, and for the briefest of moments she felt lonely, as though she had lost her closest friends.

Full of wonder, Gabriella sat in silence, holding the Lapis in the palm of her hand, waiting for the dawn, which came suddenly and gloriously, illuminating earth, sky and sea in one spectacular wash of light. Later, when the sun had risen, Gabriella could see a narrow path directly across the summit, leading to an opening in the side of the Mountain.

Could it be the place of my first dream? Is it true? Did my dream foretell of a real place in actual time and space? Is Mama there? Her mind raced ahead with unanswered questions, but then, all thought stopped as abruptly as it had begun, for, in her initial excitement, she realised that she had forgotten she would have to cross the path that lay ahead.

She could see it was wide enough for her to cross. It was even wide enough for her to cross, using the hazel wood rod for balance. However, on both sides of the backbone of the summit, the Mountain disappeared, sheering away almost vertically, dropping straight down to the sea below. The heights were dizzying, she had no reason to believe it was possible for her to make it safely to the other side, yet, somehow, she knew she could, knew she would. And she knew this from the very depths of her being.

Placing the Lapis in her pocket with the other stones she had a talk with herself. *No looking down,* she said. *You can do this. Do not look down.* She took a few deep breaths, began to sing a melody she had never sung before, and then she closed her eyes. Having seen the path to the opposite side was arrow straight, Gabriella decided to trust her inner guidance and not allow her earthly vision to complicate the treacherous crossing. With eyes tightly shut, as if blind, and yet not, she walked, without stumbling, seeing her way from within. And she was fearless and sure-footed.

As Gabriella sensed her safe arrival, the hazel wood rod touched the earth. Opening her eyes, she said, 'I did it. All I need to do next is round a tiny curve and then at last I will be at the opening to the cave at the top of the Mountain. She did not speed her pace, but walked as she had been, steadily, and with purpose. After taking only a few steps, she saw it and sighed, 'Oh! There is a stone blocking the entrance.'

Without feeling any sense of dismay, Gabriella studied the massive stone blocking her path. It looked like a rather ordinary slab of granite, grey, with great crevasses carved upon it, but on closer inspection she saw that there was a slight pattern to one of the fissures in particular. The shape reminded her of last night's dancing stars, as there was a sort of spiral form carved into the stone, and the memory brought a smile to her lips.

Feeling the urge to touch it, she placed the hazel wood rod against her leg and allowed her hand to trace the circling shape; beginning at the outermost point and moving towards the centre. As she did, small pieces of stone began to fall away, to the ground. She was surprised; but continued to trace the spiral with her fingers, as it seemed so the right thing to do.

When her fingers arrived at the very centre of the spiral she removed her hand and looked more closely. It was then she saw that her fingers had dislodged six loose, but very specifically shaped, pieces of stone, leaving indentations where they had previously been. Closing her eyes, Gabriella touched the rock once more, pausing at each concave, moving from outward in, as she had done the first time.

It all seemed so familiar to her. 'I know these shapes. These are the shapes of the stones I have carried with me for so long. Their forms have graced my life. I recognize them.' Slowly opening her eyes, she reached within her pocket and found the Garnet. Remembering the words which had accompanied it, she reached towards the impression at the outermost point of the spiral.

Placing the Garnet within it, she said within her heart:

Commit yourself to your new goal
Release the past. Be still. Be whole.

Carnelian was next:

The outward journey starts within.
From this truth you now begin.

Then Citrine:

Rest in judgments you have made.
You listen well. Let self be stayed.

Malachite:

Use your heart and not your eyes
To seek with love, past earthly guise.

And Aquamarine:

Awaken what is pure and strong,
Lift up your voice and sing your song.

All five fitted in such an extraordinary manner that Gabriella gasped. Still one space remained, but its shape was less familiar to her than the others had been. *Could it be the Lapis belongs here?* she wondered.

Taking the final stone from her pocket, with just the smallest hint of doubt, Gabriella remembered the words:

Sea and breath and earth meet here,
Within this love there is no fear.

Then, she tenderly, placed the blue stone, with its golden starlight flecks, at the centre of the spiral, and the two met perfectly. Gabriella wondered at the perfection of it all and, as she slowly drew her hand away from the stone, the door vanished, revealing the very room that had appeared in her dream, at the top the rainbow spire of smoke.

'Mama. Mama. Are you here?' she called out. There was no answer.

With a degree of disbelief, she reached for her hazel wood rod and stepped over the threshold, thinking, *It is all here, just as in my dream. Only the carpets are more luxurious that I remember, how deep and sensuous the purples and blues of them and, how sweet, the smells of freshly baked bread and honey. But, of course, Mama is not here, I guess I always knew she could not really be here.* Then she remembered that she had never actually seen her Mother in the cave, only heard the loving encouragement of her voice, urging her to find it.

Looking to her left, she saw huge bouquets of flowers, orchids and lilies; great fronds of palm, jasmine and honeysuckle, burst forth from green marble vases on top of green marble stands. A roaring fire blazed inside a marble hearth of brilliant white. Quartz crystal lamps glowed with light throughout the room and a small couch with velvet and silk cushions of red and gold was sat next to the fireplace.

All was glowing and welcoming, but even with all this luxury, Gabriella found she could not rest. Then she knew what was missing, she had seen it in her dream, but it was not here. *Where is it?* she wondered. *Where is the mirror with the golden frame?*

Walking toward the bouquets of flowers once more, she saw steps leading deeper into the cave. She climbed all twenty-one of them and found they led her to another room. Once inside the second room, Gabriella paused to catch her breath. On each of the four walls were windows, through which were unobstructed views in each direction: North, South, East and West.

Save the four windows, she could see only two other items in the room: against the wall, opposite the stairs, was a small golden table and, on top of it, the golden-framed mirror. Gabriella could not take her eyes from it as she walked closer until, there, in the mirror before her, was the silvery-grey hair she had seen in her dream, only this time she saw more than just a glimpse. The hair framed a face with silver-blue eyes; they were deep like the sea, yet bright as the heavens, and as Gabriella gazed into them, they, in turn, gazed back at her.

This is the woman who has guided me, she thought. And without a word she reached toward the mirror, to touch the face looking back at her. As her fingers came to the cheekbone of the precious countenance before her in the mirror, Gabriella felt a gentle touch upon her own face. Tenderly stroking the old woman's hair, Gabriella felt a caress upon her own temple.

This is no reflection of another. This is me. The realization came to her in waves, the voices, the songs, the dreams, the encouragement, the lessons, the fears; all had been the adventures that had made up her journey. And her journey had taken a lifetime.

She was no longer a child. She was now an old woman and, an old woman with a story to tell. She walked from the mirror, down the stairs, to the entrance of the cave, and said:

What I have seen, high above all the earth,
Is not about death, not at all. It is birth.

The Laws and the wars and the hatred of men
Will happen all over and over again.

Until we can see past our own little world,
See all of the beauty and splendour unfurled.

Miraculous beings, each creature, each life,
Demanding each one be the same, creates strife.

We all are connected. We all are entwined.
Like diamonds in carbon, we all need to find

The beauty, that comes from the pressures and pain,
A universe playing a joyous refrain,

Composed of all life, as it ebbs, as it flows.
Then inside, each person, will know as it grows,

No matter the colour, the size or the form,
There is no perfection; there is no set norm

You are what you are. And like each shining star,
The life that you dance; it is not happenstance.

A plan is unfolding, beyond wildest dreams.
The path you are on, is not all that it seems.

So, open your Self to the truth that you know.
Release all the fears and the doubts. Let them go.

Rejoice in surrender, there is no great fight.
The far side of shadow, is pure radiant light.

Gabriella sang these words from the door of the room, in the cave, at the summit, on top of the Mountain of Remembrance, and with each word of her song her left side throbbed with a violence she had never known. Still, she sang to the heavens, as tears, part from pain, part from joy, streamed down her face. And then, as quickly as the pain had begun, it ceased.

As her song ended, as her pain ended, Gabriella turned her face toward the light, with her right arm fully extended. And then, out of the corner of her eye, to her left, where nothing but sky had been, she beheld a glorious wing of purest white.

She moved her arm, and then; she moved her wing. She crossed wing, over arm, over chest, and then, arm, over wing, over chest. With great care and amazement, she opened and closed the feathered extension of her Self and, from her depths, she realized, *I wasn't born deformed. I was born not yet formed.*

That glorious day, in the setting sun, Gabriella stood, wing and arm outstretched, embracing all she saw, her heart, wide open to the Land that had rejected her, the Land which had nearly destroyed her.

And she felt nothing but love.

THE LIGHT

For the people of the Land of Never Forgetting, the day had begun like any other, with their heads covered, their faces towards the ground and no one looking at one another, no one looking up.

There are those that say a mighty sound, a roaring noise, came from across the River of Dreams and commanded their attention. Others say it was more like a whisper.

It was late in the day, the sun well past its brightest shining, when the sound was first heard. Initially, people tried to pay it no heed; some picked up the pace of their walking, others worked with greater diligence in an effort to ignore it. A few carried on conversations with themselves, if they could find no one else to talk to, trying to occupy their minds with anything, other than the sound. And perhaps, a very few heard nothing at all.

But all efforts to remain deaf, to deaden the sound, to avoid paying attention, were in vain. So persistent, so dynamic, so uniquely specific to each of them was the intrusion that it demanded their response. The sound continued to fill the air until each one, every single person in the Land of Never Forgetting, ceased doing whatever it was they were doing, and began to listen.

No matter the quality of the sound that reached their ears, the message was singular. 'Look up. Look up. Look up to the source of the sound!' it said.

And putting aside ancient fears and habits, judgments, and worries about how it might appear, one by one they began to raise their eyes towards the Mountain of Remembrance. As they lifted their faces, attempting to locate the source of the sound, to follow the instruction they had been given, their dark hoods fell from the crowns of their heads, and the Light shone upon them. And what glorious light it was. Such magnificence, few would speak of, and those that have tried, say words could never fully express the exquisite radiance they bore witness to that day.

For the summit of the Mountain, so long a symbol of darkness and dread, was ablaze with golden splendour. It was as though the very stones were glowing, illuminated from within. No longer was the familiar form of the granite rock face visible to the eye; in its stead, there appeared to them an orb of pure, gleaming light, like nothing any had ever seen.

Long past the setting sun, even as the sky darkened with the approach of nightfall, the light continued to shine. It grew in intensity and size until it seemed it would burst. Slowly, at first, it began to spin, and then, before their very eyes, the people saw the single light become a mass of luminous vibrations that began to separate from one another, sending sparkling, glittering fragments into the indigo sky, until, at last, there was no longer a single light, but a multitude of small, shimmering beacons.

As the one Light became many, the focus of the people changed. It was as though each one of them felt connected to their own sliver of light in the sky that night. And, in silence, each man and woman and child studied his or her singular gift with gratitude and awe.

In dividing, the Light did not diminish. Rather, they say it grew brighter as the vigils were kept. Upturned, unblinking eyes gazed unceasingly upon the dazzling luminescence. And then, the Light became a warmth within each of them.

Some spoke of the brightness passing through their eyes, into their minds, bathing their very thoughts; others said it was as though the glowing enveloped all of them, their seeing, their hearing, their touch, every aspect of them, set ablaze by the resplendence given to them that night.

The Light pierced the darkness of their humanity, illuminating the hidden corners, the places of fear, their long forgotten and often rejected individuality.

It knew every story, every hurt, every unlived dream and as the golden beams ignited the hearts of those gathered, they saw themselves in a new way.

And in truly seeing themselves, they began to see one another.

With a fervour, they lowered their eyes from the sky, needing to behold each other. And as they did, for the first time, they saw not what was different between them, but rather what was the same. For within the eyes of each, a spark of recognition had been set alight. No more could they see the essence of one another as anything but brightness and beauty, for each had been enlightened that night. They were not separate from the whole and it was not separate from them.

They, each, in their profound uniqueness, were bright glimmering facets of its glory.

And from that day, they were forever known as The People of Light.

In Gratitude

I would like to thank so many people, it is difficult knowing where to begin. So, I shall start by firstly thanking you, the reader. Thank you for sharing this journey with Gabriella, for investing the energy necessary to read this book, to follow her story, to imagine yourself in a different world. If you have been blessed in this experience, please tell someone else, so that this story of the Light might shine more brightly.

To the many wonderful friends in England and the USA who have supported this book pre-publication and held both it, and me, in various moments along the way; my profound thanks to:

Kim Moore, Linda Dilks, Susie Gowenlock, Gill Deane, Fi Mulligan, Lesley and Dave Carpenter, Renée Van der Vloodt, Siobhan and Rob Nolan, Simon and Sarah Matthews, Katharine Patel, Wendy Saunders, Marie-Christine Hunter, Sarah Slade, Eve Ellis and Annette Niemtzow, Geoffrey Blaisdell, Michael Slade, Rebecca Kaye, Jan Colville, Elise Thoron and Oz Enders, Sophia Bartleet, Marsha Levy-Warren, Laura Bass, Serenna Davies, Philly Knowland, Annie Ayton, Kilburg Reedy, Tracy Ludlow, Bill Pindar, Don Schutt, Anita Nelson and John Brady.

To the amazing women of the Mews, who have sustained me on a daily basis during this season of my life: thank you to Helen Henley, your laughter and your smile brightened my spirit when it flagged; to Louis Wycherley, your integrity and gentle encouragement helped me to finish what I had begun; and to Jacquie Moulder, beautiful lover of books, your unwavering commitment to this story has inspirited me beyond measure.

Tom Evans, thank you for all of your suggestions, especially for the one that put me in contact with Discovered Authors and Jennie Paterson. And thank you Jennie, for seeing the potential in Gabriella; for being supportive and positive every step of the way.

Jon Stewart and Anna Pointer, thank you for your intelligent and insightful responses to the story. Graham Bass and Irene Marks, for listening to those first words on a hillside in Greece. Lucy Simon, thank you for telling me to pick up paper and pencil and begin, and for hearing the lyricism in my prose. Diana DeVegh, thank you for your utter commitment to helping me recognize my own voice, and for knowing that you would be enchanted by Gabriella's story, even before you had read it. Susie Shew, I am so thankful that you have always heard my heart.

To Victoria and Keith Knights, thank you for your support and invaluable input. Tony and Susie Valentine, thank you for your wonderfully cogent responses and for celebrating this process so freely with me.

Chris and Richard Pointer, where do I begin? Thank you for the hours and hours of editing, writing, reading and re-reading. The final stages of completing Gabriella have been joyous and could not have happened so painlessly without your friendship and your encouragement.

Thank you, Sheilagh Jevons, for creating such a magnificent painting. I am so very grateful to have your unique interpretation of the story as the cover art for the book.

Mem, Dad, Sarah, Phil, Ellen and Anna, thank you for being excited, for listening to snippets of story across the five years it has taken to write it, and for creating space to read it when it was completed. Ellen, a very special thank you to you, for reading it cover-to-cover, in one sitting, at age 11.

Mom and Daddy, thank you for always believing in me. Your love has been a constant source of strength and encouragement. You taught me to aim high and to never be afraid of failing. That has allowed me to dream really big dreams, and to see many of them come true. To Phil, thank you for your support, Tommy and Robbie, for your bubbling laughter, and Susie, thank you for your constancy, for your astute feedback, and for writing the first poems I ever truly loved.

Five remarkable women have partnered me in these new waters since 2002 and have read so many drafts between them along the way, that I have lost count. I absolutely could not have arrived at this shore without each of their unique gifts:

Sue Brady, thank you for reading this book with the genius of your actress-self. Your insights helped to define and shape the characters in this book; what a gift you are to me my beautiful friend.

Mac Mahoney, thank you for sharing your journey with me, your life has inspired me in the writing of this story. In the darkest moments, your unique and steadfast light has brightened my path.

Suzie Jennings, thank you for holding Gabriella so carefully. Thank you for championing her, and me, in this season. Your warrior spirit has given immense strength and determination to every step I have taken.

Sue Bouder, your commitment to seeking the spiritual in the everyday is a wonder to me. Thank you for lending your profound insights not only to this book, but also to my life.

Marian Murphy Powell, thank you for knowing me so well, and loving me, no matter what. Thank you for listening to me read newly written sections over the phone, across the ocean, across five years. Thank you for helping my seed of an inspiration become a book, and for never, ever, letting me doubt that I would complete it.

And lastly, my beloved Nicholas, the inspired work you have done in designing the cover and the layout of the text has made Gabriella look beautiful, inside and out. From the depths of me, I thank you for your gentle and profound care of me, in this, and in all things. Know that in you I have found my way home. Always, anam cara, always.

Judy Malloy is a storyteller.

She began her career telling stories on the stage and spent twenty years in New York City performing on Broadway, off-Broadway, and in regional theatres, ultimately culminating in the production of her own award-winning, one-woman show, Angel's Unawares. Also a recording artist, she is featured on numerous theatrical albums, the highlight of which, being her own solo CD, The Missing Peace, which has received critical acclaim.

Along with her work as a singer/actress, Judy is a healer. A graduate of the Swedish Institute in NYC, she had a successful private healing practice in New York from 1995-2000 and it was during this time, inspired by the words of Caroline Myss who said, 'Your biography becomes your biology', that she began to develop and lead workshops exploring the necessity of finding the language of one's own story and learning to recognize the singularity of that story as it manifests in the body, the mind, and the spirit.

Her New York life came to an end in June 2000, when Judy got married and moved to Dorking, Surrey, to live with the love of her life, Nicholas Down.

Here in England Judy continues to have a thriving healing practice and has begun to lead workshops once more.

She can be contacted at: www.gabriellathemyth.com